L. C. TYLER was born in Southend-on-Sea and then educated at Oxford and City Universities. His day jobs have included being a systems analyst, a cultural attaché and (for a few weeks one summer) working for Bomb Disposal. He has won awards for his writing, including the Last Laugh Award for the best comic crime novel of the year. He is Chair of the Crime Writers' Association and has been a CWA Daggers judge. L. C. Tyler has lived all over the world, but most recently in London and Sussex.

*lctyler.com*

# Cat Among the Herrings

## L. C. TYLER

Allison & Busby Limited
12 Fitzroy Mews
London W1T 6DW
*allisonandbusby.com*

First published in Great Britain by Allison & Busby in 2016.
This paperback edition published by Allison & Busby in 2016.

A CIP catalogue record for this book is available from
the British Library.

10 9 8 7 6 5 4 3 2 1

ISBN 978-0-7490-1996-9

Typeset in 10.5/15.5 pt Sabon by
Allison & Busby Ltd.

The paper used for this Allison & Busby publication
has been produced from trees that have been legally sourced
from well-managed and credibly certified forests.

Printed and bound by
CPI Group (UK) Ltd, Croydon, CR0 4YY

*For 'Cat'*

*'Murder, like talent, seems occasionally to run in families'*

G. H. Lewes

# CHAPTER ONE

It was not the happiest of funerals.

A spiteful gale, gusting fitfully from the Channel, flung needles of sleet at our faces. I heard the rector utter that most final of instructions: 'Commit his body to the ground, earth to earth, dust to dust, ashes to ashes'. Then, for a page or so of the burial service, nothing reached me but the howling of the wind in the trees. Half blinded and more than half deafened, I stood, feeling the rain soak slowly through to my skin. No adjustment that I might make – turning up my collar, pulling my coat more closely about me – could do anything but bring an even colder, wetter layer of clothing into an even closer contact with myself. Black, billowing clouds were fleeing inland, but we had nowhere to run.

'. . . forgive us our trespasses . . .' blew in my direction. We were almost there, then. I counted to ten slowly and said an 'Amen' that nobody else could have heard.

A little to my left I caught the glance of young Tom Gittings. He gave me a quick smile – I think he would have winked if he had been sure nobody else was watching. The irony of the living being made to suffer for the questionable benefit to the dead had certainly occurred to him too. But we were both aware that the slightest suggestion of levity would be out of place. This was a dreadful and momentous occasion. We were burying the last of the Paghams.

The service that had preceded the interment had been another matter. Quite different in every respect. We were warm and dry then, inside the church, listening to a storm that rattled the windows but that seemed as yet to have little to do with us. The rector had spoken at length of the Pagham family. He reminded us that they had been significant landowners in the Middle Ages. One had been a bishop who had advised Richard II slightly too well and become collateral damage during the Peasants' Revolt. Another had fought with Drake, sinking a Spanish galleon (it was said) within sight of his own tenants, who were assembled on the pebbly coastline, curious to discover whether their landlord would return to collect the next instalment of their rent. Another had been knighted by Charles II on the very day of his glorious Restoration, possibly in mistake for somebody else with a similar name. Their later decline, the gradual sale of their lands to pay gambling debts or bribe electors or invest in the South Sea Bubble . . . these things the rector passed over quite quickly. Members of the congregation who were unfamiliar with local history would have been bemused at how the Paghams of the nineteenth century had found themselves living in a small thatched cottage close to the village green, catching herring and mackerel for a living and never quite free from the smell of rotting fish. But this too had to be mentioned in passing, or how else could the rector praise the meteoric rise that had followed? It was, if you were prepared to overlook their previous ignominious fall, a genuine tale of rags to riches. Robin might have been the last of the Paghams but he had been able to go out in style.

The rector spoke warmly of Robin's father, Roger Pagham. A good man and a regular churchgoer. He did not draw any comparison with Robin Pagham in this respect. There was no need. We all knew Robin.

It was tragic, the rector said, that only a year or so after burying the father, we were now assembled to bury the son. But we should be thankful that he had died doing what he most enjoyed. The congregation turned, almost as one, to look at the woman in a tight black dress and lace veil in the front row. Some of us had already noted that deep and sincere mourning did not preclude a skirt well above knee level.

'Sailing,' added the rector quickly, but perhaps not quite quickly enough. Robin, he went on, had not been the first son of West Wittering to meet a tragic end at sea, nor would he be the last. Experienced yachtsman though he had been, and unthreatening though the winds had seemed, he had perished. Though some had said it was inexplicable, those who knew the sea and its ways well understood how conditions could change in an instant, how a moment's inattention could prove the undoing of the wisest mariner. He did not add that everyone's first assumption, on hearing the tragic news, had been that Robin must have been drunk. Robin had undeniably gained solace from alcohol in a way that he had not from religion. It had, you might say, been a contest between his many hobbies to see which would eventually kill him.

The rector had hoped, he said, that the next event here at the church relating to the family would have been a joyous one. Robin had finally, after many years, found somebody that he wished to spend the rest of his life with. As most of them were aware, he and Catarina had been about to announce their engagement. The rector did not have the pleasure of knowing Catarina well, but she was clearly (he consulted his notes) a very special person. He looked up and gave a slightly wary smile to the lady in black.

The smile was not returned. Robin's fiancée, as we now knew her to be, continued to stare straight ahead. Her small hand clutched a black-edged linen handkerchief, which she occasionally applied to her eyes, uncovering her face as little as possible.

It was gratifying, added the rector, to see such profound and genuine love, in spite of the difference in their ages. At this point somebody at the back of the church had a coughing fit, but the rector pressed on regardless. He was a good man and this was not the first funeral at which the deceased had been allowed considerable benefit of the doubt. I noticed that the rector felt no need to mention any of Robin's convictions for the possession of drugs, nor his caution for breaking his then-girlfriend's nose. (But this was five or six girlfriends before he met Catarina – more than two years ago, in fact.) Robin had, the rector continued, not been a *regular* member of the congregation but . . . he paused as if wondering what it was fair to try to make us believe . . . Robin had possessed Christian Charity in abundance. He would, in the rector's opinion, have made a wonderful father.

This last drew a brief but very audible sob from Catarina, which brought the proceedings to a sudden if temporary halt. The rector opened his mouth as if to expand on the theme of Robin and fatherhood then, apparently thinking better of it, quickly turned the page. 'Thus,' he announced, 'the ancient line of the Paghams comes to an end. The family was well respected and well loved within our community and will be missed by us all.'

At this point, Catarina was heard to mutter something from behind her black veil. None of us spoke the language in question, but it did not sound as if she was agreeing that the village had been universally well disposed towards Robin. The rector took another deep breath and announced that we would now sing Robin's favourite hymn. It proved to be 'For Those in Peril on the Sea'.

Afterwards there were prayers, which Catarina was prepared to take as read. Then we sang 'Guide Me O Thou Great Redeemer', though the rector wisely did not attempt to claim that Robin liked, or even knew, more than one hymn. And that was that.

Apart from one thing.

Just as we were all preparing to troop out into the rain, Catarina turned to the congregation and lifted her veil so that she could observe us the better. Her dark eyes glowered. She raised her hand and pointed a gloved finger in our direction, sweeping it from left to right and taking in every one of us.

'One of you bastards murdered Robin,' she said in heavily accented tones, 'and, whoever it was, I'm going to have your arse. You losers have messed with the wrong lady.'

The rector consulted his prayer book for a moment, as if he had temporarily lost his place in the order of service. Then, in total silence, he led us out of the church and into the rain.

# CHAPTER TWO

It was not the liveliest of wakes.

The rector had announced that we were all invited to refreshments at Greylands House after the funeral. There was some uncertainty in our minds as to who would host the event, Robin, as I have said, having no immediate family. We drove along the rutted lane to the Paghams' residence, a mile or two outside the village, with a mild curiosity to see who would take charge in the absence of any living Pagham. We had speculated that it might be the Paghams' solicitor as executor, or perhaps some distant relative. In the event, Catarina took pride of place, though she condescended rather than hosted. She stood by the door as we trooped in and she shook hands with each of us. There was a surprising firmness to her grip that was completely at variance with the fragile, black lace gloves.

'Thank you much for coming,' she said to me. Or perhaps

she said it to somebody else entirely. It was undoubtedly my hand that she pressed, but she was looking beyond me, over my shoulder. It was rather as if I had been hoping to meet the president and had found myself shaking hands with one of his bodyguards. Polite, professional but honestly not too interested in me as a person.

'I didn't know Robin well,' I said. 'I moved into the village only a couple of years ago – hardly any time in a place like this. But I'd met him a few times at the sailing club. He was a very warm-hearted and generous man. We'll miss him.'

Though she had not let go of my hand the whole time, only now did she turn her head and look at me properly.

'You are the writer?' she asked.

'I suppose so. I write crime novels,' I said.

She nodded. 'That is right. Crime. I have heard of you.'

'You've read my books?'

'No. I think not many of your books in the shops. Not any more. But are still some old reviews on Internet. I have read reviews – they are very amusing. I laugh. But maybe not so funny for you.'

I said, I hope convincingly, that you got used to bad reviews.

She shrugged. '*You* will miss Robin?' she asked.

'Yes,' I said. 'Robin was what you might have described as a character. He was pretty wild when he was younger, by all accounts, but he had mellowed.'

'Robin was not old man,' she said.

'Not young, of course . . .'

'Not old to die,' she said. 'Not old not to know how

sail boat. Not old not to make much love. Two, three times every night. How about you?'

'I'm not much of a sailor,' I said.

She looked me up and down. 'No,' she said. 'Not so much, I think.'

I left her to interrogate the rector, who had just arrived with his wife. I overheard him answering: 'about five times a week, except at Christmas'. But I think that referred to the services he took in the village.


A number of the local youths had been employed as waiters. Since most of us sipped our sherry slowly, and since none of them had any experience in this field, they frequently lapsed into chatting to each other in the kitchen or texting, having little else to do.

Once or twice Catarina, noticing that she was paying them for doing nothing, snapped an order at the staff and they quickly circled the room again with trays of sweet and dry sherry. Like the rector, they were not quite sure what to make of Catarina and were taking no unnecessary risks.

Drinks were served in whatever glasses they had been able to locate. Measures were variable, arbitrary and sometimes surprisingly generous. One of the children had been able to negotiate for herself a tumblerful of sweet sherry and now sat on the floor, slightly befuddled but not yet actually vomiting. Catarina nodded approvingly in her direction. 'Cute,' she said. 'When Robin and I had our children . . .'

In the long pause that followed I said: 'The rector was right: Robin would have made a fine father.'

'Perhaps,' said Catarina. 'He would have beaten the children, of course. But perhaps he would be too drunk for other things that a father must do. He must teach hunt. Robin would not have been safe teach hunt. Small child with loaded gun and drunken father – not good I think. But I would have been a fine mother. You see these titties? I will have strong, healthy babies. What you say?'

I examined Catarina's cleavage for as long as politeness demanded. 'Ah . . . yes,' I said. 'They would have been very healthy.'

'You are like me,' she said. I must have looked puzzled because she added: 'You not live here long.'

'About two years,' I said.

'But these people – they all live here *for ever*.' She waved her hand at her guests. 'Look at them. They are proud that their parents and their grandparents never leave this place. Like peasants in my country. You know what they think of me?'

I had a pretty good idea, but I shook my head.

'They think I am common woman with short skirts and big titties. They think I not love Robin. They think I want his money, not his dick.'

Well, that seemed a fairly accurate summary of what the village thought.

'I'm not sure that's entirely true,' I said, nevertheless.

'Which bit not true?'

'I don't think any of it is true, really. I'm sure you did want his . . . I mean that you wanted him for himself. Not his money. The rector said that Robin had finally found true love.'

18

'Huh!' she replied. 'He does not mean it. As you say in your country . . . it grinds my goat to hear it. But I am not deceived. Robin's family is oldest in the village. He is rich. I am not worthy of him. So they kill him.'

'They killed him to stop him marrying you?'

Catarina looked into the distance as if seeing something that I could not. 'Yes, I think so.'

'You mean the whole village?'

'Of course not. You really think a whole village plots to kill somebody? Is that what is in your crime books?'

Actually I *had* used that plot, sort of, but it didn't seem terribly relevant now. I couldn't see why anyone would actually want to prevent the marriage – let alone kill Robin to do so. Who could possibly gain by it?

'Sorry – it makes no sense,' I said. 'How does killing him help anyone?'

'Honour,' she said obscurely. 'In my country they kill for honour. Even the priests.'

I followed her gaze to where the rector, clutching half a pint of dry sherry, was in conversation with one of the local councillors. The councillor made a whirling motion with his hands and then placed them over both ears. They were probably discussing the proposed wind farm, then. Even so, neither looked likely to commit murder.

'Not here,' I said. 'Not in Sussex.'

'Everywhere,' she said. 'The church protects them. But perhaps here they would not make the priest an archbishop afterwards. That was bad. To make him a bishop, yes, of course. But an archbishop . . .'

Perhaps she had been reading too much Dan Brown.

That seemed likely. Nobody was quite sure which country Catarina came from. Most countries in Eastern Europe had been canvassed since the village became aware of her, but one of the former Soviet republics seemed likely.

'The coroner said it was an accident,' I said. 'What makes you think it wasn't?'

'I say too much in the church?'

'Gosh, no. Well, maybe a bit. It's just that it isn't normal in England . . .'

Catarina looked round the room as if suddenly worried that, by speaking to me in a loud voice about somebody present – possibly about everybody present – having murdered her fiancé, she might have attracted undue attention. 'Meet me in garden in ten minutes,' she said. 'I will explain you. I go. You follow. Not good we are seen going into bushes together. Not at funeral.'

Then she was gone. I stood for a moment, wondering which of the little groups of sherry drinkers to join for the required period of time. Before I could decide between the rector's wind farm discussion and some people I knew from the film club, Tom Gittings wandered up, clutching an orange juice.

'That was a very earnest conversation you were having with Catarina.'

'She thinks Robin was murdered,' I said.

'Yes, she mentioned it in passing during the funeral service. Did she say much more than that to you?'

'Are you asking me in your capacity as a journalist or as a friend?'

'Strictly as a friend. I've done all the reporting I'm

planning to do on Robin's death. I can't say I enjoyed having to cover the inquest for the *Observer*.'

I nodded sympathetically. Tom had known Robin well. Too well to be comfortable producing dispassionate copy for the local paper. 'She's going to explain it to me in the garden,' I said. 'But she thinks the family wanted him dead rather than married to her.'

'What family? Robin was the last of the line.'

'No great uncles? No third cousins?'

'Nobody that I know of. Robin was the only child. His father was the only survivor of a number of children – he had brothers but they were killed in the last war. Same with the previous generation – you can check out the village war memorial for the exact names. There was also a daughter – can't remember what she was called – died in the influenza epidemic of 1919. The succession of Paghams has been hanging by a thread for some years. Maybe if you did some genealogical research back into the nineteenth century you'd come up with something, but the chances of their even knowing about the engagement would be slim. I doubt they'd have any legal claim to the estate. Not good enough for it to be worth committing murder on the off chance a court would find in their favour.'

'I knew you were a friend of Robin's,' I said. 'I didn't know you were so well up on his family history.'

'Difficult not to be. We're both local. His family and mine have lived side by side for hundreds of years, ploughing furrows on adjacent strips of land, mending hedges, stealing each other's cattle.'

'Actually stealing cattle?'

'Well, sheep at least.'

'All very neighbourly.'

'Yes, most of the time,' said Tom. 'Dad and Robin certainly got on well. They both sailed. They shared a love of the sea . . . and other things. But our two families haven't always seen eye to eye, as you probably know – and I doubt if we know all the Pagham family secrets. Still, I can assure you absolutely that there are no known relatives. And that the coroner said it was accidental death.'

'There were rumours that he had been drinking,' I said.

Tom shook his head. 'I was there for the whole inquest. Nothing said about alcohol.'

'I read your report,' I said. 'But editors cut things.'

'It's one of the hazards of the trade,' said Tom. 'And you're right, of course. What I wrote was much longer and the editor cut it to a couple of paragraphs. But he cut nothing of any real interest. Anyway, even without an autopsy report, I knew Robin. So did my father. Dad would have told me if Robin had ever set sail under the influence. According to the coroner, he'd eaten a good meal and drank some coffee. No booze at all. His death is odd because nobody knew the coast round here like he did. But there's no reason to believe it wasn't an accident. It must have been a freak wave or something – overturned the boat.'

'He would have had a life jacket on?'

'Yes, of course. He was still wearing it when his body was washed up two days later.'

I paused and wondered what the body would have looked like. Perhaps it was as well that Tom had been restricted to a couple of paragraphs, leaving out much of the detail he'd had to sit through. Not that he wouldn't have made it interesting. He was, in fact, a talented writer with ambitions that went beyond his current rather junior role in Chichester.

'How's the book coming on?' I asked.

'Almost finished. I suppose you couldn't put in a good word for me with your agent?'

'I don't have an agent,' I said.

'I thought you dedicated one of your books to your wonderful agent, Elsie Thirkettle?'

'I switched to somebody else. But it didn't work out – the new agent, I mean. I always felt I was a bit too much under Elsie's thumb but the new one was . . . even more difficult. It's a long story.'

'I'm sorry to hear that. So, no agent at the moment. Could you go back to Thirkettle?'

'I doubt it, but I don't need an agent. I'll let you have Elsie's contact details, if you like. I can't pretend I have any influence with her these days – if I ever did have any. She'll probably just say, send in a covering letter, three chapters and a synopsis.'

'Is that standard practice?'

'It used to be. I'm out of touch. It's a while since I had to do that sort of thing. You have to remember you are at the beginning of a glorious career in literature. I'm at the end of one and it wasn't especially glorious.'

'But you're still writing books?'

'Yes, you never stop writing books.'

'Catarina's out in the garden,' said Tom. 'She seems to be waving at you.'

'It's time to go and meet her inconspicuously,' I said.

'Good luck with that,' said Tom.

The garden was more than a little overgrown. Robin had discontinued the services of his father's gardener as soon as he decently could. The grass must have been cut by somebody sometime in the autumn, but wet bushes overhung the lawns and weeds snaked thick stems across the unswept gravel. In the distance, beyond the perimeter hedge, I thought I could make out the dark water of Chichester Harbour and, far beyond that, the misty line of the Downs. Once, with its winding paths, its summer house and its hedged seating areas, it must have been a place where two elegantly dressed people could have an assignation under the stars. Not so now. Fortunately the light was good enough to avoid the obvious snares and only one of us was elegantly dressed. I was still in a damp Barbour, but Catarina's black dress was uncreased and spotless. I wondered if she had had a second one to change into on her return to the house. I was sure that she had worn no coat for the interment. Though she had sheltered under a large black umbrella, the rain at the church had been almost horizontal at times. She must have been as wet as the rest of us.

Here in the garden a low sun had broken through and for a few moments we had that heady spectacle of dazzling light on dark-grey clouds.

'Very attractive grounds,' I said. 'I've always liked azaleas.'

She looked around as though she had not previously noticed. 'Good soil. Good for sugar beet,' she said, knowledgably. 'Good for red cabbage too. I think so.'

'Robin owned a lot of the land round here.'

'He did not farm it.'

'He rented it out,' I said. 'I don't know who to.'

'To the peasants.' She spat these last words over the euonymus in a way that should have made its roots wither.

I wondered again which country she came from. It must have had a communist government within her lifetime. If so, she seemed to be largely untouched by the usual prejudices of Marxism–Leninism.

'Are you saying that it was one of these people – his tenants – who killed him?'

She shook her head. 'I do not know who – only that he was murdered.'

'How do you know?'

'Two things.' She held up a forefinger and thumb. 'First, the coffee cups. And second the old man.'

'You've lost me,' I said.

'But soon you will find. On day Robin was killed, I go into Chichester. I have not planned to go, but Robin said he is sailing and I should go shopping. He give me money and say, go buy things.'

'He was always very generous.'

'No. He was not. He was mean bastard. He does not like to spend money. But that morning he give me. So, why give me? Why say go? Why not be mean bastard?'

'I don't know,' I said. 'But you went?'

'Yes, I go. I buy some few small things. I have lunch. I come back. Robin has gone sail. But there are two cups on the table in the sitting room.' She looked at me significantly.

'You mean somebody visited him while you were out?' I tentatively suggested.

Catarina regarded me in much the same way that she had when I suggested that the whole village might have killed Robin.

'Of course. What else? One man may drink much coffee but he needs only one cup. This is true everywhere, I think.'

'And he didn't say he was expecting somebody?'

'No. But I think he knows this somebody person is coming. That is why he give me money to go to Chichester. That is why he is not mean bastard. He wants me gone. Even if costs money.'

'Maybe he made a note somewhere of who he was expecting. Did he have a diary?'

'On his phone. He had it in boat. Is gone.'

'So, on the morning he died, somebody visited him here? Somebody he didn't want you to see?'

'Yes.'

I considered this carefully in the light of what I knew of Robin. 'Any lipstick on the cup?'

'None,' said Catarina.

'You checked?'

'Of course. Any woman would check.'

'Maybe he might have wiped it off?'

'You can always tell.'

'So a man . . . or a woman without make-up, of course.'

'What woman does not wear make-up?'

'Some don't.'

Catarina shook her head. Such a woman was no threat to anyone. 'A man, I think.'

'Is this the old man you referred to?'

Catarina shook her head again. 'No, that is I think another somebody. What does it mean in your language: "the old man"?'

'In what sense?'

'Robin – like I say, he is always mean with money. He is man in Christmas story who meets ghost, but Robin not believe in ghosts. One day we argue about it. He say, don't worry. When Old Man dies we will have plenty. And he smile. Like this.'

The smile was crooked and faintly lecherous. I had no doubt it was an accurate portrayal of Robin's expression, but it still gave few clues as to whom the 'old man' might be.

'His father?' I suggested. 'I mean, colloquially "the old man" might mean "my father" or equally "my husband" – you know, "my old man said follow the van".'

Catarina looked at me suspiciously. 'You have husband?'

'Sorry – forget the husband bit. In Robin's case, and indeed in mine, only the former of those would apply. So maybe he meant when his father died he would inherit . . .'

'Father already dead then. Cannot be him.'

'Yes, of course. An uncle, then? A godfather?'

She shook her head impatiently. 'No uncles. No godfather I think.'

'But Robin was waiting for somebody to die, who would leave him some money?'

'Yes. That is what I say. You not listen so good?'

'My hearing is fine, actually. And I do see what you mean. But what I don't understand is this: wasn't Robin

27

actually pretty well off? I mean, we all assumed he had plenty of cash – the land, this house. He was one of the richest men in the village – for all I know, one of the richest in the county.'

'He need to pay tax when his father died. I ask: why not bribe officials? Is easy. Is cheaper. Always. Only idiot pays tax. But he says his lawyers say he must pay. They have already informed government how much money his father had. Fools! That they should tell them such things! I say, maybe lawyers lie to government? But Robin say these lawyers do not know how to lie. Can you believe that? Did they learn nothing at law school? So Robin has much land but no money.'

'What about the rent he was getting?'

'He owes it all to the government because of idiot lawyers.'

'He could have sold some land to pay the inheritance tax.'

'You never sell land,' said Catarina. It seemed the one point that she and Robin had been agreed on. 'Land is for always.'

'Somebody who was about to leave him money would hardly kill him,' I said.

'So, who is the person? I ask Robin's friends, but they do not know. What do you think, Ethelred – why does Robin believe he will get money when Old Man dies?'

'Maybe not a legacy, then,' I said. 'Maybe something else . . .'

'What?'

'I don't know,' I said. 'Perhaps his lawyer could tell

you? I agree that it's odd Robin died just before this legacy or whatever it was arrived, but it doesn't mean the two things are connected. It's odd he died, full stop. He was an experienced sailor.'

'Yes, much too odd. That is why you must investigate.'

'I'm a crime writer, not a detective.'

'But somebody tell me you have investigated crime before?'

'In real life? Once or twice. I'm not good at it. Tell the police about your suspicions – they're much better at real-life crime than I am – much better all round.'

'I have told them. Police ask for the cups. I say, in dishwasher. Do they think I leave dirty cups around house? Police say who is Old Man? I tell police, is their job to find out. Police say, they don't take orders from me. Police say they don't take orders from me even if I bribe. They say coroner says accident. Police say, is good enough for them and don't try to bribe coroner or big trouble.'

'They're probably right,' I said.

Catarina's shrug left it unclear exactly how much she had offered the coroners. 'So, you won't help?' she demanded.

'I can't,' I said. 'I'm sorry.'

The sky had darkened considerably while we had been talking. The clouds menaced above us. Before, they had been brilliantly grey and had shimmered in the late afternoon light. Now they were dull and threatening. A sudden gust of wind animated the bushes and sent an empty plastic watering can skittering across the lawn, where it came to rest against the sundial.

'We'd better get inside,' I said.

'Yes, you go,' she said. 'It is too hot for you.'

'Cold,' I said, thinking to correct her English, but she just looked at me.

I felt it was unchivalrous to leave her standing in the middle of the lawn, but it was, after all, her lawn and her choice. The first drops of rain had started to fall by the time I regained the house. The party was, I noticed, already over. Only a few stragglers remained. Most were clearly about to leave but one was peering out into the damp garden as if searching for something. He was a large man – not fat or muscular, but simply large. He moved slightly awkwardly, as if sixty-odd years of being that size still took him by surprise, but that he might get the hang of it eventually. I knew him slightly. He fell into that annoying category of people whom I've met too often to be able to ask their name but not often enough to actually remember it.

As I entered, he sort of shuffled round to face me. 'Is Catarina out there?' he asked.

'She was a moment ago,' I said.

'Is it raining?'

We both looked out of the window, making any reply redundant.

'A bit,' I said, as we watched the cold drizzle splash against the grimy glass.

He nodded. 'I might go and find her – just to thank her. For the sherry, you know . . .'

'Of course,' I said.

As I watched him step ponderously and cautiously through the long grass in the fast-fading light, I finally remembered – he was called Barry something or other. Barry

30

*Whitelace*, that was it. Like me he was a new-ish arrival. And his wife's name was Jean – I remembered that because on most of the occasions we'd met he'd apologised that Jean wasn't with him. And others in the village had mentioned him to me, because he had the reputation for being a bit of a busybody. He had taken up cudgels on behalf of his new village at every possible opportunity, whether the village had wanted his help or not. He'd been at the anti-fracking demonstrations earlier in the year. The threat had been to a field on the other side of the county, but that was, as he'd once said to me, still too close. I'm not sure what constituted far enough away – Kent possibly, or Lithuania. He'd also spoken out against the wind farm proposal that I'd seen the rector talking about. Whitelace felt strongly about all sorts of things. I didn't know what Jean thought about anything. She clearly didn't get out much.

Through the window I could still just see Whitelace making his way across the garden in search of his hostess. It occurred to me that I hadn't thanked her myself, but the rain was becoming heavier and I didn't fancy getting wet all over again. Even more to the point, I didn't want to resume our discussion of my skills as a detective. In the absence of anyone else to say my farewells to, I nodded in a friendly way to one of the waiters, who looked up briefly from his phone and then returned to texting. I found my way to the front door without further assistance.

My first thought was to get into my car and drive back to the village. Then I noticed a sailing boat on a trailer, parked by the side of the house. I had been told that the boat had been recovered but I had not heard where it was.

Somebody had delivered it back home, where it now looked somewhat forlorn. I pulled up the collar of my Barbour and walked over to it.

An inch or so of greenish rainwater in the hull suggested that it had been there a few days. It had clearly washed up on the beach bows first – the front end bore numerous gouges and scratches. The sails had gone – perhaps they had been removed before it had been transported back to the house. The mast, to my eye, looked a little bent. The centreboard was damaged and the rudder was wholly missing. Still, mast apart, it looked repairable, if anyone had wanted to repair it. But in all likelihood it had undertaken its final voyage. So who had called for coffee on the day it set sail for the last time? And what was the money that Robin had stood to inherit?

I glanced around to see if there was any sign of Tom. He might just know who this 'old man' was. Not that it was any concern of mine, of course. None at all. But he had gone. I could catch him tomorrow. I had an excuse for dropping by.

# CHAPTER THREE

'I checked the website,' I said. 'It's all electronic submissions now, apparently. Still three chapters and a synopsis, though. I'll email her and ask her to look out for your submission.'

'She probably gets a lot of them,' said Tom.

'About two hundred a week, so she claims.'

'How many does she take in a typical week?'

'None at all,' I said. 'Maybe half a dozen a year.'

'That's encouraging.'

'Sorry. I hate to disillusion you so early on, but it really is as bad as that. Welcome to the world of publishing.'

'No, I meant it. It's encouraging. I can be one of those half-dozen.'

I looked at him. Once, I thought, I had been like that. Now, if I'd been told that Elsie accepted ninety-eight per cent of submissions, I would have just assumed I'd be one of the two per cent rejected. I'd probably be right, too. Elsie had not forgiven me for deserting her and signing up with one of her rivals.

'I had an interesting talk with Catarina,' I said. 'She wanted me to investigate Robin's murder.'

'Do you do that sort of thing?'

'No, I don't do that sort of thing. Well, hardly ever. And definitely not this time.'

'Quite right. If there was anything suspicious the police would have picked it up. It would have been mentioned at the inquest.'

'Absolutely. One thing she said was odd, though – Catarina thought Robin was about to inherit some money – "when the old man dies", he had apparently said. You've no idea who that could be?'

'None at all. I said that Robin had no close family.'

'It didn't need to be close family. They just had to be . . . well . . . old, I suppose. A friend perhaps?'

'Robin had plenty of friends. The crowd he hung around with in London – I doubt many of them had money or that they would have left it to him if they had. As for Sussex . . . one or two members of the sailing club are fairly rich, by most people's standards, but they have families to leave their cash to. They might include a favourite charity or two in their wills, or their old college, but they'd hardly hand it over to Robin to fritter away.'

'So nobody who would willingly leave him a life-changing sum of money?'

'Not willingly.'

We were both silent for a moment.

'Unwillingly?' I asked.

'Blackmail, you mean?'

'It would be a motive for murder.'

Tom shook his head. 'Not Robin. He wasn't the sort to stoop to that. At least, I don't think so. He'd have probably tried almost anything short of blackmail to raise funds, of course. He'd talked to Dad about creating a wind farm just outside the village. That didn't make him popular round here.'

'The wind farm? The one Barry Whitelace was objecting to? How did your father fit into that?'

'I think Dad was going to sell him the land. Robin was going to build the windmills and run it. But it won't happen now.'

'That could be what Barry Whitelace wanted to talk to Catarina about,' I said. 'He'd have wanted to know if there's any chance she would still go ahead with it.'

'It's definitely off,' said Tom.

'Are you sure?'

'Absolutely. Even before he died Robin had gone cold on the idea. You think the village might have clubbed together and bumped him off to prevent a wind farm? That's perfectly possible, of course. If you decide to take this on, you'll need to question everyone.'

'The whole village? I don't think so,' I said. 'Catarina's already ruled that theory out, at least. Of course, I don't think Robin was murdered at all.'

'Nor do I. But if he had been, then I wouldn't necessarily ignore the whole-village scenario. Feelings are still running very high indeed.'

'So I gather. Anyway, I'm not investigating anything. Catarina mentioned one other thing, though . . .'

'About the case you're not investigating?'

'I can still be curious about it, can't I? She said that Robin had persuaded her to go into Chichester that day. While she was out, he'd had a visitor – just before he set out in the boat.'

'That wasn't mentioned at the inquest, either,' Tom said.

'I think the police didn't follow it up.'

'Why?'

'I doubt they would have thought it relevant to a sailing accident some hours later. I also don't think they were impressed by Catarina's attempt to bribe them.'

'Probably right about its relevance. I mean, Robin was alone in the boat, as far as we know.'

'Any idea who the visitor was, though?'

'Why should I know that?'

'You covered the inquest. You heard all of the evidence. You probably know the village as well as anybody. You know who Robin's friends were. You are probably better qualified than anyone to make a guess.'

'Like I say, it didn't come up at the inquest at all – not in any form. As for the rest, Dad knew Robin much better than I did.'

'So I should ask your father?'

'You could. He's getting a bit deaf these days, so you'd have to be patient. And he forgets more than he remembers. But I'm sure he'd try. And you mustn't be put off if he gets irritable – he's like that a lot.'

It was not very encouraging. Anyway, I already knew Colonel Gittings a bit – we'd met at the monthly film club a couple of times, and once at a village fete. He hadn't been very friendly on those occasions – a fact I'd put down to my being a new arrival, though he may have disliked me for all sorts of reasons. I'm not sure he rated writers very highly. On each of those occasions, we'd exchanged only half a dozen words. Later, when we'd passed each other in the street, he had shown no sign of recognising me and my half-hearted greeting had gone unacknowledged. I wasn't that keen on trying to renew the acquaintance. And I wasn't sure what good it would do me to know, anyway. I wasn't getting involved. I'd made that clear to Catarina.

'But your father was a close friend?' I asked.

'Yes – very much so – they saw each other quite often at the sailing club.'

'But . . .' I tried to remember what Tom had said before. 'You mentioned something about the families not always seeing eye to eye?'

Tom looked at me blankly.

'When we were at Greylands,' I said.

'Oh, that . . .' said Tom. 'But you must know the story – it's in at least one of the local history books. I was forgetting you're a newcomer.'

'I'm rarely allowed to forget it,' I said.

'The Gittingses have owned land in the parish since the seventeenth century at least,' said Tom. 'But we're recent arrivals compared with the Paghams. It's recorded that Sir Walter de Pagham held three fiefs by knight's service in Pagham, Earnley and West Wittering during the reign of King John.'

'Fair enough. I'll have to stick around a bit longer before I qualify as a local. So what was the cause of friction between you? Punch up over a leylandii hedge? Or was it the sheep stealing you mentioned?'

'No, nothing that serious. Just murder.'

'Murder? What, one of your ancestors killed one of his?'

'The other way round, according to the judge. One of his killed one of mine. Actually it was a great-great-great-great-uncle in my case. It's quite a well-known story in the village, because it occasioned the last public hanging in these parts. I could tell you all about it if you're interested. There's a possible miscarriage of justice angle to it. It might make a good plot for your next book – that could be more profitable than acting as Catarina's gumshoe.'

'Yes, in the sense that Catarina's offering me no fee of any sort. You don't want the story for a book of your own?'

'I don't write crime novels. Anyway, delving in family history like that for fun and profit seems a bit in bad taste. And of course, you may decide there's not much to it. Lancelot Pagham's motives were never revealed. If he really was guilty, then it was just a bit of senseless Victorian violence.'

'Most real crime is,' I said. 'Senseless violence, I mean. It's only in books that there is a decently convoluted motive, disputed wills, missing relatives and proper red herrings.'

'You find that a convoluted plot and lots of red herrings are a winning formula?'

'Not so far,' I said. 'But I'll keep trying. I'll also email Elsie and let her know your manuscript is on its way. She may not represent me any more, but at least she'll recognise the name.'

# CHAPTER FOUR

## Elsie

*Dear Mr Smith,*
*Thank you for your recent letter enclosing a copy*
*of your manuscript* OUT OUT BRIEF CANDLE. *I am*
*grateful to you for telling me that you were writing*
*in the style of Hilary Mantel, because I would never*
*have guessed that from the book itself. By the same*
*token, there was no need at all to tell me that it had*
*already been rejected by twenty other agents.*

*All great literature raises questions in one's mind*
*and the question your book raises is what you were*
*doing at school when everyone else was studying*
*English? You must have had an awful lot of fun*
*behind the bike sheds. Even by today's lamentable*
*standard your grammar and spelling are pretty*
*average. Your plotting makes me wonder if you have*
*actually read a novel, other than your own, from*
*beginning to end.*

*You ask if, in the unlikely eventuality of my rejecting it, I could give you some feedback on your book. Perhaps you are already realising that this may not be as good an idea as you thought. But I should be delighted to give you some advice.*

*First, before you approach any agent, do take a look at their website. Mine says first three chapters, covering email, electronic submissions only. But you have sent me an envelope full of what appears to be the complete novel on heavy-duty paper. And no return postage. Perhaps you believe (many people do) that agencies are run on charitable lines and that I have a fund for returning unsolicited material and that you will get it back shortly. I don't and you won't.*

*Second, before you approach any agent, do take a look at their website. Mine says to use double spacing and Courier or Times New Roman for your typescript. What is that quaint typeface that you managed to find? It did at least distract me from the abysmal storyline, so I suppose all was not lost.*

*Third, before you approach any agent, do take a look at their website. Mine says read through your manuscript for errors before sending it out. Of course, what I should have said was to read through the manuscript for errors and then correct them. So that one is entirely my fault. I apologise unreservedly.*

*Fourth . . .*

'Sorry, Elsie, can I interrupt you?'

'You have interrupted me, so clearly yes, you can do

that. Was there anything else you wanted to know?'

Tuesday looked at me blankly. 'Sorry . . .'

'I was writing a rejection letter,' I said. 'It is important to write them with care. I like to let the authors down gently.'

'Me *too*. I think that's *so* important. Did you find a few nice things to say to him?'

'The letter is every bit as nice as he deserves. What did you want me for?'

'Oh, Ethelred Tressider has just emailed. He said you would remember him . . .'

'Ethelred who?'

'His surname's Tressider.'

'What's his first name?'

'Ethelred.'

I paused briefly and frowned. 'Does he write crap police procedurals set in the fictional town of Buckford, a place that has not changed since the mid-50s in any respect at all, a bit like Ethelred himself? Does he also write historicals featuring Geoffrey Chaucer, which give him unrivalled opportunity to spout Middle English poetry, thus lowering the tone of an otherwise average crime novel?'

'Yes,' said Tuesday, brightening up, as she always does given the slightest encouragement.

'Nope, still can't place him,' I said.

'He used to be one of our authors,' said Tuesday, 'but he left us for Janet Francis.'

'Oh *that* Ethelred Tressider,' I said. 'What does he want? I suppose he's come crawling back, asking us to represent him again?'

'Why?'

'Because Janet Francis dumped him – or he dumped her. That's the word on the street. One or the other. He's well dumped, anyway. Just tell him to piss off.'

'He's not asking you to represent him.'

'No? What does he want then?'

I opened my emergency chocolate drawer and rummaged around, while Tuesday chattered happily to herself. Mars Bar or Kit Kat? A tricky choice. If I was to have to consider Ethelred's problems then the extra glucose in the Mars Bar would probably help. So, Mars Bar it was, then. But possibly with the Kit Kat in reserve? All of the carbs in that biscuit base to keep my brain ticking over . . .

'And a friend of his has written a book,' Tuesday continued. 'He's planning to send it to you.'

'Brilliant. A bigger slush pile. Just what I need. You've made my day.'

Tuesday pulled a face. I'd taught her about irony. She no longer assumed I always meant it when I said she'd made my day, in the way she did when she first joined me as my assistant. For some weeks she must have thought I was very, very easily pleased. And that most manuscripts we received were brilliant. Now she knew better. 'He thinks you'll enjoy it,' she said cautiously.

'Yeah, right. As if.'

'Ethelred says his friend writes for the *Observer*.'

'The *Chichester Observer*?' I said, unwrapping the Kit Kat.

'Ethelred doesn't say. Shall I tell him not to send it?'

I hesitated. You need to kiss a lot of frogs in this business. 'Say I'm looking forward to it with excitement,' I said.

'Is that irony?'

'You're learning.'

I looked at her, standing there, so eager to please anyone in any way.

'Just in passing,' I said, 'did you mean it when you said it's important to let rejected writers down gently?'

'Yes, of course.'

'No, really.'

'Yes, really.'

'OK,' I said. 'Just checking.'

# CHAPTER FIVE

'So, did you investigate my murder?'

I looked at Tom blankly for a moment. I had just been emphasising again the synopsis and three chapters thing and the importance of following Elsie's directions to the letter. In particular I had been explaining that, while Elsie would never rule out anything on a technicality if it looked likely to make her money, failure to observe her instructions at the outset would never be entirely forgotten. It would be stored away, in a safe, dry place, for Elsie's future use. He might expect, perhaps many books into their relationship, to receive an arch observation that he'd never been able to count up to three. But Elsie rarely killed an author who might still have a book or two in them, and I didn't think that could be what the threat referred to.

'*Your* murder?' I said. 'You mean . . .'

'My ancestor. John Gittings. I said I thought it would make an interesting subject for a book.'

'Yes, of course,' I said. I wondered if by ordering another round I could change the subject, but our glasses were both almost full. The problem is that people imagine all sorts of incidents will make an interesting subject for a book, but most won't. The thing that is so amusing encapsulated in two hundred words quickly palls when expended to seventy or eighty thousand, just as the startling headline in the paper – 'Scandal Hits Chichester Council', say – often promises very much more than it is able to deliver. The trick for the fiction writer is to take the mundane, the everyday, and write it so that it grips the reader's attention. Most real-life murders are depressingly similar. Tom had said himself that his ancestor's death had appeared motiveless. Just one of several thousand murders between 1837 and 1901. A golden age in some respects – Sergeant Cuff, Mr Whicher, Sherlock Holmes. But in other respects not so much . . .

'So, you think you can use it?' Tom asked, for some reason misinterpreting my guarded silence as wild enthusiasm.

I sighed. This was, after all, his own family. I had to show a bit of polite interest. 'Why don't you tell me a little more about it?' I said.

Tom nodded and took a preparatory sip of beer. Then, in a practised manner that owed perhaps to his being a reporter, he began. 'OK. Well, my ancestor, if an uncle can properly be called that, was found stabbed to death in the Herring Field – that's a parcel of marshy land down by Chichester Harbour, where in the distant past they smoked herring. Or so the story goes. Possibly they did just that – it's not much use for anything else. These days, it's used for nothing at all. He – my ancestor – was found face down in the long grass. A fisherman's knife was discovered close by, in a pool of stagnant water, blade uppermost, half hidden in a patch of reeds.'

He paused and looked at me.

'OK so far,' I said. 'The stagnant water with the blade sticking out of it is a nice touch – a sort of Excalibur moment. Were there any suspects apart from this Lancelot that you referred to?'

'Lancelot – Robin's ancestor – was the owner of both the field and the knife. He never denied either fact, but said he had missed the knife the previous day. He thought he might have dropped it on the village green while he was mending his nets. He hadn't been to the Herring Field for about a week, so he couldn't have left it there.'

'It wasn't entirely cut and dried then?' I asked.

'No, it was the herrings that were cut and dried . . . Sorry, I'll steer clear of the puns, shall I?'

'It's your story,' I said. 'Cheapen it as much as you wish.'

'What I meant to say,' Tom continued, 'was that you are quite right. It was all very far from proven. But there was never more than one suspect. And the only hard evidence was the knife.'

'Witnesses?'

'No.'

'So, you think they got the wrong man?'

'The evidence wouldn't have convicted somebody these days.'

'And the name of the murdered man – your ancestor?'

'John Gittings.'

I took out my notebook and jotted both names down,

47

then closed it and allowed the elastic to snap back into place. 'So, in the absence of any real evidence, how did they prove that he'd done it?' I asked.

'As far as the jury was concerned, the fact that it was his knife was pretty much conclusive. No DNA then or fingerprinting. No CCTV. A bloody knife thrown down in haste beside a lifeless body was plenty – that and the fact that the Gittings were the richest family in the village in those days. If we swore it must have been one of them there Paghams, then it must have been one of them there Paghams.'

'So your family swore under oath that it was Lancelot Pagham?'

'Yes, they did swear – and very much under oath – but not intentionally.'

'So how do you swear under oath accidentally?'

'John's brother George gave evidence at the trial that, the same morning, he'd seen Lancelot Pagham walking towards the church – in the opposite direction to the Herring Field. He actually tried to say that it couldn't have been him.'

'That was helpful under the circumstances – it was after all his brother who had been done in.'

'I'm sure he intended to be helpful but, as the judge pointed out, there was a shortcut from the church down to the coast. All George had done was to prove that Lancelot was out and about just before the time of the murder. The detour via the church might have cost him five minutes, but not more. Plenty of time to do the murder and get back home.'

'Not as helpful as all that, then.'

'Not to the accused, anyway. George tried to protest that he had been misunderstood, but was told to sit down.

The jury seems to have placed some weight on George's testimony, albeit not in the way he meant it. They say George was guilt-stricken for the rest of his life. He was never quite the same man after the trial. He died in 1875 – exact causes unknown.'

'George didn't believe Lancelot Pagham was guilty then?'

'I suppose not. Or if he did believe it, he'd still tried to save him and failed miserably.'

'But why would he particularly want to save him if he didn't have good reason for thinking him innocent? Lancelot Pagham was a fisherman, you say?'

'Yes.'

'And John Gittings was the lord of the manor or something?'

'Not quite. He was a farmer and a big landowner.'

'But still – not likely to be close friends with a poor fisherman.'

'No. But Lancelot's brother, Perceval Pagham, worked for the Gittings family. He was a labourer on their farm.'

'OK – that makes a bit more sense, then. So, George tried to save the brother of one of his employees, who had been wrongly accused? I can understand that. But, and I have to come back to this, the person murdered was still *his own brother*. He'd have had to be pretty convinced they'd got the wrong man.'

'Yes, as you say, he'd have had to be fairly certain to have intervened like that. Otherwise, he should have been shouting for Lancelot Pagham to be strung up, as everyone else was. But family tradition holds that, after the trial, he never smiled again. So, we have to assume he knew something. Maybe something he couldn't reveal at the trial.'

'Did Lancelot Pagham appeal?'

'I don't think people did in those days. Once convicted you were hanged in short order. Justice was a lot more efficient then.'

'At least two Sundays had to elapse between judgement and hanging,' I said. 'I think I remember reading that somewhere, anyway. Time for repentance.'

'Very useful if you were actually guilty,' said Tom. 'Not so much if you were innocent.'

'True enough. And how exactly are you related to George Gittings, the brother who gave the helpful evidence? Another uncle?'

Tom frowned and counted on his fingers. 'He was my great-great-great-great-grandfather.'

'That's quite a few greats attached to both the grandfather and the uncle. When was the murder? 1850s? 1860s?'

'1848. It's mentioned in the local guidebooks.'

I took out my notebook again and jotted down the year and the date of George's death – 1875. George had had twenty-seven conscience-stricken years, then. Plenty of Sundays for repentance if he had indeed concealed something at the trial.

'So, you think you can use it?' asked Tom.

'I didn't think so at first. To be perfectly honest, Tom, I was listening only out of politeness to begin with. But maybe, after all . . . It's an interesting case, if it really was a miscarriage of justice. Particularly in view of George's failed attempt to save the man accused of killing his own brother. And the idea that he knew more than he told the court. But why not just denounce the real killer if he knew what had happened? What was stopping him? And if he was only guessing – that somebody else *might* have done it – why did he take it so badly that he failed to save Lancelot?'

'There would be more on it in the library in Chichester, of course.'

'Yes, I suppose there would be.'

I noticed Tom had finished his beer. 'My round,' I said. 'I think I can use that after all.'

'Excellent,' said Tom. 'Has Catarina spoken to you again about investigating Robin's death, by the way?'

'She phoned me,' I said. 'I made it clear there was nothing I could do.'

'Quite right,' said Tom. 'The coroner's verdict was very clear. No room for reasonable doubt.'

'Why do you want to know that? Were you expecting her to ask me again? Has she said something to you?'

'No, not at all. It's just that, from what I've seen of her, she seems a bit persistent. She strikes me as the sort of person who usually gets what she wants. A husband, for example. Dad says once she got her claws into Robin he was never going to escape. Anyway, I'll have a pint of whatever you're having, since you're offering. Then I'll get that manuscript off to your agent.'

'My ex-agent,' I said. 'She's my ex-agent.'

# CHAPTER SIX

## Elsie

*Dear Mr Jones,*
*Thank you for submitting your manuscript. Much of it is every bit as good as* Fifty Shades of Grey. *Indeed, whole pages appear to have been copied from it word for word.*

*As for the part of the book that you may actually have written yourself – it seems to be about an exceptionally attractive author having a great deal of sex. Could that possibly be wishful thinking on your part? Many of the things you describe are, I suspect, not physically possible. They do not happen in real life. More important, they do not happen to writers in real life and your describing them in such detail will not make it any more likely that they will happen to you. I am sorry to be so blunt, but nothing in your manuscript suggests that you understand subtlety.*

*You ask for feedback. One of the most often quoted pieces of advice is to write what you know. Clearly you know* Fifty Shades of Grey *very well indeed, but that is not quite what is meant. And sadly, early nights with a hot-water bottle for company do not make for exciting reading, as I know only too well myself. That is why I do not attempt to write bonkbusters and so my advice to you, Mr Jones, is to take your laptop and stuff it . . .*

'Am I interrupting you?' asked Tuesday.

'OK,' I said. 'Let's pause and look at the evidence. There is my laptop on the desk and here's me not using it. There's a half finished sentence, sadly sitting there on the screen. I was not holding out any hopes that it would be completed by the Rejection Letter Bunny. So, two guesses as to whether you were interrupting.'

'I mean do you *mind* if I interrupt you?'

'What do *you* think?' I said.

'Shall I come back later?'

'I've no idea. You would know your intentions better than I do. If you mean do I want you to come back later . . . will you be bringing me some fatuous query from a writer that would have been easily dealt with had he or she just looked for a nanosecond at my website?'

'No.'

'Will you be bringing some fatuous query from a writer that would have been easily dealt with had he or she just looked for a nanosecond at their contract?'

'No.'

'Does it concern anyone currently under contract to us in any way?'

'No.'

'OK. Then you may try me with your question now, since you have already interrupted me and there's not much point in your going out and coming in again.'

'I've had an email from Ethelred. He says that he passed on your instructions to his friend, who is called Tom Gittings, and the manuscript will be with you shortly.'

'And he actually thinks I want to know that?'

'I assume so. He sent an email.'

'Time must weigh heavy on his hands down there in Sussex.'

'No, he seems to be very busy. He says that he is researching a miscarriage of justice that happened close to where he lives. Somebody murdered back in the 1840s. He thinks it might make a good book.'

'True crime?'

'I'm not sure. Do you want me to check exactly what he said?'

'Nope. Life is much too short. Let's just assume it's more fictional time-slip rubbish. Somebody investigating a contemporary murder who makes important discoveries using parallels with a murder long past. Honestly, it's the lowest form of mystery writing. Absolute crap. No publisher would be remotely interested.'

'Contemporary murder? No, he says that he's definitely having nothing to do with Catarina's case. She's asked him again but he's refused.'

'Catarina's case? What is that?'

'I was telling you about it the other day.'

'No, you weren't.'

'You were rummaging around in your chocolate drawer,' said Tuesday primly. 'I didn't think you were paying attention.'

'I *was* paying attention,' I said. 'But I was paying attention to *chocolate*. What is Catarina's case, when it's at home?'

'As I told you before,' she said in the same prim tones, 'somebody called Robin died recently in a sailing accident. His fiancée, Catarina, thinks it was murder. She wants Ethelred to investigate it.'

'She's asked him to do that?'

'Yes.'

'And he's said no?'

'Yes.'

'Twice?'

'Yes. That's why I said he'd refused again.'

'Tell her to get breast implants and have another go at persuading him.'

'Isn't that just a little cynical?'

'Yes, sorry. You're right. It's only a little cynical. Tell her to get breast implants *and* dye her hair blonde, then have another go.'

'I can't tell her. I don't have her email. Just Ethelred's. Unless that was irony, of course.'

'What do *you* think?'

'Was that irony too?'

'No, that was sarcasm. So, why does she think it was murder?'

'There's a lot of money involved. The whole village hates her for a number of reasons – it doesn't sound as if she needs breast implants, by the way. Some mysterious stranger visited Robin before he died. And there's a nagging doubt that Ethelred has and can't quite put his finger on.'

'Can't he? No change there then.'

'The coroner says it was an accident.'

'Coroners? What do they know about murder, eh? So, does Ethelred say that he needs my help with the impending investigation?'

'No.'

'No in what sense?'

'No in the sense that he doesn't refer to needing help from anyone at all.'

'But he'd like it anyway, deep down? He just can't quite bring himself to ask, poor lamb?'

'I don't think so. He says he's not going to investigate it.'

'Well, how could he, without my help?'

I opened my emergency chocolate drawer. It was empty. I looked accusingly at Tuesday.

'Sorry,' she said. 'I thought that I refilled it last night.'

'The chocolate drawer has to be checked twice a day,' I said. 'It's in your contract of employment.'

'Sorry,' she said. 'Shall I nip out . . . ?'

'Yes,' I said. 'You most certainly shall nip out. But first, check on hotels in West Wittering. I think I'd like a little break by the sea.'

'Won't it be cold at this time of year?'

'If winter comes, can spring be far behind?'

'The BBC was forecasting snow,' said Tuesday.

'Fair enough. Shelley always was a crap weather forecaster. I mean, if winter comes it obviously isn't spring *yet* – it's still winter. The fact that it's sunny tomorrow doesn't stop it being brass monkeys today. And what sort of weather forecaster has the middle name Bysshe? Presumably the hotels in West Wittering have heating of some sort.'

'So, I'll check hotels, then go out and buy chocolate?'

I hesitated only for a fraction of a second. 'Chocolate first,' I said. 'Then let me know all about the hotels.'

Solving murders is of course important, but they will, in my experience, often wait half an hour or so.

# CHAPTER SEVEN

I rubbed my eyes. Viewing page after page of early Victorian newspaper print on screen is tiring. At least digitisation allows for easy searching. The relevant articles hadn't taken long to track down, even if I had to squint at the screen. The trial had been well reported.

One Jane Taylor had given evidence first. She had, she said, been betrothed to the murdered man. They were due to be married later that year. Early on the day in question, she had met John Gittings in the churchyard and they had had some small disagreement. (She had burst into tears at this point and the judge had courteously given her some minutes to collect herself.) John had left her in order to return to the farm, which he had recently inherited from his father. Sometime later she had briefly seen John's brother, George Gittings. George had gone on some errand to Chichester, where he had spent the rest of the day. She was expecting to see John later, for he often visited her at her parents' house in the evening, and they would go on walks together when the weather was fine. When he did not arrive, she put it down to their earlier argument. She did not start to worry until George showed up, asking after his brother, who had not returned to the farmhouse. She knew of no quarrel between Lancelot Pagham and John Gittings. It was true that Lancelot Pagham had spoken to her a few times in the village, but there was no harm in what he had said to her – none at all, whatever people might think. She was a respectable woman. And it was well known that she was betrothed and would shortly be married. John Gittings had no enemies in the village that she knew of. He was popular with his workers, unlike his late father.

Perceval Pagham, Lancelot's brother, had next taken the stand. He had worked for the murdered John Gittings. He knew both parties well, and did not know of any reason why Lancelot and John should fight. He thought that the knife found by the body could be anyone's – it was just a fisherman's knife – but Lancelot had certainly possessed one much like it. It was always kept well sharpened. It was a good blade. He said that Lancelot did own the Herring Field though it was of little use to anyone – it flooded in the winter and nothing would grow there. It was the last remnant of the Paghams' ancient estate and Lancelot would not sell it, though John Gittings had asked him for it, since it connected two parcels of land owned by the Gittingses. But there was no dispute over the field as such. Lancelot had objected to the Gittings' cattle being driven across it, but no damage had been done because no damage could be done to such a useless patch of reeds and thistles, flooded half the year. He too was asked if John Gittings had had any enemies and replied in the negative. He had been a good man and a good master. So was his brother George, now he had in his turn inherited the farm – a very good man. He was honoured to serve him.

Oliver Cate, another fisherman, gave his evidence. He knew, he said, of no falling-out between Lancelot and John Gittings. He thought Lancelot was a proud fellow with a name that was above his station in life. He did not know if Lancelot's ancestors had previously been rich, but Lancelot often told him that they had. Somebody had once pointed out a tomb in the church as being one of Lancelot's ancestors; but, since he couldn't read, he couldn't say for sure that it was so. It was a fine tomb, though, with a knight in armour, lacking only part of his sword and his nose. The knife was certainly Lancelot's. He'd seen him use it. There was a notch on the handle that he recognised. On the day of the murder, he'd seen Lancelot Pagham on the green in the morning, but not later. He hadn't seen John Gittings at all. The following day, when the search for John Gittings had commenced, he had been the one to find his body in the Herring Field. It had been dragged into a reed bed. John Gittings had been stabbed several times, once through the heart. The knife had been abandoned close by, as if thrown there in guilty haste. The reeds and thistles close by had been trampled down, pointing to a mortal struggle on that spot. He had reported the discovery to George Gittings and then to the constable.

George Gittings then took the stand. The judge had to ask him to repeat the oath, because he had been unable to hear him the first time. Perhaps the proceedings had become a little raucous by that stage. Lancelot Pagham had called out to him from the dock: 'Look at me, George Gittings!' The judge had called for order. Gittings then proceeded to give his evidence. He was unaware of any animosity between his brother and the accused. He confirmed that 'harsh words had been spoken' about the Herring Field. But rumours of anything more than that were completely untrue, however many people may have said it. The accused was known as a haughty man but he meant no harm by it. This too must have provoked a reaction because the judge said that he would clear the court if there were further disturbances. In any case, George had added, in the phrase that would haunt him ever after, when he had last seen Lancelot Pagham he was heading *away* from the Herring Field and towards the church. Some other man must have killed his brother. Later, George said, he had gone into Chichester to purchase a plough, which had been delivered some days afterwards. When he returned home he had found the house in a state of some agitation because John had not come back. He had ridden a tired horse to Jane Taylor's cottage but all she had been able to tell him was that they had quarrelled bitterly that morning and she had not seen him since. The family had waited up all night. In the morning, search parties had been sent out. When the body had been found, he went to the Herring Field and helped bring it home. He hoped he would be excused further questioning, because he was still unwell.

A doctor gave evidence that he had examined the body and that the cause of death was a stab wound to the heart.

There were other more superficial wounds to the chest and arms. The victim's knuckles were bruised and his hands cut, as if he had resisted for a while before the fatal blow was struck.

Finally, Lancelot Pagham was questioned. It was true, he said, that his family had once been more important than it was now – there were in fact two tombs of his ancestors in the local church. Unlike Mr Cate, he could read both English and Latin, and so was in no doubt. But he set no great store by any of that. The Herring Field was his, and he had as much right to it as anyone else did to their land. The Queen herself would have to ask permission to drive her cattle across it. On the day John Gittings was killed he had gone to Itchenor on business. He had heard that a boat was for sale cheap, but when he got there nobody knew anything about it and he had returned home. Plenty of folk would have seen him in Itchenor, as they would know if the authorities had bothered to enquire properly. He knew that the constable had visited Itchenor, but suspected that he had spent all his time there in the alehouse. ('That's a lie!' from the constable.) He had not been to the Herring Field for some days. He had lost his knife the day before – he thought on the green, where he had been mending nets. It was a good knife and he had been sorry for it. Nor had he been near the church that day, even if George Gittings claimed to have seen him there. He had certainly been there the previous day. He had laid flowers on the grave of his sister, Morgan Blanch, recently deceased in childbirth. But he had not been there since.

The judge asked who had told him that a boat was for

sale. Pagham replied that somebody had left a note at his cottage. The sea was too rough for fishing that day, so he had walked over to Itchenor. Along the coast? asked the judge. No, by the Chichester Road, he replied. He had been nowhere near the field. Where had he learnt Latin? asked the judge. Pagham said he had taught himself. He didn't claim to know a lot. The judge commented that it must be very useful to him in the classification of the fish that he caught (laughter). Pagham asked the judge if he knew the Latin name for mackerel. The judge said that he did not and he very much doubted the accused did either. '*Scomber scombrus,*' said Lancelot Pagham. No reply from the judge is recorded.

The judge, having been put firmly in his place by the defendant, proceeded to instruct the jury. They were, the judge said, to bring a guilty verdict only if they were certain of their facts. There was some dispute as to whether Lancelot Pagham had been seen at the church that day – they had to decide whether to believe the testimony of the wretched man accused of murder or that of a prominent local landowner, whose respectability had been vouched for in court and who had no possible reason to lie. Had the accused walked by the church (perhaps inspecting Latin inscriptions on the way) and not directly to Itchenor as he claimed, then he would have had every opportunity to go via the bleak field that had been the scene of the murder. But it was the jury's decision. He, the judge, would not try to influence them in any way.

At this point George Gittings seems to have made some protest because he was told to be seated. Order restored, the judge continued. The existence of a continuing dispute over whether Mr Gittings' cattle could be driven across Mr Pagham's field seemed to be admitted. The jury might, if they chose, find that as a fact. The accused had, as they knew, said that he would not let the Queen herself drive cattle over his land. That seemed improbable (much laughter) but they might conclude from it that he was a proud and overbearing man, quick to take offence, and with too high an estimation of his own worth. That alone did not mean he was a murderer, of course. Nor did the fact that his parents had named him after a knight of the Round Table have any bearing on the matter. (Laughter.) Nevertheless, there was no doubt that his knife was the murder weapon. It had been identified by the notch on the handle. It had been thrown down in haste. It was for them to decide whether Pagham himself had used it or whether he had, as he claimed, rather conveniently lost it the day before. Was it likely that a fisherman would lose a valuable possession of that sort and not look for it high and low? A fisherman's knife was, they might think, like a knight's sword, a trusted companion. But Pagham had merely noticed its loss and taken no further action. Moreover, the jury should ask themselves who had benefitted from the murder – *cui bono?* – a phrase that Mr Pagham could doubtless translate for them. Mr Gittings was well loved within the village. They had ample evidence that he had no enemies. But they might think that his death relieved the accused man of a troublesome neighbour. No evidence had been given on whether the accused resented the wealth of the Gittings family and whether he might have a hatred of

John Gittings for that reason. It was probable that that was the case, but no evidence had been produced so that should not influence them in any way.

The judge paused and surveyed the jury. It was a grave duty that they had, he continued, but murder was a grave matter. Throughout Europe, as the jury knew, the lower orders were in rebellion against their betters. The King of France had been driven from his throne. Chartists had threatened to create anarchy in London. Young women in America had started wearing trousers. It was important that the murder of a prominent landowner was dealt with firmly to show that such things would not be tolerated here by the good and sensible folk of Sussex.

It was probably the threat of women wearing trousers that tipped the balance. It took the jury less than half an hour to return a guilty verdict. Lancelot Pagham was hanged before the end of the month.

I had arranged to meet Tom for lunch. He was reporting on assorted cases of shoplifting and small-scale drug-dealing and the court was not far from the library. As I was walking past the cathedral I was slightly surprised to hear my name called out. I turned. A woman in her twenties casually dressed in jeans and a warm sweater, was waving at me.

'I thought it was you. I'm Sophie Tate. We met at the funeral.'

'Yes, of course,' I said. To be specific we had met just before. She had asked me if she had come to the right place for Robin Pagham's funeral. I had told her she had. We'd agreed that the clouds looked ominous and rightly predicted that it might rain later. I must have told her my name then, because (as I now recalled) somebody else had stopped to chat and Sophie had disappeared into the church. Afterwards none of us had hung around in the churchyard. 'Yes, of course,' I said. 'Do you work in Chichester?'

'No, I'm on holiday – staying in West Wittering. I came into town to do some shopping and gawp at the cathedral. I used to go out with Robin, in case you are wondering. A bit of a coincidence my being back down here on the day of the funeral, but there you are. I always used to come here before I met him – I couldn't see any reason why I should have to stop just because we'd split up. Quite a shock to hear that Robin had died, though. I'd known him a long time. I had to be there to see him off.'

'I didn't see you at Greylands afterwards,' I said.

'No, I didn't fancy it – not with Catarina, or whatever she's called, playing the lady of the manor. I wouldn't have seen her as Robin's type, but there you are. So, I went back to the place I'm renting, had a hot shower and changed into dry clothes.'

'Did you and Robin go out for long?'

'About nine months – better than par for the course. Engaged to be married for the last two.'

'Oh, so Catarina . . .'

'Wasn't the first to receive a proposal? Far from it, I'd say. Might not have been the last, either. Robin could change his mind pretty quickly. Still, she was the one who was able to grab the seat when the music stopped. I'm told the entire Pagham estate is hers for keeps.'

'I'd wondered about that,' I said.

She shrugged. 'Well, that's how things go. You win some, you lose some. And at least he didn't break my nose.'

'You heard about that?'

'I think you'll find it's common knowledge in West Sussex. Is it true that Catarina has asked you to investigate Robin's death?'

'That's common knowledge in West Sussex too?'

'It must be, mustn't it?'

'Well, this time West Sussex is wrong,' I said. 'I'm not investigating anything.'

'Did Catarina say why she thought it was murder?'

I wondered how much to tell her. The rumour mill in the village had clearly already been working overtime. 'Nothing much,' I said. 'She just thought it inexplicable that he would have drowned like that.'

'Even if he was high at the time?'

'He'd stopped taking drugs,' I said.

'Not when I knew him.'

'It would have shown up in the coroner's report.'

'How do you know it didn't?'

'Tom Gittings covered the hearing for the *Observer*.'

She raised her eyebrows. 'Fair enough. If that's what Tom Gittings of the *Chichester Observer* says. Or what he doesn't say.'

There was a touch of contempt in this last statement.

'You know Tom?'

'A bit. He's never mentioned me, then?'

I wondered if I could rescue Tom from this omission.

'Actually, thinking about it, maybe he did mention you once or twice . . .'

'Nice try, Ethelred. But he clearly hasn't breathed a word. Another case of what Tom hasn't said. Still, I am happy to reveal I know Tom, even if he is remaining silent on the matter.'

I looked at my watch. I was already late for lunch.

'Here's my address in West Witt,' she said, scribbling something on the back of a business card. 'Drop by if you do decide to investigate on Catarina's behalf. I might actually be able to help.'

'Thanks,' I said. I gave her one of my own cards in return. It wasn't entirely a waste. She might just look at my website and maybe buy a book. But that was the most I expected to come from the conversation.

Obviously I was wrong. I mean, I'd hardly be telling you now about a chance meeting with somebody who proved to have nothing at all to do with Robin's disappearance, would I?

# CHAPTER EIGHT

'How was your morning?' I asked.

'Dull,' said Tom. 'I have detailed notes on a series of shopliftings and car thefts that I have to turn into news. The problem is making one shoplifting sound superficially different from another, or any of the shoplifters better than a two-dimensional caricature. I take your point that most real life crime is tedious in the extreme. To the extent crime fiction is based on reality, I don't quite understand its popularity.'

'It's all a question of how you tell them,' I said. 'I've done a short story on a shoplifter that worked quite well – at least, I thought it did. The motive, at least, was amusing: to return something shoplifted from another store the previous day.'

'Why?'

'He feels sorry for the shopkeeper he stole from the first time round. He no longer has the thing he stole, so he steals another one from elsewhere.'

'And he gets caught the second time?'

'No, he gets caught as he smuggles it into the first shop to place it back on the shelves. The shopkeeper recognises him. Crime writers like irony and injustice. Most crime writing isn't about crime, of course. It's about detection. It's a type of puzzle that just happens to be about murder. What makes murder a convenient vehicle is that one of the two people who know for certain what has happened is dead and the other isn't letting on – indeed the other is usually lying through their teeth.'

Tom nodded, as if storing that information away on one of the remoter shelves in his memory. Then I added: 'I ran into an old friend of yours outside the cathedral. Sophie Tate? She said she used to go out with Robin? She was engaged to him?'

The expected smile of recognition did not come. 'What else did she tell you?' he asked.

'Not a lot. But you *do* know her?'

Tom looked over towards the bar, then paused for a long time before saying: 'Yes, of course. Sophie Tate. I noticed she was at the funeral.'

'And she was engaged to Robin before he met Catarina?'

'Sort of.'

'Not officially?'

'I don't think so.'

'She also said she thought Robin was still using drugs.'

'He told me he'd given them up,' said Tom. 'Why would he say that if he hadn't? Is she around long?'

'She said she was on holiday.'

'Not just here for the funeral, then?'

72

'Complete coincidence apparently.'

'I doubt it.'

There was a hint of contempt in that last remark that was reminiscent of Sophie's observations on Tom. And I remarked that he had merely noticed her at the funeral – not actually spoken to her, which was odd if he did know her and hadn't seen her for a while. I waited to see if he would expand on his last comment but that seemed to be all he had to say on the matter. On reflection, it didn't seem worth telling him which of the cottages in the village Sophie was staying at – not if he couldn't be bothered to cross the churchyard and say hello. Perhaps they had had some past disagreement. Or perhaps it was simply that she and Tom had known each other less well than Sophie had implied. I studied the menu for a while. The sausage and mash with onion gravy looked good.

'So, how are your investigations into true crime coming on?' asked Tom, putting his own menu down.

That, rather than a discussion of the nature of crime fiction or Robin's exes, was the reason for our meeting. Tom had promised to fill in, as far as he could, any gaps in what the papers had reported back in 1848.

'I have a vague sense of unease about the whole thing,' I said. 'There was no firm evidence at all – just that George Gittings said he saw Lancelot Pagham by the church – and that the knife was Lancelot's. The argument over driving cattle across the field doesn't sound enough to occasion a murder. And where was George Gittings? Jane Taylor says quite explicitly that he was in Chichester all day. But his own testimony is that he stayed in West Wittering long enough to see Lancelot Pagham heading for the church. One of them is lying.'

'Or the reporter got it wrong,' said Tom. 'You can't assume everything was really said the way it was reported. It would have been a long day in court. You don't always catch everything – especially when you're struggling to get it all down in your notebook.'

'That's true. The judge had to warn everyone several times about the noise they were making, which can't have helped. I'm not sure what to make of the rather odd remark about Jane having talked to Lancelot Pagham. It was a small village. Everyone would have talked to everyone, surely? Was something slightly more than talking implied? Jane seems just a bit too keen to stress that she was a respectable woman about to be married to a leading landowner. The judge didn't follow it up, anyway, so I suppose we'll never know what she meant by it.'

'Not precisely,' said Tom.

'The judge seems to have taken against Lancelot Pagham quite early on. Fishermen weren't supposed to be called Lancelot or to know Latin.'

'I think Lancelot's parents were painfully aware of how much they'd come down in the world. Giving their children fancy names may have compensated a little, though I don't envy either of the brothers at school. Look at the tombstones of that period and everyone's called William or John or George, with maybe the odd Isaac or Jacob. Lancelot seems to have taught himself Latin. It was said he knew Greek as well. He'd have probably been a university professor if he'd been alive today. But the life chances for fishermen weren't that good back then, whatever they'd been baptised.'

'But it's George's behaviour that I really don't understand,' I said. 'I think he lied about having seen Lancelot at the church. He goes out of his way in his evidence to stress that rumours about Lancelot were untrue. He tries to intervene when it seems that his evidence is being misinterpreted. And yet everything he does and says seems to land Lancelot more deeply in trouble.'

'Indeed. So it does. And, as you say, where was George all day?'

'In Chichester, if Jane Taylor is to be believed.'

'But is she to be believed?' Tom opened his bag and took out an envelope from which he extracted a photograph. He passed it to me. Judging by the voluminous sleeves, the tight waist and the elaborately feathered hat, the picture dated from the last decade of the nineteenth century. The woman was, I judged, in her sixties. She was smartly dressed – clearly somebody who both cared for her appearance and had the money to buy the latest fashions. The clothes were dark – perhaps black – it was difficult to say. The sepia tones also did not reveal if her hair was blonde or grey, but not a strand was out of place. Her head was tilted slightly to one side. There was nothing in her face that constituted a smile, but her expression left you in no doubt that she was pleased with herself. Her gaze challenged the camera to do its worst.

'Jane Taylor,' said Tom. 'There's a note on the back saying that the picture was taken in 1895. She would have been sixty-four then. Her husband had died twenty years before.'

'She looks quite . . . spirited.'

'We'd probably say "feisty" these days. It's a shame we don't have one of her in 1848. I bet she turned men's heads then.'

'How did you get the picture?'

'From the family album. She's my great-great-great-great-grandmother. She married George Gittings about four months after his brother's death. George was by that time a prosperous farmer himself, having inherited everything from his murdered brother.'

'Married within four months? Quick work for those days,' I said.

'Quick work by any standards.'

'So, let's get this right: after John's death, George gets the girl, the money and the farm?'

'Exactly. *Cui bono?* as the judge so rightly asked.'

# CHAPTER NINE

Lancelot Pagham's hanging was a disappointment to everyone. It lacked the drama of the trial and gave me no further insight into the murder, even if it did strengthen my respect for the purported murderer.

Large crowds had gathered outside Horsham gaol the night before and, by the time designated for the execution, the crush in the street threatened to occasion more deaths than Pagham's alone. Enterprising citizens had rented out seats in any rooms they had overlooking the scaffold. There had been much singing and jollity up to the moment that Pagham had appeared. Sellers of cakes and ale had done a good trade. Then, according to reports, a ghastly hush had descended on the assembled multitude. Men and women gazed at the condemned man in awe. Pagham, conversely, had surveyed the crowd with something resembling contempt. He had been offered the chance to speak some last words, but declined with a shake of his head. The only thing that he was heard to say was an instruction to the executioner to get on with his task. A person in the crowd called out: 'He is innocent!' At that point Pagham turned and for a moment his eyes searched for somebody; then he went to his death 'as bravely as any man could'. The crowd dispersed apparently with grave frowns. Whether those who had paid 'upwards of five Guineas' for their seats felt they had had value for money is unclear. It had all been mercifully quick. It was devoid of any confession or of a last protestation of innocence.

Was it George Gittings who had cried out at the last moment? There was no way that I or anyone else would ever know.

It took a moment for me to realise that the noise I could hear was my phone ringing. I hurried towards the exit, muttering apologies to everyone that I passed, struggling to extract the handset from my jacket pocket as I did so.

'Hello?' I said, as soon as I was in the corridor.

'Why you not return my call, Ethelred?'

'I sent a text,' I said. 'There's nothing I can do, Catarina.'

'A text?'

I wondered if, in whichever part of eastern Europe she came from, a text was some deadly form of insult, akin to refusing to eat the eyeballs of a goat that has just been slaughtered in your honour. That seemed likely.

'I tried to phone,' I lied. 'I thought a text would be faster.'

'Faster than what?'

'I'm sorry . . . perhaps I should have come over to you . . .'

'Yes. You should come here. That is what a man would do. You are afraid of me?'

'No,' I said. But that too was a lie.

'You come tonight. I shall be waiting. I have found things that will blow your head.'

'But . . .' I said.

It's difficult speaking to somebody who has hung up. It was always one of Elsie's tricks, in the days when Elsie's tricks had anything to do with me. Of course I would go. Surely I was not afraid of visiting her? Or was it that I was more afraid of not visiting her? My phone rang again.

'What are you playing at, Ethelred? I've been trying to get through to you for ages.'

'Elsie?' I said.

'What is your phone telling you?' she asked.

'Yes, sorry,' I said. 'I can see it's your number. And your picture, because you showed me how to put that on the phone but not how to take it off. Sorry – it's just a while since we spoke. How are you?'

'Busy. Very, very busy. Busy, busy, busy. Doing deals on behalf of those fortunate enough to be represented by me. Answering fatuous queries from former clients about mates who want to write books. But I thought I might take a short break somewhere on the south coast. I was trying to decide where. What would you suggest?'

'Brighton is lively. Lots to do there. The Pavilion. The pier. Restaurants. Antique shops.'

'Too noisy. I need somewhere quieter.'

'Eastbourne?'

'I'm saving it for my old age.'

'Bognor?'

'Too pebbly.'

'Pebbly? Is it?'

'Yes. Pebbles everywhere you look. I need sand dunes. Lots of them.'

'Littlehampton is—'

'No it isn't. Littlehampton isn't anything at all. Let me think, let me think . . . That place you live in – what's it called?'

'West Wittering. You know that. You've been here before. And you still send me royalty statements, so you have the address.'

'So I do. Though not statements for your latest books, obviously, because you found another agent for those. Until she dumped you. Do you have any sand dunes in West Wittering by any chance?'

'Yes. Lots of them. For example there's—'

'Excellent. Well, if you recommend it so strongly, I'll give it a go.'

'Dorset's also very nice. For beaches.'

'Dorset? Not edgy enough. Too many yokels in smocks. Too many mayors selling their wives to passing sailors. Too many women standing on the breakwater and staring out to sea, waiting for the return of the man who cruelly betrayed them. It's a county ruined by literature. Are there any big luxury hotels in West Wittering these days?'

'No. None at all. The Beach House does B and B and has a good restaurant.'

'Is it close to the beach?'

'It's in the village centre. It's not as close to the beach as I am.'

'That's kind of you but I couldn't put you to that much trouble.'

'Sorry? What trouble?'

'"What trouble?" he says. That's so sweet. OK, if you insist.'

'Insist what?'

'If you insist it's no trouble, I'll stay with you, closer to the beach.'

'Did I say that?'

'More or less. I'll see you tomorrow afternoon, then. I'll have one of the bedrooms overlooking the garden.'

'What time are you arriving? I was planning to be in Chichester . . .'

But, as I've possibly observed before, it's tricky speaking to somebody who has hung up.

I took a deep breath and dialled. Tom answered straight away.

'Tom, I'm going to see Catarina tonight.'

'Is that wise?'

'No, but she won't stop phoning me until I do.'

'I'd be careful.'

'That thought had occurred to me too. Just one question, though – something that I've been wondering about. Do you by any chance know for certain who inherited Robin's estate? Sophie thought it was Catarina. Can that be right?'

'Yes. That's right.'

'All of it?'

'Robin changed his will shortly before he died. She got the lot. *Cui bono*, eh?'

# CHAPTER TEN

## Elsie

*Dear Ms Brown,*
*Thank you so much for submitting the summary and*
*first three chapters of your novel. The covering letter*
*was a model of what it should be. It sets out clearly*
*your background and previous writing history (well*
*done with the Bridport Prize long-listing). It is also*
*helpful to know that I am the only agent that you*
*are approaching. Sadly – it's so easily done with cut*
*and paste, isn't it? – you address the letter to Bill*
*Hamilton at A. M. Heath . . .*

'May I interrupt?'

'Yes, Tuesday, you may. I think I've already said all I
need to. As I tell my writers, you don't need to explain
every little detail. I'll email it to you to pp and send.'

'You don't want to sign it personally?'

'You think the author might prefer that?'

'Yes, I do. Absolutely. They'd know they had been taken seriously. It might lessen the pain of rejection that they're bound to feel. They will have worked on their book for years. They will be sitting there waiting for some tiny bit of praise that will make their day. And it's such a small effort on our part.'

'True, but I can't be arsed. Was that all?'

'No. I wanted to tell you I've checked hotels in West Wittering. There are in fact one or two places doing B and B—'

'Don't worry. I'm going to stay with Ethelred. He insisted.'

'Ethelred . . . ?'

'Ethelred Tressider. He used to be one of our authors. Do keep up, Tuesday.'

'Yes, of course. I just thought—'

'Just thought what? That I would cold-shoulder some author just because, having had his career carefully developed by me over many years and having had his nose wiped and his various gripes and whinges put up with, he leaves us on a whim to join some clearly inferior agency?'

'No. Absolutely not. We wouldn't be so petty – would we?'

'Do you think I would bear a grudge against Janet Francis because she stole, perhaps not my best or most respected, but certainly one of my oldest authors?'

'You did steal three of hers.'

'They had minds of their own.'

'Unlike Ethelred?'

'Your words, not mine.'

'So are you planning to sign him up again? That would be great. I've always enjoyed his books.'

'Have you? You actually *liked* some of them? Which ones?'

'I love the Master Thomas series.'

'Really? The Master Thomas series? Even though they're full of Middle English poetry?'

'Yes. I did Chaucer at uni.'

'And that didn't put you off for ever?'

'Gosh, no! Love Chaucer to bits.'

I looked at her. Either she was serious or she was getting very, very good at irony.

# CHAPTER ELEVEN

I had driven into Chichester by car and so stopping at Greylands House on my way back was easy enough. I swung off the main road shortly before it entered the village and drove along the muddy track towards the estuary. After a while the track split into two, the left-hand fork being marked 'PRIVATE', the right unsignposted. Somebody had not planned to be helpful to the merely curious. But I had been here before and needed no additional directions. The last few hundred yards to the house were on good, clean gravel, edged with overgrown grass and weeds.

Greylands was a half-timbered farmhouse, which had grown in fits and starts, a room or so on average every generation, sometimes extending laterally, sometimes making an experimental stab in some other direction. It had ended up with a broadly Tudor front, facing the track and the farmland, and a broadly Victorian rear, exposed to the salt winds and with distant views over the sleek, green marshes and tidal flats. I parked close to the front door and rang the bell.

Catarina had prepared some refreshments – strong tea flavoured with mint and very sweet cakes dripping with honey. A knowledge of eastern European cuisine might have helped me locate her place of birth.

'You are late,' she said, before I could even sit down.

'I wasn't aware we had agreed a time.'

'How long does it take to get here? Not so much, I think.'

'I had work to do. I am researching Robin's ancestors.'

'That will help find his killer? You think maybe some family feud? Yes, perhaps . . . It is like that with us too. Is not good kill somebody's grandmother. Is worse than steal horse.'

'A family feud? No. That's not how things are here. Tom thought I might be interested professionally – as a crime writer.'

'*A crime writer?*' Elsie herself could not have said the words with greater disdain.

'It's what I am. You know that. Look, if the police won't help, maybe you should employ a private detective?'

'They do cheating husband. They do divorce. They do fraud by bastard you thought was friend. Not murder.'

'You've tried them, then?'

'They are no good. Nor are Mafia.'

'You've tried them too?'

'Of course. But I need somebody who lives here. I need

somebody people will trust. People here do not trust Mafia. But if it is somebody they think is friend . . . Then maybe they say stupid thing and we catch them.'

'You want me to cynically exploit my neighbours' trust in me?'

'Yes.'

'Why should I?'

'Because Robin is your friend. You are at funeral.'

'Yes,' I said. I was at funeral.

'You would not wish his murderer to escape justice.'

'Even if Robin was murdered . . .'

'He was.'

'Even so, I still don't think I can help.'

'But you will try.'

'You don't think the Mafia might like the first shot at it, anyway?'

'You are afraid?'

'I have no idea what I am getting into.'

'If you are killed, I will make sure you are avenged. Ten will die in your place.'

'You could really arrange that?'

'Of course. Why not?'

'Which ten would die?'

'Any ten you wish. Send me text with names.'

I sighed. This conversation was not going as planned. 'You said you have new evidence?'

'I think so. Is like this. This morning I go to see Robin's lawyer. He is working on the will. I want to make sure he is not doing stupid thing – telling government how much money Robin had. He say he has good trick – quick something or other. We not pay much tax. I say good – you learn. Then, like you tell to me, I ask: who Old Man? Why Robin say we have money when he die? He look at me odd, then say: no more money. I say, why? He say, all that finished now – Old Man and money – finished; Robin must have tell you that. I say: *who is Old Man*? He say: so, Robin *not* tell you who is Old Man? I say, maybe. Yes, maybe he tell me. Of course. He tell me everything. I just want to know if there is money and if *you* know who Old Man is. He shake his head and say can't tell me any more. I say, yes he can if he doesn't want balls cut off. He say nothing. I say: I can have him killed – before or after balls cutting, whichever he prefer. He makes very worried but he say nothing. Then he look at me and say: you pregnant? What, I say, *you mean I fat*? No, he say – you not fat but maybe have baby? I say I not some stupid village girl – I don't just *have baby*. After wedding, then maybe yes. Six, seven babies, why not? But not before wedding. He think I try to trap Robin into wedding with making baby? He say no, no, no – not that. I say: what, then? Nothing, he say. Just wondering – maybe you have baby soon, even though definitely not fat. No, I say. He say: you sure? Yes, I say. You think I not know if I have baby coming? OK, he say. Just asking.'

'You think he did know who the "old man" is? And wouldn't tell you even under threat of having his balls cut off?'

'He say Law Society will cut off his balls if he tell me.'

'So he knows but can't divulge what he knows? Maybe this Old Man is also a client and he can't reveal what he has on him?'

'Maybe Old Man pay him more than I do?'

'Well, he's not saying, anyway. As for whether you are pregnant – could Robin have made provision in his will for a child? Or maybe his father set up a trust for the benefit of grandchildren as yet unborn? If so, the lawyer would have needed to know whether there might be such a child in order to carry out his work. Hence the question about pregnancy.'

'So, why not just say me that? You think lawyer is bullshit to me?'

'I think there's something he's not telling you.'

'Why?'

'I wish I knew.'

'I wish too. So, you will help me?'

I thought about this. There was a lost part of the jigsaw. Something obvious I was missing. I chewed on the last of my sticky cake and took a sip of tea. It was tempting in a way to take up Catarina's offer, but what was I supposed to do – arrive at her solicitor's office and demand to know full details of his clients' affairs under the Freedom of Information Act? Bribe him to tell me? Kidnap the solicitor and extract the information by force? Tell him he was on my list of ten? Catarina had already tried naked threats of violence – Sussex solicitors were tougher than I thought. Anyway, intriguing though this proof of the existence of the 'old man' was, we were miles from connecting him with a sailing accident off the Sussex coast.

'The Mafia would do a much better job for you,' I said. 'And they're not constrained in any way by the Law Society. I'm sorry, Catarina. I really am. But I'm not the person you need for this.'

I do not know what the translation might be of the words Catarina muttered to herself as she showed me out, but I do not think they were in any way complimentary. And if I were to be gunned down on the way home, the guarantee that ten villagers would die was almost certainly now invalidated.

# CHAPTER TWELVE

## Elsie

*Dear Ms Green,*
*Thank you for sharing with me your* MS, THE BELLS
OF HELL GO BLING-A-LING-A-LING, *or as much of it as*
*you can be arsed to write.*

*There is, as you probably know, much good*
*advice on the Internet for writers. There is also a*
*great deal of crap. I think I know which you have*
*chosen to read.*

*First, it is not my job to (as you put it) sort*
*out the spelling and grammar 'and stuff'. If you*
*were a brainless celeb with a wish to have your*
*name on the cover of the book, then you would*
*of course find many people willing to do just that.*
*But (and I have googled you, Ms Green) you are*
*not. So the spelling and grammar are down to you.*
*All of it. These are basic skills for anyone who (for*
*reasons I will never quite fathom) wishes to be a*

*writer. Would you employ a plumber who said that he'd never quite got the hang of pipework? No, I thought not. I need writers who have all their tools on the van.*

*Second, you say that you have only written the first three chapters and will write the rest once you get your advance. Again, I have googled you and you are not JK Rowling or Hilary Mantel. I ask for three chapters because that's as far as I'm going to read with most submissions. If I like it I will ask to see more, but I won't want to wait another six months before I get it. You don't get any money until you finish the job. (See note on plumbers.)*

*Third, you ask for a meeting so that you can explain the book to me. Is that the only way that I will understand it? Will you offer to do the same for everyone who buys a copy? Having read the first three chapters, I think that you really might have time to meet each of your readers personally, but readers are busy people and they conversely may not have time to meet you.*

*Fourth, if you are going to express admiration for the writers I already represent, do try to spell their names correctly. You might also try looking at Amazon rather than making a wild guess about the sort of thing that they write. And of course, you should not assume that because I represent writer X I really want somebody else exactly like him.*

*Fifth . . .*

'Sorry – are you writing to accept an author?'

'Why would you think that?'

'It was just that you looked quite happy.'

'There is always satisfaction in a job well done. As you may discover yourself one day. As for accepting Ms Green, I would rather be stranded on a desert island with nothing to read but that manuscript we enjoyed so much yesterday.'

'The one I had to go to the post office to collect because the author hadn't put any stamps on the envelope?'

'That's right.'

'The egg and chips diet book?'

'Precisely. Three hundred and sixty-five variants on egg and chips, one for each day of the year. And with no trace of irony. So he may not quite understand my reply saying that it was well worth paying for.'

'I could do you a standard rejection letter. It would save you so much time. We used to have them at Francis and Novak. The letter just said that we loved the book but that we didn't think we were the right agency to represent it. Sometimes we added a nice PS.'

'Wouldn't that just give the writers encouragement?'

'Yes.'

'So . . . why would you want to do that exactly?'

'Because it's a nice thing to do.'

'Nice?'

'Yes.'

'You think you should be nice to writers?'

'Yes, don't you?'

Sometimes you know it's going to be just too much effort to explain something properly.

'Yes, of course,' I said. 'But only if all else fails. I'm off now, anyway. Ethelred is expecting me, and I don't want to disappoint him, poor agentless little lamb. A few days by the sea await me.'

'Wrap up warm,' said Tuesday. 'The weather forecast is for wind and rain. Are you planning wintery walks on the beach? I always think you need a dog for that.'

'I've got a writer,' I said. 'That's almost as good.'

'It's quite a big house,' I said. 'I'd forgotten.'

Ethelred put my tea on the table in front of me, next to the biscuits. 'Not as big as some,' he said.

'Lucky you inherited that money a few years ago,' I said. 'I doubt that your royalties would have paid for that conservatory. Not with your last agent. What was her name – Janet something . . . ?'

'My royalties are fine,' he said.

'The two books that she placed have sold well, then?'

'You can look them up on Nielsen.'

'I have. I just wondered if you were planning to lie about it. It was a bit of a mistake switching to her, wasn't it?'

'My earlier books didn't sell that well either,' he said.

'As I know to my cost,' I said. 'You wouldn't believe how many times I've had to calculate fifteen per cent of nothing. I meant more from the point of view of mixing business with pleasure. Sleeping with your agent. I doubt if there actually was that much pleasure, of course.'

'I have no complaints,' he said, trying to look daggers, a thing that he has never done that well.

'I didn't mean from your point of view,' I said. I took a

ladylike sip of tea and selected another Jammy Dodger.

'Elsie, have you come here just to insult me? And there's no need to pretend to be thinking deeply about that question. When you were my agent I had to put up with all of your snide remarks, but I don't any more.'

'Not even in return for my assistance in solving a murder for you?'

'There is no murder to be solved. And if there were, which there isn't, I wouldn't be asking for your help.'

'But you did ask.'

'No, I didn't.'

'Tuesday said that you'd told her about this friend of yours – Robin Pagham – who may have been bumped off. I think his so-called fiancée with big tits is the most likely suspect. Tuesday said there was a lot of money involved. Does the fiancée get any of it?'

'All of it,' he said.

'Then we probably don't need to look much further. Case solved. You see how useful I am?'

'Catarina *wants* me to investigate. She can't be the murderer.'

'I beg to differ. Oldest trick in the book, that one.'

'The coroner has already said it's an accident. If she does nothing then she's completely in the clear. She's got the money. Nobody is accusing her of anything. If she killed him, then reopening the case is the last thing she'd want.'

'Is she blonde?'

'No. Why?'

'I've just noticed that, in the past, a sachet of hair dye seems to cloud your judgement.'

'Well, she's got black hair. Brown eyes. I think she's eastern European.'

'You are still putty in women's hands, Ethelred. Not all women, of course, because not all women like handling putty. But merely because she has brown eyes doesn't mean you're safe. Far from it. Who are the other suspects?'

'There aren't any. It's not a murder case. You don't get suspects when it's accidental death.'

'Who does Catarina think did it?'

'She thinks it was somebody who wanted to stop her marrying Robin and inheriting the money.'

'But Robin's death means she *does* inherit,' I said.

'Yes,' said Ethelred. 'So there was no point in killing him. While Robin was alive he might have called the whole thing off. But killing him made it certain Catarina would get the cash. Her premise is fatally flawed.'

'Did Robin have enemies?'

'Not really. He was one of these rather idle but amiable people who have no need to make enemies. I think some people – the police for example – disapproved of his drug habit. And others felt that he didn't treat his girlfriends that well – but there's only the one proven case of actual physical violence. Plenty of people would disapprove of the way he behaved, but not so much as to contemplate killing him.' Then he added: 'One of his ex-girlfriends was at the funeral – Sophie Tate.'

'Did she dance on his grave?'

'I think she was quite upset that he had died. She happened to be staying in the village when she heard about it.'

'Pure coincidence?'

'Yes. Of course.'

'Yeah right.'

'I believe her. And don't ask if she's blonde.'

'But she is?'

Ethelred pulled a face. He seemed not to subscribe to my putty theories, but he clearly did not believe everything that Sophie had said either. 'Tom thought she was a bit of a fantasist. She told me that she'd been engaged to Robin, but Tom reckoned not.'

'Why did she and Robin break it off? If they were engaged.'

'She didn't say,' said Ethelred. 'Just that they were.'

I thought about that for a bit, then said: 'So what did Robin do for a living? When he wasn't sailing or beating up his girlfriends?'

'Not much. He was supposed to be an actor – I mean he studied at Bristol Old Vic or somewhere. He was on television quite a lot fifteen or twenty years ago. He was in a series with Richard Briers or Tim Brooke-Taylor or somebody. He played the son of a neighbour. It wasn't a big part, but it was regular work. Then he was in a Bond picture as a British agent who gets killed ten minutes into the film. He did a short stint in *EastEnders* as somebody's posh cousin, who turned out to be a conman. Finally there was a toothpaste ad that ran for quite a long time. After that the work dried up a bit. Thinking about it, the rector didn't even mention his acting at the funeral. A lot of people here possibly don't remember it at all. Even Robin brushing his teeth and spotting blood on the bristles is now a forgotten masterpiece. He was still asked to open the occasional village fete, when all else failed. But the hurdle you have to jump to be a celebrity is a low one these days. He'd have been a natural for *Celebrity Big Brother*.'

Ethelred grinned smugly, like he was a candidate for celebrity anything.

'So, do *you* ever get asked to open fetes?' I asked.

The smile faded. 'I haven't lived here very long,' he said, guardedly.

'But, thinking about it, you didn't get asked in the other place you lived either, did you? You were there for ages and ages. And, correct me if I'm wrong, you also didn't get asked in Islington before *that*, and you must have been there for quite a while too. And before that—'

'Anyway,' he said, 'I suppose Robin's father kept him while the father was still alive. After that Robin inherited the Pagham estate, but there would have been death duties to pay. Catarina said he claimed to be short of cash. He was apparently expecting to inherit some money soon.'

'From . . . ?'

'That's not clear. He talked to Catarina about getting the cash when the "old man" died. It meant nothing to her. Catarina even asked the lawyer about who that might be.'

'And . . . ?'

'The lawyer said there was no more money from that source.'

'No *more* money?'

'Yes, that's what he said. That was finished.'

'So there must have been money from there before?'

'Clearly. But Law Society rules prevented him saying any more than that.'

'Meaning?'

'Client confidentiality or something. Catarina was as persuasive as she reasonably could be.'

'So, a nice regular source of income that cannot now be revealed. Could Robin have been blackmailing somebody?' I asked.

'I did wonder about that. But he was to get the money *when the old man died.* Dead men pay no blackmail. And you'd hardly do it through your family solicitor, anyway. It has to be legit, but the lawyer still wouldn't tell Catarina anything about it.'

'Maybe if I had a word with him?'

'I don't think you could come up with any threats Catarina hasn't tried,' he said. 'The lawyer also asked Catarina if she was pregnant.'

The answer to this last puzzle seemed fairly obvious, to me at least. 'A clause in the will leaving money to a purely theoretical and as yet unconceived heir of his body? Or a family trust?' I suggested.

'Again, that's precisely what I thought,' said Ethelred. 'But you'd have expected the lawyer to say that up front, wouldn't you? Anyway, Catarina would have seen the will and would know if that was an issue, so to speak.'

'Just a thought, but could Robin have had heirs of his body that he didn't know about?' I said. 'I mean, you say he was a bit of a lad. There could be all sorts of Pagham offspring out there. Would they have a claim on the estate?'

'I suppose they might. But surely they would just pitch up and make their claim? Catarina hasn't mentioned anyone who has done that. This is getting a bit hypothetical, isn't it?'

'It's called lateral thinking. What about the two teacups thing?'

'Coffee cups. Tuesday mentioned that to you as well, did she? It's no more than that, unfortunately. A visitor on the day he died. Again, I don't think it goes anywhere.'

'OK – so, what are your theories then, Lord Peter?'

'I don't have any theories, Elsie, because this isn't murder and I'm not investigating it. I do realise that one of the many clichés of crime fiction is the amateur detective who says they won't investigate a case and then does just that. But that isn't going to happen here. I am not Lord Peter or Miss Marple or Albert Campion. I am a mid-list writer, trying to produce another book with as few distractions as I can manage.'

'This is the historical miscarriage of justice thing?'

'Yes, an ancestor of Robin's, coincidentally, was hanged in 1848 for a murder that I am almost certain he did not commit.'

'True crime or fictionalised?'

'I was thinking of turning it into a novel, but now I'm not so sure. It's an interesting story as it stands.'

'So, who did it?'

'It may have been the murdered man's brother, George Gittings. Actually that seems very likely. He was certainly the one who benefitted most. I still need to do more research.'

'And it has no bearing on Robin's death?'

'How could it? It was more than a century and a half ago. It marked some sort of low point in the Pagham family history. They were down to owning just one small field that nobody else wanted – except to drive cattle from one plot of land to another.'

'And after that they got richer?'

'Not immediately. The Paghams gained nothing directly or indirectly from the murder. It was later they built up their fortunes by hard work and diligence and so on – though if Robin had lived I can see that he might have blown it all again on drugs and booze, given time. Strangely, I think Catarina might have saved him from that. For all her claims to having links with the Mafia, she seems remarkably down to earth. She might just have turned things around.'

'Does she really have links with the Mafia?' I asked.

'I've noticed a lot of people are quite wary of her . . .' Ethelred began. Then he shook his head. 'But it's not very likely, is it?'

'If she really had links with the Mafia, she'd hardly be asking *you* to investigate, would she?'

'People apparently trust me,' said Ethelred. 'Well, more than they trust the Mafia.'

'People dump on you,' I said. 'Women especially.'

'I don't think so,' said Ethelred. 'The rain's stopped. Do you fancy a walk?'

'Why not?' I said.

Well, as I'd said to Tuesday, if you don't have a dog with you . . .

# CHAPTER THIRTEEN

Some smells have colours. The odour of the marsh, carried in on a brisk breeze, was dark green – salty and pungent. At low tide only a narrow winding stream crossed the sleek mudflats. The sea had retreated to a point where it was no more than a grey streak on the horizon. Green posts marked the navigable channel, the first two quite clear, the others vanishing into the misty distance. Wading birds, dotting the shingle, were the sole living things in view.

'There aren't many boats,' said Elsie, viewing the few that were still moored by Snow Hill, some floating in the deeper water of the channel but most resting, high and dry, at precarious angles on the mud.

'In the summer there are sailing boats chained up all along the sea wall,' I said. 'You could hardly get a cigarette paper between them. In the winter they are all hauled up the slipway and parked at the sailing club over there or in their owners' front gardens. Some people like Robin sail all year round. They usually wheel the boats down on trolleys and push them out into the creek over there.'

'Nobody's out today,' said Elsie, pulling her coat round her.

'It was only Robin, the day he died,' I said. 'It was cold and the sea was fairly rough. But if you like sailing . . .'

'So, nobody saw him set sail? Nobody saw what condition he was in?'

'He wasn't drunk, if that's what you mean,' I said. 'That at least was clear from the inquest.'

'What about the houses over there?' Elsie pointed to the residences overlooking the creek.

'Mainly weekenders,' I said. 'That pink one and that one just there are owned by local residents. They would have been around that day – I mean around in the village. But nobody has said they actually saw him bring the boat down and launch it. The trailer was left by the sea wall just there.' I pointed to a spot at the bottom of the slipway, where the sleek, oozy, brown mud met hard, ridged concrete.

'Where is the boat now?'

'Tom Gittings' father took it back to Robin's house – he towed it on its trailer.'

'How far?'

'A couple of miles. But on the day in question the boat would have been stored over there in that parking area owned by the sailing club. The bushes round it give the boats a bit of protection, I suppose, that they wouldn't get if they were left on the shore where we are now. And there's a lock on the gate.'

Elsie surveyed the shoreline. 'Do you get the feeling that there's something obvious we're missing?'

'Yes,' I said. 'That's just what I feel. Not that I'm investigating anything. It just bugs me that I can't see it.'

'Maybe if we take a walk along the sea wall,' said Elsie. 'Where does it go?'

'To the dunes,' I said.

'Lots of rabbits?'

'Yes,' I said.

'You'll like that,' said Elsie, inexplicably. 'Come on, boy. Next time I'll try to remember to bring a ball.'

I might have queried what we were to do with the ball, but Elsie was already striding off, as well as somebody of her modest height and generous waistline can ever stride, towards the rolling dunes of East Head.

The following day, I made my excuses to Elsie and left her reading by the fire. I needed to finish my researches into Lancelot Pagham's conviction.

This time I was checking marriage records. Could Jane really have married George so soon after John's death, as Tom claimed? Today I was trawling through microfilm, but it did not take long. It was faster even than Tom had implied. Two months, to the day, after the execution there was the parish register entry for the marriage. George Gittings, bachelor married to Jane Taylor, spinster. George's father was recorded as being a farmer, Jane's as a coastguard. So, the match was probably something of a move up for Jane. Then I looked at the names of the witnesses who had signed the register that day. One of them was Perceval Pagham – brother of the murderer, who gave evidence at the trial. Perceval would of course have been working for George by then. It was not so odd that he would attend the wedding – perhaps the whole village did. But why was he selected out to be one of the witnesses?

Then another thought occurred to me. I ordered up the microfilm of the parish records of births. Five months after the marriage a birth was recorded. A son, John. Father George Gittings, Farmer. Mother Jane Gittings née Taylor. Godfather – Perceval Pagham.

So Jane was about two months pregnant when John Gittings was murdered. At that stage Jane would have been fairly certain she was with child, though it might not have been obvious to others. On the morning of John's death they had met and quarrelled. Had she told him what she knew? But they were already engaged. A pregnancy might be awkward but it was no disaster. Unless John knew the baby could not be his. I thought back to Jane Taylor's evidence. Was the baby Lancelot's? Or more likely George's? That would explain why he was so ready to marry her. I sat tapping the desk with my finger until a glance from a neighbouring reader suggested I was tapping harder and louder than I thought. I smiled a quick apology and stared again at the screen. George had married Jane as swiftly as was decent to avoid any scandal. He would scarcely have done that if he suspected that the baby was not his or John's. And it was very understandable if he had known for certain the baby was his.

So, what if . . . my neighbour coughed pointedly – I

had started tapping my finger again . . . what if *that* was what the argument between Jane and John had been about? What if Jane had seen George, as she said she had, and told him to clear off to Chichester or somewhere for the day, until John calmed down? Of course, it was unlikely that he would have calmed down much over the course of the day. Did the brothers arrange to meet at the Herring Field to discuss matters out of the way of the rest of the village?

'Excuse me,' said my neighbour. 'Would you mind not doing that?'

'Sorry,' I said. 'But I have to go now, anyway.'


Once outside I phoned Tom.

'I'd like to check out the Herring Field,' I said. 'Could you tell me how I get there?'

'I can show you myself next weekend. Give you a tour of it, in fact.'

'That's kind, but I'm sure I'll find it. I'd like to take a stroll down there this afternoon if I can.'

Tom gave me directions.

'I suppose I ought to get Catarina's permission to go on it,' I said.

'Why?'

'It's her land now. It would be part of the Pagham estate. It was the one piece of land they kept all the way through.'

'No, it's ours,' said Tom. 'We bought it . . . oh, I don't know . . . in 1848 or 1849 – shortly after the murder, anyway. It's been ours for ages.'

'Perceval sold the bit of land that his brother had been desperate to hold on to?'

'Why not? After his brother's hanging, you could see that it would have had unfortunate memories for Perceval Pagham. And we wanted it to connect two parcels of land we owned. And Perceval worked for George by that stage – he'd have wanted to keep in with him. It would have been difficult for him to say "no". John wouldn't sell but there's nothing anywhere to say that Perceval wanted to keep the land. All in all it's not surprising that the field was sold.'

'No, I suppose not, if the price was right. Did George pay much for it?'

'No idea, I'm afraid. That sort of detail would be lost in the mists of time. The land was as near worthless as you could get. A few pounds, or even a few shillings? Agricultural labourers didn't earn much then. Even five shillings might have been more useful to him than a weed-choked field. My father might have records. I can ask him if you really want to know.'

'Did you know that Jane was two or three months pregnant when she married George? I've looked up the birth records.'

'No, I didn't. That sort of thing was probably more common in remote country districts than we think. People would have noticed but I doubt it caused much of a scandal. But she was engaged to John then . . .'

'Exactly. So, was the child George's or John's? The baptismal records say George, of course . . .'

'Well, that is an interesting question. If it was John, then it was my however-many-greats grandfather who was murdered – not an uncle. If it was George's, then my however-many-greats grandmother was a bit of a goer. Well,

well. That side of it certainly wouldn't have gone without notice at the time. I wonder what the consensus was in the Dog and Duck? Parish registers would be so much more interesting if they had also recorded the local gossip.'

On my way home, I turned off the main road and followed a straight and narrow lane that led, first over tarmac then over dirt, to the estuary. The track ended close to three low cottages, huddled together, overlooking the mudflats. They were all weekend homes, shut up for the winter. I parked and pushed open a new-looking wooden gate that took me onto the coastal footpath. A few hundred yards later, out of the sight of these or any other homes, I caught sight of the Herring Field, as Tom had described it for me. I realised I had passed it many times before on my way to Itchenor – an hour and a half of brisk walking, ending at a pleasant waterside pub and with the option of a bus home, at least on Mondays, Wednesdays and Fridays. But I had never chosen to pause here, not knowing what the field was. It was just a poorly drained piece of coastal land. In the last hundred years it had been enclosed with a sea wall on one side but it was still mainly thistles and reeds that grew there. I stood on the wall, looking down at the lank vegetation and the untidy hedges that bounded it on the landward side. Had somebody really been killed in an argument over this? Or had this been where two brothers met to fight over the already pregnant girl one of them would later marry?

I noticed that I was not alone. A solitary walker was heading in my direction. He was in late middle age and dressed consciously for a country walk – a heavy tweed

111

jacket, of the sort sold at county shows, heavy corduroy trousers, solid, shiny leather boots. He ambled along, limping very slightly, his bulk seeming to occupy the whole width of the path. As he drew closer, I realised that it was Barry Whitelace. At the same moment, he finally noticed me and blinked uncertainly as if he too had problems in remembering names and mine was troubling him. Then he smiled smugly.

'Admiring the site of the wind farm, Ethelred?' he asked.

'Here?' I replied.

'Right here.'

'Is there enough wind? Wouldn't further round the coast be better?'

'Offshore would be best of all, but that doesn't seem to have been the plan. Here would be dreadful. It wouldn't have been a good idea at all. But Catarina says she has no plans to go ahead with it in any way shape or form.'

He leant on his stick and took in the view. He seemed pleased and I was sorry to have to disillusion him.

'I'm afraid it doesn't belong to Catarina,' I said. 'It's owned by Derek Gittings. It would be his decision.'

Whitelace's face dropped. 'I thought it was Robin's project.'

'He and Robin apparently had some sort of plan for a joint venture. But the good news is that Tom says it's all off now, anyway. If you really wanted to make sure, though, you'd need to check with Colonel Gittings, not Catarina.'

Whitelace frowned. 'I might do that. Catarina just said that Robin had been thinking of putting some windmills in here but had decided not to. She never mentioned that he didn't own the land himself. But now he's dead of course . . .'

It was like a stone being dropped into a deep, still pool. Robin was dead, and the ripples of that fact continued to spread outwards.

'It's a pleasant spot,' I ventured.

'So it is,' he replied. 'One of our favourites – Jean and me.'

'I'm sure Robin wouldn't have gone ahead with it,' I said. 'Or Colonel Gittings. Both families have lived here for centuries. They wouldn't have wanted to spoil a place like this.'

'That's right,' said Whitelace. 'I wonder why their plan fell through, though? Robin did need the money. I'm sure he was the driving force behind it. Maybe it's as well things worked out as they did.' The fact that I had been at Robin's funeral did not seem to have suggested to him that I might have been a friend of Robin's and might not think it was all for the best.

I stayed for another few minutes after Whitelace had gone on his way and watched the grass waving gently in the breeze. Perhaps the landscape remembers things long after we have forgotten them. Perhaps the imprint of lost deeds lies dormant in the soil for generations, to rise from time to time as what we choose to call ghosts. Today the sun shone and the trees made a gentle swishing sound. Whatever the land knew, it was not prepared to share.

I turned round and walked slowly to where the car was parked.

*　*　*

When I got back to the house Elsie was waiting for me. The fire had been allowed to go out. She had had other concerns.

'I've been to see Catarina,' she said. 'Nice pad she's got. I rather think we've made some progress, you and I.'

# CHAPTER FOURTEEN

## Elsie

Greylands House was, if not a short walk from Ethelred's, then closer than he had led me to believe. When I had dropped hints over breakfast that I might help him in his enquiries he had looked at me suspiciously and said that Catarina's residence was some way off.

'On the edge of the village, then?' I had asked.

'I wouldn't say it was in the village at all,' he had grunted, through a mouthful of toast and Oxford marmalade.

'But drivable?'

'Sort of. It's not that easy to find.'

'But you could describe it to me?'

'It's not that easy to describe.'

'But you are – please excuse me if I am misremembering – a writer. Describing things, using words, is what you do for a living. A foggy evening in the fictitious and slightly improbable town of Buckford flies from your pen. A description of the wounds inflicted by a serial killer is meat and drink to you. A criminal cleverly avoiding Sergeant Fairfax's questions – this is skilfully worked so the reader has no idea what lies are being told. But telling me how to recognise a turning off the Birdham Road stretches you too much?'

'I don't use a pen. I haven't used a pen for years.'

'No? Let's just cut to the chase then. Is the house before or after Sheepwash Lane?'

'After.'

'Is it before or after the Lamb and Flag?'

'Before.'

'Then I'll find it.'

'There's a tricky fork in the road after you turn off.'

'Do I go left or right? I'm assuming those are the only options?'

'Left. I think you'll find the track a bit bumpy in that Mini of yours.'

'I probably will. But into every Mini's life a little rain must fall.'

'Any more rain and it will fall apart with all that rust.'

'I'll make sure I get there before it rains.'

'Catarina may be going out.'

'Do you have her number? I'll phone and check.'

The lie that had followed was so convoluted and unlikely that I shall not even begin to describe it. It deserved the response I gave.

'Fine.' I said. 'Your superior male logic has finally defeated me. I won't even think of going there.' I picked up and placed a piece of Ethelred's toast in my mouth. The butter did not melt.

'OK,' he said, actually believing me. 'I'll be back at lunchtime.'

\* \* \*

Up to a point, though, Ethelred was right. The first two drives I turned down were interesting but (according to the owners of the houses concerned) I had no business to be where I was. In each case I was ordered to depart at once. I contented myself with making very, very slow three-point turns, while they gave me increasingly frantic instructions. Men always assume that, because you are a woman, you have no idea how to manoeuvre a car and that you have just demolished their herbaceous border by accident rather than design. Which was fine by me.

Still, third time lucky. I parked very carefully in front of an olde worlde farmhouse and rang the bell. The lady who opened the door was clearly Catarina – certainly there was nothing in her attire or demeanour that hinted at a life spent cleaning and polishing for others. I was in no danger of mistaking the home help for the lady of the house. She, for her part, looked at me suspiciously. Well, obviously a well-dressed and attractive, if slightly plump, woman pitching up just after the death of her fiancé . . . I could have been some young girl on the make. Young-ish anyway.

'I not buy anything from gypsies,' she said. 'Goodbye.'

'I'm not here to sell you anything,' I said.

'No?'

'No. I'm a friend of a friend.'

'What friend?'

'Ethelred.'

'You come here in that?'

We both looked at my car.

'The garage said the tyres should last until the next MOT,' I said. 'At least, as long as I didn't do more than twenty or thirty miles on them. The track to your house won't have helped, of course.'

'No point new tyres. Too much hole in bodywork, I think. Is death trap.'

'To be fair, the garage said that too. Still, it gets me from A to B if I change gear carefully. But I didn't come here to talk about the conservation of classic cars. I came to talk about Robin.'

'So Ethelred can help? He change mind?'

'Absolutely. He change mind. But maybe we should discuss this inside? I'll leave the car where it is?'

'Yes, I not like that flower bed anyway.'

Those familiar with my previous investigations will know that it has been necessary for me to tell the occasional fib and claim to be Ethelred's assistant in order to gain access to people or things that Ethelred had forgotten to tell me about. I have to stress that this time I did not stoop to any such deception.

'So Ethelred works for you?'

'In a manner of speaking,' I replied. 'I have a number of people under contract at my agency.'

'Like Ethelred?'

'Not exactly like Ethelred, I'm pleased to say, but similar in some respects.'

'This is proper detective agency you run? You talk me straight answer.'

I gave her a straight answer. Had she asked for a straight and truthful answer it might have been slightly different, but it was straight enough.

'So, Cat,' I said, 'tell me a bit more about the day Robin died. These are very good cakes by the way. Do you have any more?'

'No. You have eaten them all.'

'Have I? Well, they were very good. What's in them – honey and what . . . ?'

'Sesame seed and some almond. Flour. Egg. Orange. Other things.'

'Could you let me have the recipe?'

'Yes, of course.'

'Or if you were making more, I could just drop round.'

'Tomorrow, perhaps.'

'Tomorrow. Excellent. Maybe with just a touch more honey next time, Cat? Or chocolate, maybe. Chocolate would be good – but you'll need the Belgian version, not the basic cooking one. Where were we? Oh yes, the murder . . . what was the weather like that morning?'

'In morning, sunny. But you cannot launch boat in morning – low tide. Must wait until midday. Then it start rain and wind.'

'But Robin went out?'

'He not mind rain. Wind good for sailing boat. Rain just water like all round boat.'

'Yes, I suppose so. What time?'

'He say he will go eleven or half past eleven.'

'But before he went, somebody came to visit him?'

'Yes. For coffee.'

'And Robin delayed going out?'

'I think so. I go to Chichester half past ten. So visitor arrive after. That is strange.'

'What is strange?'

'Here, can launch boat only at high water – three, maybe four hours a day. Bad weather coming. Robin would want to go sail. He would not want stick in the mud. He would tell visitor, I go sail – you piss off – come back another day.'

'So, you're saying that this must have been an important visitor?'

'Yes.'

'Important and unexpected?'

'Yes.'

'So, he saw this person, then went down to the sailing club?'

'Yes, I think.'

'Later you came back from shopping – saw the car was gone . . .'

'No, car still here. I think maybe he not go.'

'But he had gone.'

'Of course. That is why dead.'

'So, you thought it odd that the car was still there?'

'No. His car like yours. Sometimes it go. Sometimes it stay where it is.'

'OK, how does he get to the sailing club with a broken-down car? Does his visitor give him a lift?'

'At first I think he cycle. But later I find bike here too. So, maybe lift or maybe bus into village.'

'There's a bus?'

'Every half hour. End of lane. Get off at church.'

'Did he often cycle or get the bus?'

'Sometimes. Bus not so much – I think he does not like use bus – is for peasants and old people. But cycle good.'

It was a point of view I was familiar with. Catarina was clearly one of those brought up to believe that blessed are the ostentatious, for God shall say unto them: wow, I saw that on *Top Gear* last week – is it the 3.5 litre petrol or the 2.7 litre diesel model? But a really flash bike costing a couple of grand is OK too. The streets of London are full these days of cyclists who could afford a modest little four by four but prefer two wheels. There is, as my father would say when somebody asked at his fruit and veg stall for one of these new-fangled courgettes, no accounting for taste.

'And he sailed alone?' I asked.

'Yes. It is just small boat. One person can sail.'

'Did you ever sail with him?'

She shook her head. 'If I want get cold and wet, I can stand in garden in rain. Not seasick in garden and can come in any time I like.'

'Would anyone have seen him at the sailing club? A barman or a steward or something?'

'No bar. Just parking for boats and hut to store things in.'

'So, he leaves here and simply vanishes from the map? And the last person that we know sees Robin before he dies is this mysterious stranger, who possibly gives him a lift to the club because his car has broken down. Then, nobody sees him again until he and his boat . . . sorry, this must be tough for you, having to go through it all again.'

Catarina glared at me. 'You think I not tough? I go through it as many times as I need to. I want killer found. I want killer found and hanged.'

'We've stopped hanging people,' I said.

But maybe she didn't mean hanged legally.

On the way out I suddenly had a thought.

'Do you have the keys to Robin's car?'

'He leave them in car, always.'

'Have you used it?'

'No. I have my own car. BMW. Purple. White leather. Has much class.'

So, just out of interest, I went to the garage and tried to start Robin's Saab. The key was in the ignition, as Catarina had said. I turned it. The engine burst into life straight away.

Of course, that proved nothing on its own. Still, it was interesting all the same.

# CHAPTER FIFTEEN

'That was what was bothering me,' I said. 'Tom's father had collected the boat and towed it back to Greylands. But nobody had said they had driven Robin's car back. It wasn't still parked at the sailing club, so what had happened to it? Of course that is the obvious answer – he never took it there in the first place.'

'But why?' said Elsie. 'It was working perfectly well. Instead, he apparently accepts a lift from this mysterious stranger who has dropped by for coffee. Maybe he wasn't in a fit state to drive?'

'I told you: the coroner's report says no alcohol – anyway, it would have been a bit early even for Robin. And he wouldn't have gone sailing if he was drunk.'

'Drugs?'

'Robin stopped that years ago. Sophie thought not, but I believe Tom. He knew Robin right up to the end.'

Elsie looked doubtful, but I did believe Tom on this and most other things.

'OK, then,' said Elsie, 'why do they drive down together? Not to enjoy the facilities at the sailing club, which are apparently zero.'

'Yes, it's very basic at Snow Hill – just a place to store your boat and equipment. In the summer they sometimes have parties there, but at this time of year it's pretty deserted. Maybe Robin was keen to get down to the water but they still had something to talk about on the way? So somebody came to him to discuss something that wouldn't wait.'

'Who might that be?'

'Possibly Barry Whitelace,' I said.

'Who's he?'

'He's somebody who is very concerned about a wind farm Robin was planning to build – somewhere near the Herring Field. He was very keen to talk to Catarina after the funeral . . . so, he'd have been keen to talk to Robin too. But that's only a guess. I don't know that.'

'You don't? No shit? We'd better cancel the arrest warrant for Barry Whitelace, then. Why did Robin want to construct a wind farm, anyway?'

'Money,' I said. 'It seems that, contrary to what everyone thought, Robin was always short of it. He certainly wasn't getting much from acting.'

'But then he decided not to build it?'

'So Tom says.'

'Because he suddenly had another source of funds?' asked Elsie.

'That's a logical conclusion. It would certainly explain the facts as we know them.'

'In which case, how else would he make some easy

money? Even if he'd stopped taking drugs, he'd have still had contacts, wouldn't he?'

'You mean he was dealing?' I asked.

'Could be. All these trips out in his boat.'

'It's not big enough to get over to France,' I said.

'He wouldn't need to. He just has to rendezvous with a bigger boat and bring the stuff back with him. There are no customs officers at Snow Hill, are there? There's nobody much around to see him come ashore. Anyway, with all that stuff sailors carry backwards and forwards – sails and rudders and life jackets and sheets or whatever – who's going to notice a modest little package wrapped in heavy-duty plastic? He was pretty keen to make sure Catarina was out of the way that day. So, somebody turns up at the house – they have coffee together, drive down to the sailing club and pick up the drugs from wherever they've been stashed. He does the deal. Then, he sails off to another appointment with a boat somewhere off the Isle of Wight, but this time something goes wrong. There's an argument over the price, perhaps. He gets knocked on the head and dumped in the water. Later his body is washed up in Bracklesham . . .'

'Very good,' I said. 'You should be the crime writer.'

'Crime novels? Piece of piss,' she said.

'Maybe we should focus on what really happened,' I said. 'I mean something remotely possible that fits the facts as we know them.'

'Fine, do it your way, then,' she said.

Still, unlikely though her smuggling scenario was, she had a point. Robin had been strangely keen to ensure that Catarina was out of the way. And there had been no need, on a wet and windy day, to accept a lift to Snow Hill, knowing that he would need to walk or catch a bus back. If I didn't know sailors, I'd have said there was no need to go out at all in that weather, but Robin liked a challenge.

I've mentioned this before, I know, but there are strange similarities between solving crimes and crossword puzzles. Often you will look at a jumble of facts and they seem no more than that. Then suddenly you will see a pattern and you cannot believe that you had not made the connection before. Sometimes – I am talking about puzzles now – I will find a word, any word, that is the right length and happens to fit the letters I already have. It may not be the correct answer, but it gives you a better feel for what other words might also go there. Often the real answer is only a letter or two different. Elsie's solution might be far-fetched, but maybe what really happened was only a minor truth or two away from it. Could Robin have been dealing drugs? He would have had all the connections. He had the boat. He lacked the sort of conscience that would have told him that it was wrong, or indeed inadvisable. And if you wanted to bring contraband of any sort ashore, then this was the place to do it. But nobody had even hinted before that Robin would do that sort of thing, however badly he needed the cash.

Nor was I sure that Barry Whitelace would murder to prevent a wind farm overlooking Chichester Harbour. On the face of it, it was at least as unlikely as the drug dealing. But it was quite possible that he was indeed the visitor who had drunk a cup of coffee and continued their conversation all the way to the sailing club. I suspected he was not an easy man to shake off.

'The fact that he sent Catarina off to Chichester suggests Robin knew something out of the ordinary was going on,' I said. 'And the fact that he got a lift to Snow Hill means there is somebody out there who knows about his final hours and who has not come forward to tell the police what they know. But I can't see Barry Whitelace withholding material evidence.'

'A woman, then,' said Elsie. 'Robin packs his girlfriend off to the shops. An old flame shows up. Maybe the activities planned for the afternoon included more than sailing. And you can see why the other woman might choose not to identify herself even after the body was found – she might be married.'

'Robin was engaged to Catarina,' I said. 'There wasn't anyone else.'

'Yeah, right,' said Elsie with the charitable compassion for which she is known throughout the publishing world. 'And pigs might sodding fly.'

Knowing that she was staying almost next door to the post office, I was not surprised to run into Sophie Tate again when I was buying some milk and a couple of packets of biscuits. (The packet that I thought I possessed had mysteriously vanished. Elsie denied any knowledge of them.) But we expressed surprise at the apparent coincidence.

'How long are you down for?' I asked.

'About a week in total. I go back tomorrow.'

'Sorry you haven't had better weather.'

'I'm used to it. I more or less lived down here for six months.'

'You worked down here?'

'I'm an HR consultant. Sometimes I have to be in a particular place, but most of the time I can do my work from anywhere.'

'You said that you wanted to talk to me if I was investigating Robin's death.'

'And are you?'

'No.'

'Then I suppose that eventuality does not arise.'

'Mere curiosity on my part isn't enough?'

'Got it in one,' she said. 'What I know probably isn't important, but it also isn't entirely to my credit that I know it. If you're not investigating, it won't be of much use to you or me to expand on that.'

I wished her a good trip back. She said that maybe we would meet when she was next down. I agreed that that was likely rather than otherwise. It was not a large village. And she left. I took my goods to the counter to pay for them, wondering whether I shouldn't have accepted the inevitable and bought half a dozen assorted packets of biscuits. I had no doubt that, with only two, I would be back tomorrow.

'I met Sophie at the funeral,' I said as I dipped into my pockets for change. 'She used to know Robin quite well.'

'Of course she did,' came the reply. 'They were engaged.'

'Really?' I asked, remembering what Tom had told me. But Josie knows pretty well everyone in the village, so her pronouncements on matters such as that were regarded as definitive. 'You mean officially?'

'Absolutely officially. I really thought she and Robin

128

would get married, but it didn't work out, as you probably know.'

Clearly I didn't know, so I waited for her to explain.

'I suppose it doesn't matter any more, not with Robin being dead, but she had a bit of a fling with that Tom Gittings.'

'That's why she and Robin split up?'

'So I heard. Of course, the thing with Tom didn't last long, but Robin had moved on too by then. Robin and Sophie stayed friends, I think. She always saw Robin when she came down here. Not so much since Catarina came on the scene, of course. No, maybe not so much lately. But before that she did.'

'And Tom knew all that?'

'That Sophie and Robin were engaged? He was at the engagement party. It would have been difficult not to notice.'

'Tom never mentioned he went out with her.'

'Maybe he's not too proud of what he did.'

'I'm surprised at him, anyway.'

'The quiet ones are always the worst. As for the quiet, good-looking ones like that Tom Gittings . . . Do you want another packet of those chocolate digestives? They're on special offer.'

# CHAPTER SIXTEEN

## Elsie

Ethelred had gone off to the library again, muttering that even if I was his guest that didn't mean that he had to provide beer and skittles 24/7. Well, perhaps I shouldn't have said what I did about his friend. But Tom's behaviour had been both deceitful and suspicious.

'I know what Josie told me,' said Ethelred. 'But that doesn't mean Tom was to blame. I mean, why shouldn't Sophie want to go out with him? Sometimes these things just happen . . .'

'With your friend's fiancée?'

'Sometimes. Yes.'

'Why,' I asked, 'did he more or less deny knowing Sophie?'

'I'm not sure he denied it . . . he just wasn't quite certain who I meant . . .'

'But of course. Why should he recall anyone called Sophie Tate? He'd only gone out with her for . . . how long?'

'I'm not sure,' he said. 'A few months.'

'A few months? Well, there you are, then. Let's say a hundred and fifty shags, tops. You'd have difficulty in remembering that, wouldn't you?'

'You are being very unfair on Tom,' he said. 'I probably just didn't make it clear who I meant.'

After Ethelred had left I made myself some coffee and had a biscuit or two. Then I checked, unsuccessfully, to see if I could find out where he'd hidden the other two packets. I do not, I must stress, approve of duplicity of any sort, especially when it comes to chocolate. So, I searched everywhere I could think of, but without success. The question then was this: should I try to put all that stuff back in whichever cupboard it came from or should I tell Ethelred that he had very thorough mice? I wrote a brief thank-you note, signed with a mousey paw print, and placed it in the middle of the mess in the kitchen. Ethelred would find it on his return and whether he believed it was up to him. Then I set off myself. I had a busy morning ahead of me. Ethelred had said roughly where Sophie was staying. I'd only need to ring two or three doorbells – say half a dozen absolute max.

'I thought Ethelred wasn't going to investigate Robin's death?'

'He changed his mind,' I said. 'He had to go into Chichester today, but he asked me to drop round and clarify a few things.'

'OK. He didn't seem that bothered when I spoke to him. His interest did not go beyond curiosity.'

'No, he is absolutely going to do it. He said you knew Tom Gittings.'

'Yes, that's right.'

'Nice boy.'

'I suppose so – he's just a bit confused about what he really wants,' said Sophie.

'Rather like Ethelred, of course,' I said.

'But slightly more toned, and twenty years younger.'

'Thirty years younger.'

'I was being kind.'

'I wouldn't bother. So what happened between you and Tom? And between you and Robin, of course.'

'Well, as I told Ethelred, I used to come down here quite a lot. My grandparents had a house on West Strand in the old days so, once I graduated from buckets and spades, I pretty much grew up sailing and windsurfing. I met Robin sailing. He was maybe fifteen years older than me – a vast yawning gap when you're ten, but less so when you're twenty-five. Still, he was always heaps better than me at sailing and the rest of it, so I idolised him a bit. For a long time he didn't take much interest in me, then one summer about three years ago he did. I was flattered. I knew his reputation, but I started to go out with him. I was working in an HR department in London then, so we saw each other mainly at weekends. I moved to consultancy so that I could spend more time down here. Robin had the annex of Greylands House as his own place, so I was able to more or less move in. Then Robin proposed. I suppose at forty he'd decided that even he needed to settle down. And as I say, I'd worshipped at his shrine for a while. So, I said yes . . .'

'And Tom?'

'I'd sort of idolised him too, but in a different way – he's more or less my age. For a while he was rather like an annoying big brother. Of course, with his looks he could get any girl in the village – which meant he could pretend he wasn't interested in any of us. So, he was just a friend. Then, out of nowhere, we started to get thrown together. We'd get invited to dinner with Tom's father, then Robin would get hauled off to look at some new bit of sailing kit or something, leaving Tom and me to our own devices. Or Robin would get invited at short notice, by some friend of Tom's family, on a boys' sailing weekend – and Tom would be available to take me off to Chichester Festival Theatre, for which he just happened to have a spare ticket.'

'You're saying that Tom somehow rigged things?'

'At the time it all seemed quite natural, but with hindsight . . . Yes, there were too many coincidences. And I think his father actively encouraged it.'

'And this was all while you were engaged to Robin?'

'Yes. In fact it started round about the time we got engaged. By the time of the engagement party I'd already slept with Tom once. Then at the party itself . . . well, making it official brought it home to me what I was doing. Robin was a lot older than I was. I was just starting my career, whereas his career as an actor was drifting away. I can't say my parents really approved . . . I mean they liked Robin because everyone did, but there were hints I should find somebody more my own age. And then there were the drugs. I mean I've never been into that sort of thing . . . Robin kept telling me he was quitting . . . But they don't, do they? They tell you that all the time. The trouble is that cocaine's a genie that won't go back in the bottle. Even so, I still might have stuck with him . . . gone along with it all . . . but suddenly there was Tom.'

'So you chose Tom?'

'At first, I dithered. Two men I really liked, both after me. I wasn't having such a bad time, after all. I reckoned I could handle it.'

'But, in the end, you dumped Robin?' I asked.

'That would have been the decent thing to do – to have been honest with him – but my sins caught up with me before I could do it. There was this anonymous note informing Robin what his fiancée was doing behind his back. He confronted me. I didn't try to deny it. In a way, I deserved to be denounced as a scarlet woman. And I thought I'd be going out with Tom anyway, so *tant pis*. It simplified things.'

'And you did go out with Tom . . .'

'For a while. Then that sort of fizzled out too, which served me right. It was as if Tom was only interested as long as he was screwing his mate's girlfriend. Once that was over he seemed to lose concentration. We split up round about the same time as Robin started going out with somebody else.'

'The one whose nose he flattened?'

'That's right. Martina.'

'And you now regret not sticking with Robin?'

'God, no! I was well out of that one. He's the sort of man girls reckon they can reform and turn into Mr Darcy, but you're onto a loser every time with the Robins of this world. He never did kick his cocaine habit.'

'Right up to the end?'

'Obviously. He was drugged to the eyeballs on his final trip.'

'His last sailing trip?'

'Absolutely. I'm not counting any travelling he did after he died.'

'Ethelred said there was no trace of alcohol . . .'

'And he was right. No alcohol at all – just a whole heap of drugs.'

'Which ones?'

'Some cocaine, like I say. And Rohypnol.'

'Rohypnol? The date rape one?'

'It's not unusual, apparently, for cocaine users to take Rohypnol too – it's good for coming down after a cocaine binge, or so I read somewhere. But it would explain why Robin lost control of the boat and went overboard.'

'Tom said nothing to Ethelred about any of that.'

'Tom's report on the *Observer* also charitably made no mention of it – his final act of friendship or contrition or something.'

'A good friend, then.'

'But a lousy reporter. The drugs were relevant to a lot of things. It doesn't surprise me that some people think it might be murder. But with what was flowing round in his bloodstream, most people would have fallen overboard, even tied up in the marina without a wave in sight.'

'Doesn't the life jacket keep your head above water?'

'Depends on the model. Robin was wearing a life preserver – less bulky but designed for somebody who can swim and is close to the shore. Not so good out at sea and in a drug-induced coma.'

'How do you know all this if it wasn't in the paper?'

'I went to the inquest.'

'Why?'

'Curiosity.'

Then a thought occurred to me.

'So, you'd have seen Tom there?'

'Yes.'

'And he'd have seen you?'

'I imagine so.'

It didn't seem worth asking whether they talked to each other. Sometimes you just get a feeling for the way things went.

'In that case, when you said you were down here by coincidence . . .' I said.

'I was lying. To myself more than anybody. It's a harmless habit, unlike cocaine. And not illegal. I went to the inquest. I knew roughly when the funeral would be. *Voila!* Here I am. And anyway . . .' Sophie paused and looked at me.

'Anyway?' I asked.

'Anyway . . . the sun is shining and I may as well go out and enjoy it. Unless you and Ethelred have any more questions?'

'No,' I said. 'You've been very helpful.'

# CHAPTER SEVENTEEN

I had no reason at all to feel guilty. Absolutely none. It was true that I had told neither Tom nor Elsie that I was planning to do this, but I had every right to be driving up this gravel track. Tom's father might, in theory at least, be able to shed more light on the hanging of Lancelot Pagham. I had as much cause to be here as in Chichester Library. And I might also chat to him, in passing, about the death of Robin Pagham. It would be odd, surely, to visit him and not offer my condolences on the death of his friend?

Colonel Derek Gittings opened the door a careful couple of inches.

'I was just passing,' I said.

'Were you?'

It was not a good start. A lean, weather-beaten face looked back at me. The hair was grey and sparse but the eyebrows were bushy and black – the eyes themselves pale, cold blue. He wore a cream shirt, checked with brown and green and an old moss-coloured cardigan. A foot, in a tartan carpet slipper, was poised ready to give added weight if he needed to shut the door in my face.

'I'm Ethelred Tressider,' I said. 'We met at the film club . . . in the village . . . and then . . .'

'I know who you are,' he said. 'And what you write. Not quite senile yet. Tom said you were researching some family history.'

'Yes,' I said with relief. 'I wondered if you had a few minutes?'

'Now?'

'I could come back.'

'Yes, so you probably would bloody well come back, wouldn't you? It may as well be now.'

The door opened a little wider and I entered. The hallway had last been papered many years ago, probably when Tom's mother was still alive, with a complex William Morris print – stylised vines snaked their way backwards and forwards. The colours had faded, other than the browns and ochres. By the door, the paper was grubby and worn, as members of the family had brushed past over many years. One or two brighter squares of paper showed where pictures had been taken down and never put up again. On the coat stand several waterproofs had been abandoned – all in need of a clean – and a shapeless deerstalker hung precariously by its strap. There was a faint smell of cabbage. I could not recall when I had last cooked cabbage or even looked for it in the shops.

'Thank you,' I said. 'I wondered—'

'You'd better come into the study,' said Colonel Gittings. 'Or do you actually like standing there?'

'Not especially,' I said.

'Nor do I,' he said. 'So, let's not.'

It felt like the first time we had met. I had expressed the view that *Butch Cassidy* had been a good choice of film for the evening. He had replied: 'If you like that sort of thing'. Which left me classified amongst those who enjoyed that sort of film, with the many other weaknesses of mind and body that such people undoubtedly possessed. Then he had turned to speak to somebody else before I could think of a reply, clever or otherwise. The following day I was still trying to work out what I should have said.

'The study . . . yes, perfect,' I said, on this occasion.

He motioned me towards the door, as if he had been trying to get me out of the hall for hours and had only just succeeded. His study, too, was very William Morris, but brighter – here birds clutching strawberries dotted the green fronds. I wondered whether after all, the design of the hallway had been the colonel's.

'It was my wife's sitting room,' he said, noticing my interest in the decor. 'When she was alive. Nothing to do with me.'

'I like the wallpaper,' I said.

'You can have it, if you can get it off the wall.'

'I'm not sure I could do that.'

'I'm bloody sure you can't. So, if you're not here for the wallpaper, what *is* it that you want?'

He motioned me towards a chair that had seen better days and which was covered with an old blanket. I suspected

141

that after sitting in it I would be picking dog hairs off my clothes for days.

'Tom told me about the murder of John Gittings,' I said.

'God knows what possessed him to do that. Ancient history. Best forgotten. I only know what you can read in the local history books, anyway. They're all in the library in Chichester. Might have one of the books on those shelves there, but I couldn't say exactly where.'

He indicated the wooden bookshelves that dominated one wall of the study, though how he hoped to find anything in the confusion of books, newspapers and folders he had stacked on them, I had no idea. His desk, too, was a confused jumble. Three dirty mugs sat on heaps of assorted letters and circulars advertising stairlifts and funeral plans. We get a lot of those round here but most of us recycle them promptly. His surroundings were as little cared for as his clothes, as comfortable in a way as the old red slippers he wore. In the distant days when he was a young subaltern he would doubtless have had to maintain himself and his kit in immaculate order. Later he would have had a batman to press his trousers to a knife-like sharpness. Was he sending out a message that all that was in the past? On the wall there was some sort of regimental plaque and a formal group photograph of twenty or so officers and men in uniform, the glossy paper slightly wrinkled now and faded from exposure to the sun.

'Northern Ireland,' he said, again following my gaze. 'That would have been our second tour of duty. Six of them didn't live to do a third. Landmine.'

'Northern Ireland must have been tough.'

'Really? You think so? What would you know about it, then?'

'Nothing. Just what I've read and seen on television.'

'Or at the film club,' he said.

'Maybe.' I smiled but his face remained stony. It wasn't a joke.

'Iraq was worse,' he said. 'The Falklands were fine. Stroll in the park. For my lot, anyway. I wouldn't have wanted to be on the *Sheffield*.'

I tried to remember what had happened to the *Sheffield*. Exocet missile? The conversation was drifting and I suspected it would be like Colonel Gittings to terminate our meeting abruptly and impatiently.

'So, what can I tell you?'

'I've read the newspaper reports on the 1848 murder,' I said. 'It was what happened later that I'm beginning to find interesting.'

'How much later?'

'After the murder, the fortunes of the Paghams took a turn for the better,' I said.

'I suppose so. They did all right for themselves.'

'Whereas . . .' I wondered whether to continue that sentence. Most things seemed to annoy him.

'Whereas we've come down in the world?' he enquired. 'It's all relative. We've still got more than most – this house and a bit of land.'

'Including the Herring Field,' I said.

Colonel Gittings looked at me suspiciously. 'Yes,' he said. 'Including that.'

'I'd heard Robin was planning to build a wind farm on it,' I said. 'Is that right?'

'I might have said I'd let him have the land,' he said.

'Even though everyone in the village would oppose it?'

'Not everyone. Just bloody fools like that Whitelace man. This isn't some rural theme park. We all have to make money somehow.'

'But why that?'

'That's my bloody business, don't you think? I let you in here because you said you wanted to ask questions about the past, not to discuss my personal finances.'

'Yes, of course,' I said. 'But you were good friends with Robin?'

'Yes. I still don't see how any of this fits in with your research.'

'Tom implied that the murder of John Gittings led to hostility between the two families.'

'Did he?'

'So that's wrong?'

'Maybe in the past. I honestly can't remember what my grandfather may have said or felt about it. I was always on good enough terms with Robin. As you pointed out, we contemplated doing business together. I'd go so far as to say he was one of my very best friends. I was devastated when I heard he'd drowned. Stupid bloody way to go. Just like him, of course. Stupid bloody man. But . . .'

He paused and looked into the distance.

'Where were you the day he drowned?' I asked.

'Here in the village. Where else would I be?'

Then, I don't know why, I added: 'And Tom?'

'Weald and Downland Museum. All day.'

'You're certain?'

'Of course. When something like that happens, you don't forget details like where you were when you heard. Or where other people were. Tom went there with that Sophie woman.'

'Sophie Tate?'

'That's right.'

'She was in Sussex the day Robin died?'

'Yes. She was with Tom. They were both at the museum. All day.' He glowered at me. 'You are here under false pretences, Mr Tressider. Don't think Tom hasn't told me that Catarina has asked you to investigate Robin's death. I know what you are implying.'

'I'm sorry,' I said. 'I hadn't intended to get onto that. It was just that you started talking about Tom and Sophie . . .'

'Oh – and it's all my fault is it?'

'I'm sorry,' I repeated.

'Are you? Well, if you've no more questions about me or my finances, Mr Tressider, I have some work to do.'

He picked up a circular on mobility scooters, which quite clearly had higher priority than I did.

'No more questions,' I said. 'Thank you. You've been very helpful.'

# CHAPTER EIGHTEEN

'So,' said Elsie. 'You are investigating the murder, after all.'

'No,' I said. 'I hadn't intended the discussion to go that way at all.'

'Not even a bit?'

'No, not even a bit.'

'Still,' said Elsie, 'that means Sophie was around on the day Robin died and she was there for the inquest and for the funeral. Coincidence? I think not.'

We were back at my house comparing notes. One of us had eaten a packet of chocolate biscuits as an aid to thought. Fortunately I had another hidden at the back of the cupboard, where Elsie would never find them unaided.

'She's a former fiancée,' I pointed out.

'So she'd definitely want to be there the day he died, then. What ex wouldn't?'

'That would take a bit of planning, I grant you. But, as

it happened, she wasn't around that day – not here in the village. The Weald and Downland Museum's at Singleton. That's just on the other side of Chichester.'

'All very innocent. Except she and Tom had split up sometime before Robin's death. At the inquest, after the event, they seem to have ignored each other completely. What the hell are they doing, on the day he vanished, suddenly going off to a museum together?'

'Because it's interesting. It's a big open-air museum. There aren't many like it. They've reconstructed lots of old buildings there from all over southern England.'

'Interesting for *you*, perhaps. But a whole day . . .'

'I've spent a whole day there.'

'Yes, as I said, interesting for *you*, perhaps. But what would Sophie be doing coming down midweek to meet an ex-boyfriend for a date at a museum? In my day a date meant getting plastered and throwing up in the gutter together. At the very least. I've had some weird boyfriends, but none of them have ever phoned me after many months of silence and suggested we go to a museum. And why have neither of them mentioned it until now?'

'Neither of them has mentioned it at all. It was Tom's father. Other than that, the museum trip is their own little secret, you might say.'

'So, how do we find out why they went off together like that?'

'I'll ask Sophie,' I said.

'Just like that?'

'Just like that. I'll call round and just ask her.'

'And what excuse will you use for calling?'

'I'll think of something.'

'The *Dr Atkins Diet Book*?'

'Yes, Elsie thought she might have left it behind after she had called on you.'

Sophie shook her head. 'I'm sure I would have noticed straight away.' She glanced quickly round the room as if in evidence of her observational powers.

'She'll be really disappointed,' I said. 'She loves that book. Of course, hiding the chocolate biscuits may work equally well. Anyway, I told her I'd try here on my way back from seeing Derek Gittings.'

'You've been to see Tom's father?' asked Sophie.

'Yes. I'm doing this research on a murder that took place back in the 1840s. One of Tom's ancestors.'

'I know about the Herring Field murder. I've spent a lot of time down here, after all. Look, do you want a coffee? I'm just making some. Sorry about the mess in here by the way – I'm packing to go back to London. I need to be gone in half an hour or they might make me pay for another day.'

Sophie went off to the kitchen. I heard the usual noises of kettles being filled and jars being unscrewed. At first I couldn't identify the additional sound – a faint buzzing at my elbow. Then I noticed Sophie's phone, presumably switched to 'vibrate', on the table by my chair. I instinctively glanced over. Mobile phones, like babies, demand attention at all times. They hate being ignored. The name of the caller had flashed up on the screen: 'Martina Blanch'. Then the buzz stopped as the phone switched to answer.

Sophie came back with two mugs of coffee.

'You missed a call,' I said.

'You didn't happen to spot who it was, I suppose?'

There seemed little point in lying and saying that I hadn't snooped. 'Martina Blanch?' I said.

'Oh right,' said Sophie, putting my mug down and taking up her handset. 'She can wait.'

The name had meant nothing to me, and yet I had a vague idea that I'd heard it before somewhere – I just couldn't think where. If it was a friend of Sophie's, Tom would have been the only person who could have mentioned it to me.

'So, how was the colonel?' asked Sophie, changing the subject.

'Grumpy,' I said. 'He's one of those people who makes me feel I'm still a naughty six-year-old.'

'He's like that to everyone.'

'Army training?'

'Most soldiers I know are very affable. But he outranks most of my university friends who went into the forces. Even the most pushy one has only just been promoted to major. Once they're all full colonels, maybe they'll be the same as Tom's dad.'

'He was in Northern Ireland.'

'I know. There was something a bit odd about his military career – I'm not sure what he did in Ireland, but it wasn't standard soldiering. Some sort of counter-intelligence, I think. Same with Iraq. I think he must have done a lot of things he can't talk about, even now.'

'Probably,' I said. I took a sip of coffee. I'd forgotten to say no milk. I'd drink it anyway. If she had to be gone in half an hour – twenty-five minutes now – she didn't have time to make another one. I was surprised she'd offered coffee at all. Maybe she needed to know something.

'Did he say anything about me?' she asked.

'The colonel? Not much,' I said. 'Why?'

'It's just . . . when I was going out with Tom, I got the impression he was really keen on the idea of our being together. Then later . . . well, quite the reverse. I think he got Tom to dump me. And I've never understood why. Somebody must have said something to him about me.'

'Robin, you mean?'

'Well, you couldn't blame him. Stirring things a bit, I mean. But he can't have told the colonel anything he didn't already know. It can't possibly matter now, of course, but I've always wanted to find out. Tom is certainly never going to tell me. He worships his dad. The last thing he'd do is to betray his father's confidence to a mere girlfriend.'

'The only time he mentioned you,' I said, 'was when he told me you and Tom went to the Weald and Downland Museum. The day Robin died.'

I put my mug down and looked at her but she was staring out of the window.

'Yes,' said Sophie eventually. 'That's right.'

'So you *are* still friends with Tom?'

Sophie turned quickly to face me. She shook her head. 'No,' she said. 'At least, I don't think so. Look, the whole museum thing was rather weird. Tom and I split up. You know that. Months later, out of the blue, I get a message from Tom to meet him at the museum tomorrow at ten o'clock. So I think – he's had a change of heart. He's realised that I am, after all, The One. He's going to explain everything in a romantic and mysterious way. Then I thought – no, that's crap. Tom doesn't do that sort of thing. Still, on balance I was intrigued enough to drop work on an important presentation and come straight down here.'

'And . . . ?'

'And nothing. Nada. Zilch. Lovely day out in spite of the appalling weather – you'd have thought Tom would have checked the forecast. We ran from building to building sheltering under his umbrella – quite promisingly squashed together, my cheek against his muscular arm. If it had been a rom com, we'd have ended up kissing under the dripping eaves of a Kentish mediaeval hall house, circa 1300. As it was, Tom bought me a nice lunch at a pub nearby and apologised non-stop for the weather. We sat on opposite sides of the table and chatted. We shook hands. I drove back to London. Never heard another word. Later, when somebody told me about Robin's death, I worked out that it must have been the same day. So, I was a bit curious to find out what had happened. I mean, it was a weird coincidence piled on top of a bizarre event.'

'You thought you'd been used in some way?'

'It crossed my mind. When Robin was setting off in his boat, Tom and I were at the pub. Perfect alibi for somebody who'd had a bit of a row with the deceased.'

'Perfect alibi for both of you, then.'

'Why the shit should I need an alibi?'

'Ex-girlfriend.'

'Hang on there . . . an ex-girlfriend with no grudge of

any sort. You reckon I'm some kind of suspect? You are joking, I hope?'

'Of course,' I said. 'I'm joking.'

'OK – just you sounded a bit serious. You have to admit it's strange, though. Tom invites me over that day of all days. Then nothing ever since. Not even a hello at the funeral. I mean, what's that all about, Ethelred?'

Sophie's phone rang again, some popular jingle I didn't recognise – it was clearly no longer on silent. She glanced at the screen and grimaced.

'I ought to call her back,' she said apologetically. 'Then I must go. Fifteen minutes before the owners arrive to do an inspection and start to get the place ready for the next occupant. I have to get the bags into the boot by then. Good talking to you, Ethelred. See you next time I'm down, maybe.'

'Yes, see you then,' I said.

But as I walked away I was still trying to remember where I'd heard the name Martina Blanch before. Like a tune that buzzes around in your head that you can't quite place, the question kept coming back to me, but I had no answer.

The next phone to ring was my own as I walked back to my car.

'You're out of biscuits,' said Elsie.

'There are some chocolate ones hidden at the back of the cupboard,' I said.

'There used to be,' she said. 'If you're close to the shop you might pick up another packet or two. Bourbons would be good.'

\* \* \*

153

'Sophie's off back to London today,' I said to Josie as I paid for two packs of plain shortbread. I thought they might last a little longer than anything with chocolate in it.

'Second home for her,' said Josie. 'She might as well buy a flat down here.'

Josie is well informed about most events in the village. I decided to drop something carefully into the conversation.

'Apparently she was down the day Robin Pagham died. She went off to Singleton with Tom.'

I waited to see if she would throw any light on this invitation. It was unlikely she would have heard, but she might have heard some gossip.

'Yes, I know,' she said.

'Tom mentioned it?'

'No, I saw her.'

'What, in the village? So that would have been . . . a bit before ten?'

I wondered if Sophie had in fact come into West Wittering and picked Tom up, though it was odd that having to give him a lift did not feature in her account – and from what she said, she and Tom had gone their own ways afterwards, implying two cars. Coming from London, West Wittering wasn't on the way to Singleton. Far from it.

Josie frowned. 'No, I remember. It was much earlier. I know because I was walking the dog down by Snow Hill. About eight – maybe eight-thirty?'

'At Snow Hill? You're sure?'

'Yes, I recognised her car, parked by the sailing club. She was sitting in it with somebody else, just staring ahead. I don't think she saw me, and I needed to get back to the shop, so I didn't stop. She went to Singleton later, did she? Nice museum but a rotten day for it. Rotten day all round, really.'

'These aren't Bourbons,' said Elsie darkly.

'Then stop eating them,' I said.

'I can't stop eating these until you get some Bourbons,' said Elsie. It is not only Colonel Gittings who speaks to me as if I were a six-year-old. 'I ask you to do *one* thing . . .'

'I'll get some tomorrow,' I said. 'I stop by the Village Stores most days.'

'Josie is a mine of information,' said Elsie. 'Maybe we should just ask her who killed Robin.'

'I think you're right that somebody did,' I said. 'I mean that it wasn't an accident.'

'Of course I'm right,' said Elsie. 'I think that Tom Gittings is behaving very oddly. We should pull him in for questioning.'

'Hold on,' I said. 'Reality check. We are not conducting a police investigation. This isn't a police station. No power on earth could make Tom Gittings show up here so that you can interrogate him.'

The bell rang. I went to the door.

'Hi,' said Tom. 'I was just passing. Do you mind if I come in?'

# CHAPTER NINETEEN

So, the three of us were seated in front of my fire, three mugs of coffee had been made and the last packet of shortbread opened. I had introduced Tom to Elsie and they had chatted briefly about his book, which I was sure Elsie had not yet started to read. From the praise she lavished on his narrative style and characterisation, I could tell that she basically fancied him. That and the way she gave little girlish giggles from time to time. For the record, she has never praised my narrative style in any way. She had promised to get back to him shortly.

'Dad asked me to drop this round,' said Tom, once Elsie had finished with him.

I looked at the bundle Tom had unwrapped. There were several newspaper cuttings covering the trial and the execution. I was pretty sure I had seen them all in the library, but I thanked him nevertheless. There was also an old map, showing the Herring Field. I got the impression that the exact line of the coast might have changed a little in the intervening century and a half, but not much. The piece of thick card wrapped in tissue was more interesting. It proved to be a photograph of a young man with bushy whiskers, dressed in a coat with a velvet collar, tight sleeves and two rows of what seemed to be large brass buttons down the front. A broad black tie or cravat was wrapped round his neck, leaving only a little white shirt showing below and a small, stiff triangle of collar above. He looked out at me somewhat suspiciously, as if he was unsure how good an idea this newfangled photography business was.

'That's John Gittings – the murdered man,' said Tom. 'It may be one of the earliest photographs taken in Sussex.'

I agreed it was a useful thing to have – it might even form the cover illustration if the book ever got that far. But John Gittings was revealing nothing about his killer – unless he suspected the photographer, which seemed likely from his expression.

'I think I may have tried your father's patience a little,' I said. 'We sort of got off track . . .'

'That's not difficult,' said Tom cheerfully. 'He apologised, in fact, for being a bit abrupt. You caught him at a bad time, he said. He'll try to dig out some more stuff. There's apparently a trunk in the attic that hasn't been opened for about fifty years – that's how it is when you live in the same place for generations.'

'I suppose you don't have any records of land sales?' I asked. 'It's clear that over the years the Paghams somehow got their hands on quite a lot of Gittings' land.'

'I wouldn't know where to look. Probably with Dad or the solicitors in Chichester.'

'And why was your father thinking of selling the Herring Field to Robin for a wind farm – another bit of your land about to change hands?'

Tom shrugged apologetically. 'Dad wasn't keen that you included any of that stuff. It doesn't reflect very well on us. I get the impression he'll cooperate as long as you stick to the Herring Field Murder. If you try to trash the family's reputation, he'll call in the lawyers.'

'I'm not sure he can sue me for saying that a piece of land was sold in 1882, or whenever,' I said.

'Well, as a friend, could I ask you not to?' said Tom. 'The way the last two or three generations have mismanaged things is a bit of an embarrassment to him. When he came out of the army and took over from Grandad, he hoped he could sort it all out, but the size of the problem overwhelmed even him. When my mother was alive, he would often mutter about having to sell the house one day – that there'd be nothing to pass to me – not that I wanted anything passed to me. To be perfectly honest, I think Dad's found what he inherited more of a burden than anything. I'm not surprised he wanted to dispose of the Herring Field if it was worth anything.'

I nodded and thought of the piles of paper in his study. Colonel Gittings didn't look like a man who was entirely on top of things. I wondered why he didn't just hand it all over to Tom. Perhaps there was too little left for it to be worthwhile. The Herring Field and the house and a couple of adjoining paddocks might be all that was left of what had been the largest estate in the area.

'And Dad didn't like you asking him where he was the day Robin died,' said Tom. 'He thought it was a bit insensitive. Robin was good friend. He's still pretty cut up about it all.'

'OK,' I said. 'Fair enough.'

'Well, Tom, you were well out of it, anyway,' Elsie interjected. She had been concentrating for a while on her biscuit intake but the plate was now empty. 'Nowhere near the sailing club. Because, on the day Robin died, you invited Sophie over to Singleton.'

Tom turned to her. 'Sort of,' he said.

'Sort of, in what way?' she said.

'Well, we did go to the museum, but it was Sophie who phoned me and left a message suggesting we met there . . . It was great seeing her again, but I never did work out what it was all about. Later she was at the inquest and pretty much ignored me. When I saw her at the funeral I waited for her to come over and explain but she didn't. She didn't bother to come back to the house afterwards, so I didn't see her there, either.'

I thought he sounded genuinely hurt, which didn't quite fit in with Sophie's account.

'Fair enough,' I said. 'By the way – do you know a Morgan Blanch?'

He frowned. 'You mean *Martina* Blanch?'

'Yes, sorry – Martina – that's it. Her name sort of came up in conversation.'

Tom laughed grimly. 'One of Robin's exes. Notable mainly for the fact that he broke her nose.'

'Of course, Martina,' said Elsie. 'She was the one he assaulted.'

'She was the one who complained to the police. When I asked him about it he said: "Well, I slapped her around a bit, the way you do."'

'So he slapped most of his girlfriends around? The way you do?' Elsie raised an eyebrow. 'Nice friends you've got.'

Tom sighed. 'As I've said, he was Dad's friend more than he was mine. And most of the time he was the perfect gent. But point taken. I wouldn't have wanted him going out with my sister. Martina wasn't the only one he hit.'

'Sophie?' I asked.

'That's partly why she left him,' said Tom. 'That and the drugs.'

'I thought he'd given them up,' I said pointedly. 'Or that's what you led me and the good people of Sussex to believe.'

'Oh hell, he tried to give it up,' said Tom. 'We all wanted to believe he had . . .'

'But he hadn't?'

'No.'

'And you left it out of your report on the inquest?'

'It was cut by the editor. Just a question of fitting the piece in. There was other more important stuff that week.'

'Really?' I said.

'Yes,' said Tom.

'Did you know Robin used Rohypnol?' I said.

Tom's face turned a little paler. The question clearly troubled him. 'Why do you ask? He didn't drug women and rape them, if that's what you mean.'

161

'Well, not to your knowledge,' Elsie said.

'He wouldn't do it,' said Tom sharply. 'He sometimes took Rohypnol himself. After cocaine. It's not unusual.'

'You didn't take any of that stuff yourself?' I asked.

'Shit, no. Dad wouldn't have liked that at all,' said Tom. He seemed relieved to be answering a straightforward question.

'But Robin, to your knowledge, kept Rohypnol around the house?'

Tom laughed. 'It was part of an arsenal of drugs that featured in the military operation that was the life of Robin Pagham,' he said.

# CHAPTER TWENTY

## Elsie

*Dear Mr/Mrs/Ms (delete as applicable),*
*Thank you so much for submitting your manuscript to me. It was much, much too kind of you. You really shouldn't have.*

*I liked many/some/few/no aspects of your book but frankly if I read any more wizards/ Tudors/mommy-porn/chick-lit/vampires/teenage werewolves/crap (tick all that apply) I shall vomit.*

*You do/don't ask for feedback. Here it is. I think that your main problem is plot/dialogue/ characterisation/description of place/literacy/ upbringing/being a total dick (tick all that apply). But basically, let's not beat about the bush: your book, over which you have slaved so long, is rubbish.*

*You could take consolation from the fact that JK Rowling was rejected by a dozen publishers, but only if you are, by some freakish chance, JK Rowling.*

*Most people get rejected by loads of publishers and agents and that's it. They never see their book in print. Fact.*

*So, I wish you every success in your chosen career and hope that one day you will indeed become an author, living off a pittance and selling far fewer books than your agent or publisher ever dreamt possible when they took you on.*

'May I interrupt you, Elsie?'

'No, Tuesday, you may not.'

'I've come to restock your chocolate drawer.'

'Technically that doesn't count as an interruption. Go ahead.'

'Have you thought about my suggestion for a standard rejection letter?'

'I've just done one.'

I showed it to her. She quibbled, as I knew she would. I listened for a bit.

'I've said I wish them every success,' I replied. 'I have given them my advice, which is worth its weight in chocolate.'

'I'll write you a proper one,' she said.

'This is a proper one.'

'It'll be on your desk in the morning.'

'Anything else?' I asked. I think I put more sarcasm into 'anything' rather than 'else' but frankly both words were pretty much off the scale.

'Yes,' said Tuesday. 'You should cut down on chocolate. It's not good for you. I'll bring some fruit in tomorrow. What sort do you like?'

'The fruit of the cocoa tree,' I said. 'And if I wanted a wife, I'd marry Ethelred.'

'I'll get some apples then,' said Tuesday.

And she was gone before I could point out that there are big health and safety concerns about apples. Just check out Genesis if you don't believe me.

The phone rang. I answered it, as you do.

'Don't lecture me, Ethelred,' I said. 'I'm not in the mood.'

There was a rather nervous pause, then Ethelred said: 'I've been thinking. Do you have Sophie's mobile number?'

'Yes,' I said. Because I had.

'Could you ask her a question?'

'Which question?'

'I was thinking about the plot of my very first book,' he said.

'It's a bit late for that,' I said. 'It was published years ago. Whatever she thinks of it, it's too late to do much about it.'

'I don't mean I want to change it. It's actually one of my better ones.'

'I agree your first book was some sort of high watermark in your career.'

'Just ask Sophie if Tom kept the bill from the museum,' he said.

'Is that it?'

'Yes, that's it. You don't remember the plot of my first book do you?'

'Absolutely,' I said.

'So you know what I'm getting at?'

'You bet.'

Thinking about it afterwards, I couldn't even remember the title of Ethelred's first book. Still, it wouldn't take long to phone.

'Hi, Sophie. Elsie here. How are things?'

'OK,' she said. 'Did you find your diet book?'

Sometimes people say things that are so weird that it's better to ignore them.

'This may seem an odd question, Sophie, but when you and Tom went to the museum, did he pay?'

'Yes, bless him. Well, it was his idea.'

'And, stranger still, could I ask if he kept the receipt?'

'Yes, he did. I remember that. He gift-aided the entrance fee. He said he could reclaim some tax or something and he folded the receipt away very carefully in his wallet. I remember especially, though, because he did the same thing with the lunch receipt – he checked it very carefully and then folded it neatly in half and put it in his wallet. I asked him if he'd gift-aided that too and he got quite irritable about it. He said he always kept receipts. I suppose some people do. I chuck mine in the bin straight away.'

'So do I, unless I can claim expenses,' I said.

'Martina thought it was funny too.'

'Martina?'

'Oh, she was down in Chichester too. I mentioned it to her. Was that it? Your question, I mean.'

'Apparently,' I said. 'Sergeant Fairfax of the Buckfordshire Police will take it from here.'

\* \* \*

Later I checked through Ethelred's books. The first was called *All on a Summer's Day*. In it Fairfax solves a case by sitting in his office in Buckford and examining some receipts that formed part of an alibi. He also goes off to the pub, drinks excessively and is rude to his colleagues, but it was obviously the receipt thing that Ethelred was on about. I phoned him back and told him the receipts were safely filed.

'It was just a hunch,' he said modestly.

'So, you don't need to see the receipts, just to know they still exist?'

'Precisely.'

'You mean the receipts are Tom's alibi?' I asked.

'Something like that.'

'How much like that?'

'Quite a lot. But I need to do some more checking,' he said.

He sounded so smug it was a pleasure to drop my small bombshell into the mix.

'You know Martina – she of the broken nose and a justifiable grievance – was down in Chichester too that day?'

'Was she?'

'Sophie let it slip. They'd had a laugh together about Tom keeping the receipts.'

Ethelred was silent for a moment. 'Josie said she'd seen somebody else in the car with Sophie.'

'There you are then, they came down together.'

'I wonder why?' said Ethelred.

'Two ex-girlfriends of girlfriend-beater Robin Pagham

167

are around in Sussex on the day he died and you wonder why that should be?'

'Yes,' said Ethelred.

'Because their being there together doesn't fit in with whatever this theory is that you won't tell me about?'

'Sort of.'

'Please yourself,' I said. 'Some of us have proper day jobs to get on with.'

I looked in my chocolate drawer. I'd been rationed to one Mars Bar, one Snickers and some round green and red things that you see in the supermarkets. Somewhere out there the forces of Evil were circling. The world was ganging up on me.

# CHAPTER TWENTY-ONE

## Elsie

If there's one thing that really grinds my goat (as my good friend Cat would say) it's chapters in detective novels where they go over the evidence yet again, trying to work out who the killer is. They sift through all the stuff you already know and add nothing to anything. Pillocks.

Still, I couldn't help wondering exactly what Ethelred was getting at. I mean, why should Tom need an alibi? He was a good buddy of Robin's, albeit mildly disapproving of his treatment of women, and his father was an even better friend of even longer standing. Tom was in no way a suspect. He was also completely under his father's thumb – he'd scarcely risk doing anything that would bring further disgrace on the venerable if slightly impoverished House of Gittings.

Returning to my more plausible theory, Sophie on the other hand was an ex-girlfriend, who by all accounts had been badly treated. And she was in contact with another ex, who'd had her nose broken – for which Robin had got off relatively lightly. And they had apparently both been around at the relevant time. Had I been there too, I might have joined them in putting drugs in his coffee, driving him to the sailing club and helping to push his boat out to sea in a storm. And how stunningly fitting that the drug they administered should have been Rohypnol. They had been spotted waiting at the sailing club earlier – maybe they'd checked the weather conditions or something. Then, as I saw it, Martina had later gone to the house – two coffee cups, one with just coffee and one with added Rohypnol – then driven Robin down. Sophie by this stage was at the museum, of course. If Tom's version of events was to be preferred, she had phoned him a day or two before and suggested a day out, as some sort of cover, relying on the fact that he (with his known compulsion for tidiness) would keep the receipts that would show the time they had arrived and the time they had eaten lunch. So, the receipts were sort of relevant, but it wasn't an alibi for Tom. It was for Sophie, who had accidentally revealed to me that Martina had been with her. A big mistake.

I reckoned I needed to go and see Martina. Half an hour of grilling from me and she'd crack. I'd need to get Tuesday to schedule it in for me. And I'd need to find my trusty tape recorder. I'd run through all of the above points and wait for her to break down and confess.

But I won't go through it all again now. As I say, I can't stand all of this recapitulation of stuff. It really gets up my nose.

That and short chapters.

# CHAPTER TWENTY-TWO

The problem with being a crime writer was that the more Tom tried to divert me from the aftermath of the 1848 murder, the more I felt obliged to look into it. It was unusual, after all, that the death of a member of the family by hanging had somehow acted as a catalyst for the resurgence of the Paghams. A day spent in the library and a little online research revealed that the change in fortunes had been gradual, but that it had actually begun very soon after the murder of John Gittings.

Perceval Pagham had, at the time of the killing, been a labourer on the Gittings' estate – that had been clearly reported in the accounts of the trial. Yet the 1851 census returns showed him as a farmer and the owner of Greylands Farm, as it was then described. Greylands had been extended in the late nineteenth century, but even in the 1850s, it must have been a substantial house. A little more research showed that he had enlarged the holding in

1875 and 1876. An obituary in the *Chichester Observer* dating from 1902, recorded him as a significant landowner. His daughter had predeceased him, without marrying. His only son, Cecil, became a Justice of the Peace and had five sons of his own – four of whom had died in the trenches in the 1914–18 war. Gawain alone, another Pagham to be named after one of Arthur's knights, came through it and succeeded his father in 1930. Gawain, too, had been a JP and had been awarded a CBE for some unspecified services to the state. He had made further acquisitions of land in 1935 and 1950, passing on the estate to Robin's father, Roger, in 1970. Roger had made the final additions to the estate with a further purchase in 1984.

These acquisitions, from first to last, had been mainly from the Gittings family. This in itself was not strange. There is a limited market for small parcels of land. You cannot show up with a trailer and pack ten acres into it and drive away. The most likely purchaser, if you are considering selling a few fields, is the farm next door. The Gittings and Pagham properties had been side by side.

What had induced the Gittings to sell was not clear, but their decline had mirrored the Paghams rise. Early census returns listed them as landowners. I knew that Tom's father had spent most of his career in the army. The obituary for Tom's grandfather stated that he was an accountant. His great-grandfather was listed as a smallholder and grain merchant. They were not impoverished but clearly needed to earn their living.

Then I noticed something odd. Each Pagham acquisition coincided with a Gittings death. George had died in 1875, his eldest son John in 1876, his grandson, also John, in 1935, and so on. It couldn't be a coincidence. So what was it?

'No biscuits today?' asked Josie. 'I'm amazed you can put that many away and stay as thin as you are.'

'My guest returned to London a couple of days ago,' I said.

'Your agent?'

'That's right. Elsie's my agent. Sorry – I mean she used to be my agent.'

'So now she just comes down . . . what? . . . to eat your biscuits?'

I pocketed my change with a shrug. That seemed a fair summary of our present contractual status. Then, seeing the shop was empty, I asked: 'Josie, you know the village as well as anyone . . . Have you ever heard anything about a feud between the Gittings and the Paghams?'

She frowned. 'Well, like I said, young Tom Gittings played fast and loose with Robin's fiancée.'

'I mean earlier – maybe much earlier. You know that a Gittings was murdered by a Pagham back in the 1840s?'

'A bit before my time.'

'But you've heard about it?'

'It's our most famous murder. It's got its own entry on Wikipedia.'

'So, did that lead to anything later?'

Josie leant forward, as she often did if she wanted to impart some local gossip.

'Not really,' she said, somewhat disappointingly. 'But I do remember my gran saying something very odd about them.' She surveyed the empty shop for a moment then continued: 'She'd have only been a little girl at the time, but she told me she'd seen Albert Gittings and Cecil Pagham outside the Memorial Hall one time – a couple years after the First War, that would have been. There'd been some sort of event there, opening the hall and commemorating the men who'd been killed. Well, Cecil had lost four sons, hadn't he? It was only Gawain, who was a bit funny, who'd survived. He'd not been called up for some reason. Anyway, Albert Gittings turns round and says to Cecil, four down and one to go, eh? Now that was a horrible thing to say at any time, and this was just after this event, whatever it was, to commemorate the dead.'

'What did Cecil say?' I asked.

'I've no idea,' said Josie with a laugh. 'Gran never told me that. She just told me what Albert said. She was that shocked – even though she was a mite herself. Four down and one to go. She clearly never forgot it. Did I give you your change?'

'Yes, thanks,' I said. 'I'd better get back. I need to make a phone call.'

'Death duties,' said Elsie, at the other end of the line. 'It's obvious. The head of the family dies. They have to sell a few fields to pay the tax. The Paghams are waiting with the cash.'

'How come it's always the Gittings who have to sell? Death duties would have hit both families. The Paghams held onto what they had.'

'You don't listen to the Archers, do you?'

'Yes,' I said. 'I do.' It was a radio programme I rarely missed.

'OK. The Gittings are the Grundys – always mismanaging their farm and lurching from crisis to crisis. The Paghams are the Archers, buying up the village bit by bit and getting all the best lines in the script.'

I thought about this. I couldn't see Derek Gittings mismanaging anything.

'The problem with that,' I said, 'is that there was no inheritance tax back in the 1870s – I've checked and there was just succession duty at about one per cent. It would have been an annoyance, but not ruinous. Death duty didn't come in until 1894 – the first time it would have applied would have been when the grandson, John, died in 1935.'

'I'm losing track of all these Johns – they do seem to have wanted to keep the memory of the original one alive.'

'That's the son of the second John Gittings and the nephew of Albert.'

'The Albert who wished the Paghams dead?'

'That's the one. And why the animosity?'

'Because a Pagham had killed a Gittings?' suggested Elsie.

'Tom doesn't think so. He reckons John was a victim of Gittings on Gittings violence, with Lancelot Pagham as collateral damage. There was a clear motive too – both Gittings boys were after the same girl and one of them had got her pregnant. George Gittings gave evidence that did for Lancelot and saved his own skin in the process. People must have talked about it.'

'Well, if it was a known miscarriage of justice, then you'd

have expected the Paghams to have hated the Gittings,' said Elsie, 'not the other way round. And it would scarcely have still been going on seventy years later.'

'Cecil Pagham was the nephew of Lancelot. Albert was the nephew of John Gittings. In one way it was all still pretty close. But I take your point that it's all the wrong way round. Unless Tom's mistaken – if the judge was right and Lancelot really *was* the killer, then it makes more sense.'

'We need more evidence,' Elsie said. 'Something that will help make sense of it all.'

But the next bit of evidence I was to unearth would prove to be the oddest yet.

# CHAPTER TWENTY-THREE

It was in the bar of the Old House at Home that the next piece of information emerged. Later I realised how crucial it was, but at the time it scarcely appeared to be evidence at all.

'Mind if I join you?'

A large shadow had been cast in front of me. I looked up at Barry Whitelace. 'Not at all,' I said, 'but I'm just planning to finish this half then I'm heading home. I still have a house guest to look after.'

'I won't offer to buy you another, then,' he said, sitting down. I doubt that he was planning to do anyway.

'It's getting a bit warmer,' I ventured.

He looked at me vaguely. Something other than the weather was on his mind. 'Have you seen Catarina lately?' he asked.

'No,' I said.

'It's just that I'm still not sure now what she's planning to do about this wind farm business. The first time I spoke to her I got the impression she wasn't following up on it. But I'm worried that my earlier discussion with her has simply alerted her to a business opportunity that she's missed.'

That sounded like Catarina.

'Why?' I asked.

'Well,' he continued, 'when I walked past the Herring Field today, what do you think I saw?'

'No idea,' I said.

'Notices pinned up about planning permission for exploratory drilling on the site.'

'Do you need to drill before you put up a wind farm?'

'I don't know. Maybe they're testing to see what sort of foundations they would need in that marsh? I'm going to phone the council anyway. I've said nothing to Jean, of course. No point in upsetting her. But I wondered if you'd heard anything.'

'Catarina's said nothing to me about reviving the plans,' I said. 'But it's Gittings' land, as I told you.'

'Maybe she's done a deal with him? Bought the land from him? Derek wouldn't start drilling there.'

'Sorry, I don't know Catarina's plans for anything. I don't even know if she intends to stay in the village. The house is a bit big for her on her own.'

'Haunted too,' said Whitelace with a smile.

'Is it? I hadn't heard that.'

'Well, of course it isn't – not unless you believe in ghosts, which I certainly do not. But that's the rumour.'

'Whose ghost?'

'Lancelot Pagham.'

'Who says?'

'Catarina. She told me.'

'She's actually seen it?'

'Yes, walking in the garden, clear as day.'

'She'd recognise Lancelot Pagham, then?' I asked.

'Apparently. She's seen a picture of him.'

'I didn't know there was one.'

'I agree – it's a bit odd – maybe there's a drawing in one of the local papers – the trial or something.'

'I haven't seen it.'

'Nor have I,' Whitelace conceded reluctantly. 'Of course, she can't have seen anything so it can't have looked like anything. Rum business, though.'

We both sat and thought about this. Then Whitelace said: 'There's a queer story associated with the Gittings' house too.'

'Ghost?' I asked.

'No, supernatural abduction.'

'Really?'

'It's in an old book I found. They don't name it, but it's pretty obvious which house it is.'

'I'd like to read that.'

'I'll drop it round. Sure you won't have another?'

Whitelace suddenly looked anxious, fearing that his rash offer might cost him half of bitter.

'No,' I said. 'But I look forward to reading the story.'


I hadn't expected Whitelace would remember to let me see the book. Perhaps the strangest thing of all the strange things was that it actually dropped through my letter box later that evening. The book was called *Curious Tales of Old Sussex*. It had been published in Chichester in the early 1900s and most of the stories, of witches and elves and pixies, stretched the reader's credulity a little more than a modern audience would have tolerated. Some seemed to have been lifted, with a few names changed, from similar volumes on Devon or Essex. There was a slip of paper marking the place of the story that I was to read. It was entitled *The Murderer and the Devil*.

# THE MURDERER AND THE DEVIL

*It is said that, long ago in the small fishing village of West Wittering, on the far side of the county and almost in Hampshire, two brothers paid court to the same beautiful maiden. The elder brother was a farmer named John and the other, named George, worked for him on the farm, receiving in return just his bed and his food and a little pocket money to buy ale or a fancy waistcoat at the fair. John was open-handed and well-beloved. George was sly and furtive and the damsel, who had considered carefully the suit of both brothers, quickly made her preference known for the handsome farmer. George saw that, while his brother lived, he would remain poor and would live off crumbs from his table. Worse still, he would need to watch helplessly when his brother brought home the bride he so much desired for himself. Day by day his jealousy grew, but at first he could conceive no manner in which his brother might be safely put out of the way. Then, one day, he was walking in a field owned by a certain fisherman. The field* was dank and choked with weeds of all sorts. Nobody came there, and the long grass and sedge were allowed to grow until they were waist-high. By and by George formed a plan: he would lure his brother to this desolate place and stab him; but he had no knife of his own and durst not steal one from the farm in case its loss was noticed. Then one fine morning he discovered a fisherman's blade on the village green. He decided this would be a fine weapon for the deed he had in mind and he could moreover leave it with the body so that perchance another might be blamed. So, slyly, he picked it up and hid it inside his coat and went on his way. The very next day he sent a note to John, as if from a stranger, requesting that he meet him at this remote field at such and such a time for a reason that he would reveal when he saw him.

On the morning prescribed, George said that he had business in Chichester and would be gone all day, but, having set off along the highway, he sneaked back in secret by the coastal path to the mournful field I have spoken of. When John at last arrived, George was hiding behind a large willow tree. He sprang out and, before the amazed brother could say a word, he plunged the keen knife deep into John's heart. George concealed the body as best he could and was about to set off for Chichester when he heard a cough behind him. He turned to see a well-dressed gentleman in a black silk coat and a black silk top hat, but how he had got there and why there was no mud on his boots troubled George a great deal.

'That is a fine morning's work for you,' said the gentleman. 'I congratulate you, my good sir.'

George held the bloody knife before him. 'You will tell

*nobody what you saw,' he threatened. 'Or I shall serve you as I have served him.'*

*'Why should I do that,' said the gentleman, 'seeing that we shall be such good friends, you and I?'*

*'Good friends? Do I know you, then?' asked George.*

*'We have never met, but you will have heard your parents speak of me often and the parson speak of me every Sunday. And many a carter with his wheels mired in the mud on the Cakeham Road invokes my name as he flogs his weary horses on.'*

*'So, you will not inform the magistrate?' said George suspiciously.*

*'The magistrate, too, is a very good friend of mine,' said the gentleman, 'but I shall not trouble him with this trifle. It can remain our secret for as long as you wish. My lips are sealed until the day you die.'*

*'What do you want from me, then?' asked George.*

*'Nothing at present,' said the gentleman. 'Indeed, it is you who want something from me, for you have some way to go this morning. I shall ensure that you get safely away from here and that another bears the blame for this. Leave that bloody knife here in the grass. When it is found, the fisherman who owns it, and who also by chance owns this field, will be accused and will hang for it. And I shall make sure that the young lady that you wish to marry will be yours. You will become rich and respected by all and live to a great age.'*

*'You must want something in exchange?' asked George.*

*'Just this. One day I shall return to this village. When I do, you will come away with me and live with me in my*

own house, which is not far from here, and you will keep me company.'

George did not know what to make of that, but he dared not refuse, for the gentleman could change his mind and turn him over to the Constable in a moment. So George agreed to do what the gentleman said and threw the knife down in the grass, where it remained.

The gentleman smiled and turned and walked away very slowly. As he went, George saw that there was a vent in the back of his trousers and a long tail poked out of it. And wherever the gentleman trod, he left behind the scorched print of a cloven hoof.

Now, George did not doubt for a moment that he had been conversing with the Devil but he thought to himself: the Devil keeps his promises, so they say, and he has promised me fair. I shall live to a great age. I shall perhaps live a good life and, if I do well by my fellow men, then the Good Lord will surely not allow me to be taken to Hell, because he forgives those who repent. Thus I may take what the Devil has offered but have no fear of him. So he set off for Chichester in fine spirits and was there in a very short time indeed because (as he later thought) it was as if his feet had wings. So, he did whatever business he had to do there and later came home again.

And it came to pass that the poor fisherman was indeed accused of the murder and taken to the gaol in Chichester to stand trial. George thought if he could make amends and save the fisherman's life, then perhaps the contract with the Devil would be broken almost at once, so he tried to give evidence to the court that he had seen the fisherman far from the spot on the day of the murder. But the Devil made the fisherman proud and speak so insolently to the judge that the judge condemned him to hang the very next day. And so the fisherman died bravely, praying sincerely for those who had wrongly convicted him.

In this wise George gained his brother's inheritance and married the girl, and together they grew prosperous. He could do nothing that did not turn out well. He and his family had all the vittles they wanted to eat and as many fine clothes as they could wear. George's wife had pearls fetched from the South Seas for her neck and diamonds from Africa for her ears and a great blue sapphire brooch from Ceylon. They had many children and grandchildren. But there was no joy in George's heart because he knew that any day the gentleman might return and beckon him away to Hell. So George set about living a good life, as he saw it. He asked the parson many times what he needed to do to be saved, and the parson, who knew nothing of the pact with the Devil, advised him (as he did all parishioners) to believe and trust in the Lord Jesus Christ and to do good works and give to the poor. And the wretched George did all of these things, but he still grew more and more fearful that he had not done enough. He gave money too, it is said, to the brother of the fisherman who had been hanged, so much indeed that George's family looked at how few coins were left in the strongbox and wondered why there was so little profit in their farm. And still George grew more and more afraid.

Then, when George was very old indeed, the day finally came. There was a knock on the door. When George opened it, the gentleman was standing there, looking *as young as when George had last seen him, fifty years before.*

'So you came,' said George.

'I always keep my promises,' said the gentleman, 'and I have come to take you away to live with me.'

'But,' said George, 'I have lived a good life. I have given money to the poor and to the fisherman's family.'

'So you have,' said the Devil, 'but that was simply to save yourself. You only had to repent sincerely – to go to the parson and tell him what you had done and that you were sorry for it. I could not have taken you then – no, not whatever you had promised me. Even if you repented in your heart as I walked up the path, I could not have taken you. Angels would have snatched you away from me. But it is too late now, for you are already dead and you are mine.'

'Can I say farewell to my family?' George asked.

'You may,' said the Devil, 'then we shall go to my house and you will live with me and do my bidding in all things.'

And so, by and by, they set off down the path towards the highway. They walked slowly, with George casting many a longing glance behind him, but the Devil didn't mind that, because he knew he had George for all eternity. George was never seen again in West Wittering or East Wittering or Itchenor or Birdham or any village in that part of the world.

Now, folk in the village thought it strange that George had gone and nobody could tell them where. They asked if he was dead and the family were ashamed to say that Grandfather had gone away hand in hand with the Devil so they said he was poorly and must stay in his bed. The parson called, for he was conscientious in visiting the sick, but they told him that the fever was catching and that it would be best if he came again later. And the parson came again later and indeed returned many times, but on each occasion it was the same. He was told George had cholera or typhus or some other thing that the parson might think too dangerous to go near. After a whole year had passed, the parson called once more and said that this time he really must see his parishioner, whatever the risk to his own health, because, trusting in God, he himself did not fear death and would do his duty and no man would stop him.

The family led him to the parlour and showed him George's empty chair. Take me then to his bedroom, he instructed. So they led him upstairs and showed the parson the empty bed, which perplexed the good man greatly. Then is he already dead and have you placed his body in the cellar, where it is cooler? asked the parson. So they took the parson to the cellar and George's body was not there. Then is he recovered and out riding his mare? asked the parson. So they took him to the stables where George's fat mare was guzzling hay.

We do not know what story the family eventually told him, but the parson was seen walking back to his house in great puzzlement and with a terrible frown. A few days later a coffin left George's house, carried in a hearse, drawn by six black horses with great black plumes. And the coffin was buried in the churchyard, with much praying for George's soul. But they say the coffin was empty.

And they say too that George's family never prospered after that, but the family of the fisherman who was hanged *grew rich and became great landowners themselves. But the field in which the murder took place and which the fisherman had owned, they gave to George's family, as a reminder of the terrible deed. And they gave it in such a way that the murderer's family were never allowed to part with it or to be free of the stain. And they still live in Sussex and still bear their cross to this very day.*

Barry Whitelace answered the phone almost straight away.

'Many thanks for sending me that story,' I said. 'Very interesting.'

'And at least partly true. The names of the two brothers. The Herring Field, though it doesn't name it.'

'And the Herring Field did change hands at some point – I'm sure it's the same place as in the story. It's the other bits that are really interesting. I think the tale must be based on some distant folk memory of the real murder.'

'Not that distant,' said Whitelace. 'The murder would have taken place about fifty years before the stories were collected. There would have been people alive who knew the various parties and could have heard the story pretty much first hand. The editor of the book was a local clergyman – Sabine Barclay-Wood. I say editor – he probably made up as much as he collected – and that probably accounts for the rather pious tone of a lot of the stories. He tried to give them a sort of rustic artlessness, but the Oxford education keeps showing through. The theology is usually very sound, and when it's not you can tell he's mocking it. He was vicar of a church in Selsey, so not so far from here, so he could have ridden over to the Witterings and talked to some of the older farmhands. Maybe even to the Paghams or the Gittings.'

'He describes West Wittering as if it were miles away – the other side of the county, he says.'

'I suspect Brighton was the fashionable bit of Sussex, where he would have preferred to live,' said Whitelace. 'He probably felt a bit cut off in Selsey. The Witterings really were the back of beyond.'

'I can't help wondering if the part about George being observed was true,' I said. 'Maybe somebody did see him and blackmailed him all his life. Maybe the charitable donations mentioned in the tale were hush money.'

'And the devil taking him away?'

'What if he finally had to flee his blackmailers?' I suggested. 'It fits with the family in the story covering up the disappearance and the parson's consternation when he hears the full account.'

'He'd have been pretty old to do a runner.'

'I suppose so. Maybe they hid him somewhere and made up a story he had gone? Maybe they even made up a tale that he was dead – hence the empty coffin and the sham funeral. The other thing that's odd,' I continued, 'is this business of the Herring Field being some sort of albatross around the Gittings' necks. One they could never shake off. How could that work?'

'Maybe that's symbolic rather than real,' said Whitelace. 'That bit of land would have been a constant reminder. And who would have bought it, anyway? It's of no value and it would have appeared cursed. You've heard the latest about it, I assume?'

'No,' I said.

'You remember I said they wanted to drill there?' Whitelace sounded very pleased with himself.

'Yes,' I said. 'Did you phone the council?'

'I did better than that. I went down there with a friend. We were going to put up a big sign – "no drilling here". Took a couple of spades. Dug holes for the posts.'

'I guess that would alert a few more people to it.'

'Don't sound so disparaging. It gets better. When we were digging the second hole, we found a dead body. They won't be drilling there any time soon.'

# CHAPTER TWENTY-FOUR

I was curious to see how the authorities had responded to Whitelace's discovery at the Herring Field, so I strolled down there the following morning. Barry Whitelace was already there, clutching a thermos, a packet of sandwiches and a pair of binoculars.

A small blue and white tent had been erected in the field and there was a police car and an unmarked van parked beside the drilling equipment. There was little activity on display.

'Somebody went in there half an hour ago,' he said, pointing to the tent.

'I'm surprised they haven't closed the footpath,' I said.

'They can't. Public right of way,' he said, as if that was some sort of personal triumph.

'I suppose the footpath is some way from the crime scene,' I said. 'They don't need to close it off.'

'I found the body,' he said. 'You'd think they'd consult me a bit more.'

'I suppose they got you to give a statement?'

'Told me I was trespassing. I told them, they were dead lucky I did. I offered to help dig up the whole thing, but they said I could leave it to them. Doesn't look as if they are doing much.'

I nodded. Though I am a crime writer, I get to see very few real crime scenes. Sometimes there seems to be a lot going on, sometimes not much.

'So what do you think you found?'

'Bones. I think it was a femur we found first. I'd have dug up the whole thing there and then, but my friend said better not. So we phoned the police.'

'Just bones? Not a very recent interment, then?' I said.

'Of course not,' Whitelace said, slightly impatiently.

I'm not sure why I was disappointed. Even if it had proved to be recent, it wouldn't really have helped with the mystery of Robin's death. It is only in novels that the second body leads to a breakthrough – the killer has been forced to strike again and this time has given something away. Another body would have just been another body – scarcely even a coincidence since Robin had died some weeks before. And his death was still most likely to be an accident.

'Sandwich?' Whitelace asked, proffering the packet. 'Jean makes them. Cheese and pickle.'

'No thanks,' I said. 'Bit early for me.'

'She's probably only got a few weeks to live,' he said, as if by way of inducement. 'Cancer. Lung. She used to smoke forty a day. Gave up too late. Smoked a pipe myself. Never liked it much. Wasn't difficult to stop.'

I realised that, though he had often mentioned his wife

before, I'd never met her, never really thought to ask after her other than in the polite, automatic way that one does. How's Jean? Fine – she couldn't make it tonight – feeling a bit tired.

'I'm sorry,' I said. 'I had no idea . . .'

'A lot of people haven't. She doesn't like to make a fuss. Doesn't like people knowing her business. Of course, the funeral will be a bit of giveaway in that respect.'

'I'm sorry,' I repeated. 'It must be tough for both of you.'

'Oh, I'll learn to make my own sandwiches,' he said.

I looked at him for a moment. Was this gallows humour or would cheese and pickle sandwiches be his greatest regret?

'We used to walk here,' he added. 'When we first moved down, we walked all round this bit of coast – up to Itchenor, over on the ferry when it was running, along the coast to Bosham, tea at a cafe, then back again. Out all day. Rain or shine. Or the Downs, over by Singleton – they're nice too – but mainly here. Then, after she was diagnosed, the walks got shorter and shorter. This was the last bit she could do – I'd park the car at the end of the road and we'd just walk down to here and back. She loved . . . loves . . . this spot. She used to quote that Hopkins thing about wet and wilderness? You know it?'

'Yes, I know it. What would the world be, once bereft of wet and wildness?'

'Let them be left,' continued Whitelace with feeling. 'O let them be left, wildness and wet; long live the weeds and the wilderness yet. I always thought that, after she had gone, this was where I'd come to remember her. Her spot – you know what I mean? She wants her ashes scattered here. I won't have them wreck it with a wind farm. I've promised her that

I won't. Whatever I have to do. I'll stop the bastards. Can I offer you some tea?'

I accepted a small beaker of tasteless, lukewarm liquid and sipped it slowly.

'I'm hoping it's Bronze Age,' he said, waving his hand towards the tent.

'Is that likely?'

'It has to be pre-Christian, doesn't it? A burial here by the sea, miles from any church. A Bronze Age burial site could takes months to excavate, maybe years. There could be dozens of bodies over there. Generations burying their dead where the land meets the sea. There could be jewellery. Grave goods. The ground hasn't been disturbed for hundreds of years – too poor to be worth ploughing, too wet to be worth trying to drain.'

I suspected that, like me, he would be disappointed when the identity of the bones was revealed. But he was as entitled to hope as I was. A man in white overalls appeared from inside the tent, glanced briefly over in our direction, then got into the driver's seat of the van. George aimed his binoculars at him.

'I can't see what he's doing,' he said.

'Tea break, probably,' I said.

'Tea break!' said Whitelace, as if that summed up all that was wrong with the country. 'Can I top you up?'

'No, thanks. I'd better get back,' I said, handing him my cup. 'Thank Jean for the tea.'

He nodded glumly. 'I'll stay a bit longer,' he said. 'Jean was asleep when I left. She sleeps a lot at the moment. Says I disturb her if I fuss too much.'

\* \* \*

I still have a contact in the police over on the other side of Sussex. Unusually (in my experience) for a policeman, he enjoys crime fiction. Some years before he'd given me a briefing on scene of crime operations. Then he'd been involved in a case concerning an old friend of mine. We still meet for drinks from time to time. I've dedicated a book to him. I gave him a call.

'So, you want to know what they've found?'

'If you can do it easily,' I said.

'Depends what they've come up with. I'll phone a friend of mine in Chichester. I can say we want to rule it out of a missing persons enquiry. Actually I do have one of those and I ought to do that, anyway.'

He called back after only a few minutes.

'Well, I don't know if this helps you at all, but they reckon the body has been there about a hundred years. Not my missing person, anyway.'

'Not Bronze Age?'

'No chance at all.'

'Could it be as early as the 1840s?' I asked. Because I had wondered if there could be any connection with the Herring Field murder.

'There'd be a bit of a margin of error – say fifty years either way, maximum. It might just about be late 1840s, but it's not likely. I could get back to them and ask if the body could conceivably date back to then, but it would seem a bit weird in the context of my own enquiry into somebody who went missing last October. And while we do cold cases, going back to the nineteenth century is pushing it a bit. I've probably asked all the questions I can without making it look suspicious.'

'OK. Thanks, Joe. We must meet for a drink soon. That pub near Worthing.'

'Give me a call when you're next over this way. Maybe you can do me a favour in return, though.'

'If I can.'

'You know the coast round your way?'

'Reasonably well.'

'Thought you might. Could I come and talk to you about something?'

Just for a second I hesitated. 'Tomorrow?' I suggested.

'Two o'clock suit you?'

'Fine,' I said.

'Back on the biscuits, then?' asked Josie.

'I don't eat them,' I said. 'I've got somebody coming to see me this afternoon.'

'Your lady friend back, is she?'

'She's not my lady friend,' I said. 'Or not in the sense that it's usually used. Elsie just comes here to eat biscuits and to try to run my life.'

Josie nodded. She'd met Elsie, after all.

'By the way,' I said, 'you haven't heard anything about a ghost over at Greylands, have you?'

'In the garden?'

'Yes.'

'It's all over the village,' she said. 'But it's mainly the kids who seem to have heard about it.'

'What – you mean it's kids larking about, trying to scare Catarina?'

'I don't think so. Some of them seem properly scared

themselves. Even the bigger ones. They'd know if it was just one of them making it up.'

I paid her and set off to walk back home. Of course there was no such thing as a ghost. So, somebody was making it up. The only question was who? And why, of course. That was a question too.


'Drugs?' I said.

Joe took a bite on a chocolate digestive and chewed a bit before replying. Maybe it was a trick they taught them in the police for ratcheting up the tension. 'We caught a couple of drug smugglers this week. They're minor players – that's all we normally catch, of course, but they've given us a picture of how they operate. A fishing boat comes over from France and stations itself just off the coast somewhere. Small boats come out and meet it and the goods are transferred. They're then landed by people who know the coast well. They mentioned Chichester Harbour – but I don't think they actually know anything about the guys who pick the stuff up. There are plenty of sailing boats round here, I suppose?'

'Hundreds.'

'So, if you share it out a bit – several small boats all heading for different bits of coast – most of it will probably make it to shore, even if the coastguards are watching. They can't check everyone.'

'You've caught some, then?'

'One. Local sailor from Worthing, who was a bit careless when trying to sell his share of the goods in a pub near the seafront. That's how we got onto the fishing boat. Who would I need to talk to round here to see if anyone was landing stuff on this stretch of coast?'

'Anything sailing in Chichester Harbour has to have an annual licence. The harbour authority could tell you who owned boats, I guess. The secretaries of the local sailing clubs would be another source of information. But if they knew anything was going on, they'd have contacted you already.'

'If they knew what to watch for,' he said. 'Where would you land stuff round here?'

'In the winter, East Head can be fairly deserted. But you'd probably be better off keeping any packets in the boat, bringing the boat ashore on a trailer, then hitching it up to the car and taking it all home. Unload round the back of the garage and you're good to go back for the next lot.'

'You have a devious mind, Ethelred.'

'I'm a crime writer. It's like being a criminal but not so profitable.'

'Maybe we could go for a walk round East Head later?'

'Yes, of course.'

But Joe made no attempt to move. He took another digestive.

'Do you know anyone called Robin Pagham?' he said.

'He was a friend,' I said. 'He died a few weeks ago. He drowned in a sailing accident. But you probably know that.'

'Yes,' said Joe. 'Sorry. I should have thought you'd know him well. Was he a good friend?'

'Yes,' I said. 'Well, fairly good. I can't say I approved of everything he did. If you've checked your records you'll have noticed he used to beat his girlfriends. You suspect him of drug smuggling?'

'It's possible. It's likely, in fact.'

'So, you were hoping I'd shop some of my friends to you?'

'I didn't know he was a friend, Ethelred. I just hoped you might have heard of him. Anyway, you expect me to use my police colleagues to provide you with information about a body we've dug up – out of idle curiosity, I assume? Chasing smugglers is at least my job.'

'I'm researching a murder that took place there in the 1840s. The body is relevant to that. So, it's my job too.'

'Ah, hence the interest in the exact date. Well, I do have a little more for you on that. 1874 as near as makes no difference.'

'That's pretty accurate for radio-carbon dating, or whatever they're using. And pretty quick.'

'It's based on the contents of his purse. Three golden guineas and about four shillings in small change, with coins dating from 1805 to 1874 – they included six 1874 pennies, discoloured from the burial but showing no signs of normal wear. Straight from the bank. From which we can draw two conclusions.'

'He died in 1874 or shortly after?'

'Precisely. And he probably had a bank account. So, not a farm labourer.'

'A farm labourer wouldn't have had the three guineas either.'

'True.'

'That's interesting,' I said.

'Even though it's thirty years too late for your murder?'

'It may not be too late,' I said. 'In another sense, it may be spot on.'

'Well, there you are then,' said Joe. 'I've done you a good turn, after all. So, in return, tell me about Robin Pagham.'

'Why do you think he has anything to do with it?'

'One of the men we caught . . . he mentioned somebody called Robin, who had a boat out this way. So we did a search of the police database. Lo and behold it came up with Robin Pagham, with a record for the possession of drugs and assault, living right out here on the coast. We had a note that he was a keen sailor too – actually we checked his Wikipedia entry. He was apparently an actor once. We showed our man Robin's mugshot and he agreed it was the bloke he'd seen. So that was a bit of a result.'

'Robin took drugs,' I said. 'You know that. I never heard that he smuggled them.'

'Since he's dead, we may never know everything he got up to,' said Joe. He paused as if about to ask me another question. Then he said: 'Well, enough about that. As you say, Pagham was a friend of yours. Do you still fancy a walk?'

After Joe had left I arranged two meetings. Then I packed *Curious Tales of Old Sussex* in my bag and set off.

# CHAPTER TWENTY-FIVE

'Robin would not smuggle drugs,' said Catarina. 'This I know for sure.'

'But think,' I said. 'Wouldn't it explain his death? If he had some sort of argument with the smugglers out at sea? I mean, it didn't make sense that he died in reasonably calm weather and it didn't make sense that somebody in the village killed him. But once you get in with drug dealers, it's another ball game, as they say. And the stranger who visited him – couldn't he be from the gang?'

'So, who is Old Man Robin talks about?'

'I don't know – the head of the gang?'

'And why money when he dies? Gang boss may cheat you all the time, but can't pay when dead.'

'OK, I'm not saying the drug business explains everything. But the police are convinced Robin was involved in shipping drugs into the country. They asked me about it.'

'What you say them?' Any mention of officialdom

provoked immediate and unqualified suspicion in Catarina.

'I couldn't tell them anything because I don't know anything.'

'They ask where he lives?'

'No, but I guess they would have that information . . . you mean there are still drugs in the house?'

'Robin not smuggle drugs.'

'OK. My advice to you, Catarina, is that there should not be drugs in the house when the police come.'

'They will find nothing.'

I nodded. My point wasn't that the police should find nothing but that there should be nothing to find. But even if the police did search and find drugs, it was unlikely that Catarina would be blamed. Robin had form, as you might say, and until probate had been granted, it was still his house. 'You know, I assume, that the police found a body in the Herring Field – it's been there a hundred years or so, though. No connection with Robin's death. But Robin was going to put a wind farm there.'

'Is not Robin's land. Is Colonel Gittings'. That man Witless . . .'

'Whitelace?'

'Him. He ask me if I make wind farm on it. I say, not mine.'

'But Robin was going to buy it?'

'He not tell me.'

'Fair enough. Have you heard, by the way, the rumours about ghosts in your garden?'

'Who says there are?'

'Everyone, it would seem. The local kids are terrified to come anywhere near here.'

'They are stupid. Superstitious peasants. They believe anything.'

'So, you've seen no ghosts?'

'There is no such thing as ghost. Just Mafia and tax collectors.'

'I suppose so,' I said.

My second meeting was at a cafe in Chichester. I had been sitting quietly for ten minutes while Tom read and reread *The Murderer and the Devil*.

'So, what do you make of it?' I asked.

'Sounds like our family, all right,' said Tom. He pulled a face. 'Judging from the story here, it would seem to have been pretty well known that George was the murderer and that Lancelot Pagham was innocent.'

'In other words, what you've always thought too. But I'm not sure that means everyone knew then. Sabine Barclay-Wood lived not far away. He might have known and talked to Perceval Pagham. Perceval might have given him the true story – or spun the good reverend a yarn. But the detail of the empty coffin is intriguing. I'm not saying that one of your ancestors was taken away by the devil but, since almost everything else seems to be true, I do wonder if the bit about the empty grave isn't based on some rumour that was going round at the time.'

'But why would they do that? And there's no evidence other than this story . . .'

'There's another detail that you don't know. That body they found the other day at the Herring Field – it dates from around 1874 or 1875. George died in 1875.'

'So you think the body is George's?'

'I think it's possible that something terrible may have happened in 1875 – something that caused the family to have George buried in unconsecrated ground by the harbour rather than in the churchyard – taken by the devil, if you like – then they went through a mock funeral afterwards for the sake of decency. And the burial was in some haste if they left three pounds four shillings in his pockets.'

'But no more than possible. We really can't be certain the body is George's.'

'No, we can't. It's a strange coincidence, of course – it's the right date and it's on his land and it sort of all fits in with *The Murderer and the Devil* story. But you're absolutely right – beyond that, it's just my speculation. I've no doubt that DNA testing could be arranged if you were curious enough.'

'It can't really be that important,' said Tom uncertainly. 'I mean, it has no bearing on anything now.'

'True,' I said. 'It was all a long time ago.'

Afterwards, I went to the library. I couldn't help feeling that if there was anything suspicious about George's death, it might come out in the obituary – not that he'd been carted off by the devil, clearly, but perhaps a suggestion that it had been sudden and unexpected. Since I knew the date he died, it was not too difficult to find.

*It is with regret that we note the passing of Mr George Gittings, one of the most prominent and well-respected residents of West Wittering. Mr Gittings had been ill for some time and confined to his bed, unable to attend to his duties on his estate or at the church or to take his usual seat on the parish council, where his words of wisdom were much missed. He has been laid to rest at the church of St Peter and St Paul in West Wittering, where many of his ancestors also lie. Leading the mourners was his son, Mr Albert Gittings.*

A list of other mourners followed – men and women with surnames that can still be found on the gravestones in the churchyard. Nothing much to go on there – certainly not some sudden and unforeseen event like a house call from Satan. But there was something odd all the same – it was George's second son, Albert, who had led the mourners, not his first son, John. Thinking about it, I had already made a record somewhere that John had died soon after his father. I checked my notebook – yes, he'd died in 1876. I called up that volume as well.

*We are deeply saddened to announce that Mr John Gittings, of Greylands House, passed away on January the fifth after a long and painful illness. His son, also John Gittings, succeeds to the estate, reputed to be the largest in West Wittering. Since John Gittings Junior is a minor, his uncle Mr Albert Gittings will become his guardian. The late Mr Gittings' father, Mr George Gittings, died last year.*

The 'long and painful illness' would explain why he was not at his father's funeral. That would also mean that, throughout 1875 and maybe for longer, both father and eldest son were in effect invalids, leaving Albert to run the farm. But there was no clue as to why this should have necessitated a burial in a marshy field near the cold, grey waters of Chichester Harbour.

George's obituary suggested, moreover, that he was, to the very last, well respected in the village, where he sat on the council and performed some unspecified duties at the church – a churchwarden, perhaps. If he were a known murderer, or even suspected of being one, it is unlikely that these things would have been the case. A fortiori if he was believed to be in league with the devil.

The more I thought about it, the more convinced I became that the final part of *The Murderer and the Devil* story was simply made up. And why not? Plenty of writers take some factual event and then embroider it a little. In this case the author had taken a little-known rumour about John Gittings' murder and added a neat gothic twist at the end.

I googled Sabine Barclay-Wood.

*Barclay-Wood (or Barclay Wood) the Reverend Sabine (1854–1945) – English clergyman and hymn-writer. Son of James Wood, brewer of Wandsworth and his wife, Joanna Barclay. Educated Charterhouse School and Keble College Oxford. Vicar of St Augustine's, Selsey, West Sussex for over fifty years. He actively sought, but failed to obtain, various posts at Chichester Cathedral, from which he later claimed he had been excluded by 'black malice and blacker jealousy'. Possibly best known for his hymn 'God of Sunshine, God of Love', formerly included in many school hymnbooks but now (like his other work) almost entirely forgotten. Also wrote Curious Tales of Old Sussex (1904), a strange anthology of folk stories, purportedly collected in the county but many of which seem to have been lifted verbatim and without acknowledgement from other anthologies, and Happy Recollections of a Sussex Clergyman (1939), which was the subject of a libel action on the part of the then Bishop and Dean of Chichester.*

There was a copy of *Happy Recollections of a Sussex Clergyman* in the library, though it took some time to locate it. It had been privately printed and was in the form of a diary, which Barclay-Wood must have maintained over a number of years (or invented – I was beginning to doubt him as a reliable source). It was chatty and anecdotal. He sounded like the sort of person who, once they had buttonholed you, would be difficult to shake off. I finally found what I was looking for in an entry nominally attributed to 3 February 1902.

*Dined with the Rector at West Wittering – a tedious journey along almost impassable roads but in the knowledge that I would drink good port and hear a good story or two after our meal. In fact I was rewarded with a tale that the present incumbent's predecessor had told him, years ago, about a parishioner who vanished without trace. My colleague would tell me only that the man's name was George and that he had been a very respectable party, a parish councillor and a churchwarden of long-standing. Then one day he had ceased to attend church entirely and failed to appear at council meetings. In a small village all sorts of rumours spread, including that witchcraft or worse was involved. By and by, the worthy rector had called at his house to enquire whether George was sick but was given many plausible stories by the family to put him off. It took a year for him to discover the truth, which so shocked him greatly. It seems that George had committed some crime many years before and blamed it on a poor fisherman who hanged for it (a story that it must be possible to verify elsewhere). At this point the tale became a little confused, my colleague having opened a third bottle of port – but he said that George died and, though the clergyman had doubts about doing so, he was given a Christian burial in the churchyard. The ending of it all was this, however: some years later the grave was reopened so that George's wife could be laid to rest. George's coffin could be made out – rotten and broken though it now was – but there was no sign of George – no shroud, no bones, not a tooth had survived. The gravediggers said that he must have been taken by the Devil. My colleague suggested that it was most likely that George was never in the coffin that they buried, but why that should be and where George went, was something he could never say. Drove back in the rain – one oil lamp gave out just after Birdham because, like the Foolish Virgin, I had neglected to have it refilled – but I got home safely, thanks be to God.*

Then a little further on, I found this:

*Out of curiosity I have examined some old newspapers in Chichester library. It would seem that in 1848 one John Gittings was murdered and a fisherman named Lancelot Pagham was hanged for it. John Gittings had a brother named George, who was present at the trial, and who may be the George referred to in the tale of The Murderer and the Devil (as I intend to call it). George Gittings attempted to give evidence for the fisherman, but Pagham's impertinence towards the court seems to have swayed the judge against him. 'A little learning is a dangerous thing, drink deep or taste not the Pierian spring'. verb. sap.*

Finally I came across this:

*At a bookshop in Chichester I found an ancient volume entitled Queer Stories of Old Cornwall. The bookseller assured me that it was rare and the stories largely unknown – he had never seen the book before in all his days. I bought it as a curiosity, thinking to compare my own Sussex stories with the Cornish ones. While I was paying, an old farmer came into the shop. On hearing him addressed as Mr Pagham,*

*I enquired if he was from the family of that name who lived in West Wittering. He said he was and, after some discussion, admitted freely that it was his brother who had been hanged, most unjustly as he insisted. I asked him about George Gittings. He said that he would not hear a word against him – that he had been very kind to the family and given them money. Then he told me something very odd indeed about the Herring Field where the murder had taken place – how it had passed to the Gittings family as a permanent reminder. By this time my purchase had been wrapped, and I went on my way. I have to say that the gifts to the family are a nice touch that I shall add to the story, illustrative of contrition. Of course, if there was no true Repentance in his heart then his Good Works would have been to no avail. And the Devil would have been perfectly at liberty to take him. I shall most certainly point out that very valuable moral.*

So there was the reference to the Herring Field again as a burden to the family that owned it. I flicked through the volume to the end, but I could find no more on the murder, other than a brief note for June 1904 that his book of Sussex Tales had been published and that he hoped it would be well reviewed and that sales would be brisk. He never mentioned it again.

It had been a long day, but I felt I had to phone Barry Whitelace to let him know that the body, whoever it was and however it got there, was not Bronze Age. He seemed a little distracted.

'Thanks, Ethelred,' he said.

'I thought you'd like to know,' I added. 'I suppose it's stopped the investigations for the wind farm for a bit.'

'It wasn't for a wind farm,' he said. 'It was for fracking. Test drill hole.'

'Derek Gittings was contemplating fracking?'

'Apparently. Or some company was willing to pay him to be allowed to test there.'

'I see,' I said. Then I asked: 'How's Jean?'

'She died yesterday,' he said.

'I'm so sorry. I didn't know.'

'No reason why you should. Life goes on.'

'It somehow puts the rest into perspective, though,' I said. 'I mean, the whole question of what happens to the Herring Field must seem wholly unimportant now.'

'Quite the reverse,' he said. 'I'll continue to do just whatever I have to do – whatever that proves to be – to preserve it for her. From my point of view, it's holy ground.'

# CHAPTER TWENTY-SIX

## Elsie

*Dear Mr Black,*

*Thank you for submitting your manuscript to the Elsie Thirkettle Agency for our consideration. We read it with great interest, but I'm sorry to have to tell you that it wasn't quite right for us. Different agents will have different views, of course, and it would be worth sending it elsewhere for another opinion if you wish. Most authors have to try a number of agencies before they are accepted.*

*Thank you again for thinking of us. We wish you every success in your writing career.*

*Yours sincerely*
*Elsie Thirkettle*

*PS Well done! This was possibly the biggest load of bollocks I have ever read – and I've been obliged to read a great deal.*

'How are you getting on with the new standard letter?' asked Tuesday, placing on my desk a china plate on which rested a neatly sliced pear and a folded paper napkin.

'You were quite right,' I said, eying the fruit suspiciously. 'It saves an enormous amount of time. I'm trying to personalise them a bit, though, with a helpful comment or two at the end.'

'Ooooh, how *sweet*!' said Tuesday. 'Can I see?'

'Too late,' I said. 'I've sealed it up.'

She looked at me archly. 'You are saying *nice* things, I hope?'

'You know me,' I said.

'Yes,' she said.

For a moment or two she tried to outstare me, but she was never going to succeed. She was a mere amateur up against a seasoned pro.

'Whatever,' I said. 'I spoke to Catarina last night. Ethelred's making no progress with that investigation at all. He's come up with a second body, but he's found it a hundred and forty years too late.'

'Oh dear.'

'Actually, thinking about it, that's quite fast for Ethelred. I mean, since he has established permanent residence in the nineteen fifties, it's only seventy years ago for him. It reminded me, though. There was a lead I have to follow up in the Robin Pagham case. Cancel my meetings for this afternoon. I've just arranged to go and see somebody called Martina Blanch. I have to get her to admit, over a cappuccino and pastries, that she's a murderess.'

'You're not going to record your conversation with her in an underhand manner?'

'Oh, for goodness' sake, that conversation of ours that I recorded is old history. Anyway, you worked for another agency then – I was entitled to use an underhand manner. And I've destroyed, or more likely lost, the tape. Do I have to go on apologising about it for ever?'

'You've never apologised about it.'

'Haven't I?'

'No.'

'How odd. I'm sure I meant to. I'll see you later, then. And don't try to open that letter I sealed. I just told him "well done". OK?'

But I bet she did. People can be so devious.

'You said you wanted to talk to me about Robin Pagham?' asked Martina.

I placed my spoon carefully in the saucer, like narrators do in books when they want to illustrate that somebody is thinking carefully and in total control of the situation. I looked at Martina through narrowed eyes.

'A plain yes or no will do,' said Martina. 'I haven't got all bloody day.'

'I bet I've got less time than you have,' I said.

'I doubt it.'

'I'm sure of it,' I said.

There was a sort of pause during which Martina pondered how much she could be arsed to play this game.

'As you wish,' she said. 'Just tell me what it is you want to talk about – and stop playing with that spoon, it's irritating.'

'Fair enough. No spoon, then. So, Martina Blanch, you were in West Wittering on the day Robin died?'

'Is that a question?'

'It's a statement with a slightly rising intonation at the end.'

'Which is a question.'

'Maybe,' I said.

'OK, just so that we can get away from this cafe before it closes, I agree a sentence with a rising tone at the end may or may not be a question, and I additionally confirm I was in West Wittering the day Robin died.'

'You went there with Sophie?'

'I drove down to Sussex with Sophie. I don't quite see where this is going. You phone me out of the blue and say you need to talk about Robin. I cancel a meeting because you say it's urgent. Since you're a lawyer, I'd assumed it must be something to do with the assault charges or the will . . .'

'Did I say I was a lawyer?'

'Yes.'

'Sorry – I meant literary agent. Slip of the tongue.'

'So you lied to get me here?'

'Yes. I thought I'd covered that already. So, Martina Blanch, why did you kill Robin Pagham? Was it in revenge for his attack on you? Or did you want to prevent it happening to other girls?'

'I didn't kill him at all.'

'Are you sure?'

'Positive.'

'A bit of a coincidence, then, your being in West Wittering that day, eh Martina?'

'I suppose so. But I wasn't there to see Robin.'

'Why were you there?'

'It's a long story.'

'I've got plenty of time, Martina.'

'I thought you said you'd got less time than I had?'

Martina looked at me as if she had scored some sort of point, the way that Tuesday looks at me when I concede that apples aren't that bad.

'Just get on with the story,' I said.

'The day before,' Martina began, 'Sophie phoned me to say that Tom had contacted her and asked her to come down to Sussex. She wanted to know what to do.'

'She was normally indecisive?'

'Quite the reverse. But Tom had been acting weirdly. I mean, they'd been going out together, then suddenly he'd dumped her. A few months on, he phones up out of the blue, almost as if nothing had happened, and asks her out. So she suggested I should come along with her.'

'Three of you on a hot date? Is that how it's done in Sussex?'

'Of course not. I would travel down to Chichester with her and she'd drop me off there and head off to Singleton to meet Tom. If all went well, I'd spend the day shopping and having lunch and then I'd return to London with her in the evening. But if Tom failed to show up or something, then we'd both shop or we'd drive out to a pub by the sea or whatever and we'd forget Tom Gittings ever existed.'

That seemed fair enough. A date with an emergency exit. I could have done with a few of those in my time.

'But you also went to West Wittering? Not just to Chichester?'

'Yes, it's always the way. You allow plenty of time so that you won't be late, there's no traffic on the roads and you arrive about an hour and a half too early. We drove down to West Wittering for a quick look at the place, just for old times' sake, then back to Chichester in time for the shops to open.'

'So, what time were you there?'

'West Wittering? I don't know – eight-thirty maybe? Nine? I didn't keep notes. I do remember we hit the rush hour traffic going into Chichester, which actually made Sophie a bit late in the end. And most of the shops were open by the time I got there, but not all of them. So, let's say around nine-thirty? Does that help?'

'And you have proof you were in Chichester all day?'

'I doubt it. Not all day. I suppose my credit card statement would show I'd paid for lunch and I did buy a necklace at Sahara. But, and this is a far more telling point, I had no reason to kill Robin.'

'He broke your nose.'

'Take a look at my nose – does it look broken?'

'No, it's very nice.'

'Precisely. He hit me on the nose, but no permanent damage. I was pretty pissed off at the time, but the caution he got was adequate retribution. I actually said in my statement that I bore him no ill will, or something of the sort. I would have preferred to leave it at that. In my position I honestly didn't want the publicity. It was the police who were keen to press charges rather than me.

218

Quite right, I suppose – you can't let people get away with that sort of thing. But it's all water under the bridge. Why on earth would I want to kill him and take the risk of going to gaol, simply in order to get my own back for something like that?'

'Fair enough. Sorry to suggest there was an ongoing nose problem, by the way. It looks fine.'

'Thank you.'

'You're welcome. And everything went well with Sophie's date?'

'Sort of. I got a text halfway through the morning saying she was having a great time, smiley face, XXX – you know the sort of thing. That seemed conclusive. I went and had lunch. It was only later, in the car going home, that Sophie said it had all been a bit of a damp squib. She had no idea why he'd invited her.'

'How odd.'

'I don't think so. Tom's completely under his father's thumb. I'd always suspected that Colonel Gittings disapproved of Sophie for some reason that I could never fathom, and that he got Tom to drop her. Seeing her again was some small act of rebellion on Tom's part, but he didn't have the guts to see it through. Letting "I dare not" wait upon "I would", like the poor cat i' th' adage.'

I nodded. 'Do you think they really said i' during the sixteenth century? I mean, it's easier just to say in. What was that all about?'

'I don't think Shakespeare was much good at accents.'

'Don't get me started on writers,' I said. 'I could go on all day.'

219

'So, in fact you do have quite a lot of time to spare?'

'Anyway,' I said, 'did Tom spend the whole date talking about his father?'

'Strangely, the answer to that question is that he did talk about his father. I know because Sophie mentioned it in the car going back to London. Robin and Colonel Gittings seem to have had quite a bust-up about some field that the colonel owned.'

'The Herring Field?'

'That's the one. How clever of you to know that.'

'Thank you.'

'My pleasure. Robin had agreed to buy it or something, then he changed his mind. I think the Gittingses would have made quite a lot of money. The field was pretty valueless, but Robin was going to have a wind farm built on it. Then he decided not to. Tom's father was furious apparently.'

A thought occurred to me. 'Angry enough to kill him?'

'He has got a bit of a temper. I wouldn't have wanted him as a father-in-law myself. But, he'd hardly do that, would he?'

'But he was in West Wittering. He could have been the person who called on Robin and gave him a lift to the sailing club. And he was in the army – I mean, he'd have known how to kill somebody. They actually teach you how to do it.'

'I suppose so. Robin didn't die in an artillery barrage, of course, but I agree that a soldier would have knowledge the rest of us lack. But – even allowing for all that – however cross you were that a deal had fallen through, you wouldn't kill somebody, would you?'

I carefully placed my spoon in my saucer. 'Unless . . .' I said.

'Unless what?'

'No, you're right,' I said. 'You wouldn't kill somebody for that.'

'Any other questions? I really don't have much time.'

'Yes, that's it,' I said, getting up and brushing the crumbs off my dress. That must have been three – no, four – chocolate croissants; I'd tell Tuesday I'd had a small green salad.

'Are you going to pay for those coffees?' Martina asked. 'I mean, you invited me here. I assume you're not expecting me to pay?'

'We could go halves.'

'No, we couldn't.'

I waved at the waitress. 'Can I pay, please? Yes, both of us. Oh, and could I have a receipt saying small green salad and Evian water?'

# CHAPTER TWENTY-SEVEN

The call came the following day. I was able to update Elsie on a few things and she was full of what she believed to be her ground-breaking discoveries.

'And I think I've remembered where I first came across the name "Blanch",' I added. 'I thought Tom must have mentioned Martina, but it wasn't that. Then I thought it was because of this firm of venture capitalists who've been in the news – you know, Blanch Capital? But it wasn't that either.'

'Fascinating,' said Elsie. 'Any more things that it wasn't?'

'No,' I said. 'There aren't. Do you want to know about this or not?'

'Tell me and I'll let you know afterwards whether it was remotely worthwhile.'

'Lancelot Pagham's sister's married name was Blanch,' I said. 'Morgan Blanch. I saw it going through the old newspaper reports of the trial again. She'd died shortly before the murder. Lancelot had been to visit her grave.'

'So Martina could be a descendent of Lancelot's sister? Is that what you are saying, now you've finally got round to saying anything at all?'

'It's possible. It's not a common name. She obviously has some links with the area.'

'Would that entitle her to any of the estate? I mean if he'd died without making a will?'

'Maybe. I think she'd have needed a good lawyer, but you can go back several generations in the absence of a will or obvious heir.'

'What if she'd already consulted one? A lawyer, I mean. What if she knew that, if Robin died before he married Catarina, then she'd inherit?'

'Did she make any reference to the estate when you spoke to her?'

'Yes, she did. She may have confused me with a lawyer at first.'

'Really? She thought you were a lawyer?' I asked.

'These things happen. She wondered if I wanted to talk to her about the will. So, for once, you could be right. Like you say, Blanch isn't the commonest name. If she is a descendant, and if she knew, it gives her a further reason for wanting Robin dead.'

'If she knew.'

We both thought about this for a moment, then Elsie added: 'Did the colonel know that one of his ancestors was buried on the site, when he started fracking?'

'He hasn't been fracking – he's just applied for permission to drill to find out whether it would be possible. But, no, I suspect not.'

'Look,' said Elsie, 'you don't suppose that Robin was blackmailing the colonel? He could be the "old man" he referred to – the one who would provide the big payday. Maybe allowing him to build a wind farm on the Herring Field was his offer for keeping quiet about whatever it was. Robin wouldn't take it – wanted more – so Gittings killed him. He was in the army. He knows about weapons. He knows about boats. He was around that day. He could have done it.'

'No, I don't suppose any of that,' I said. 'In the first place, Robin was going to get his money "when the 'old man' died". You only get to collect from your blackmail victim while he's alive. And there's no evidence at all of blackmail. They actually seemed to be quite good friends.'

'Tom succeeded in splitting up Robin and Sophie – with his father's approval. That doesn't suggest they were friends.'

'True. But you're coming up with reasons why Robin would have killed Colonel Gittings, not the other way round. I've talked to the police. Robin was involved in drug smuggling. There's every chance that was the reason he died. I'm pretty certain of it, actually.'

'Did Catarina say anything about drug smuggling?' asked Elsie.

'No,' I said.

'Did you ask her?'

'Yes.'

'Did you ask her properly?'

'Yes,' I said.

'I bet you didn't. I'd better come down to West Wittering. If you want something doing . . .'

'There's no need. The police seem to know what happened.'

'But I'll come anyway.'

'You're not planning to stay here again?'

'Thank you. I'd be delighted. That's so kind of you.'

'I may be out quite a lot.'

'I've got a key.'

'Have you?'

'Yes, I forgot to give it back to you.'

'I didn't know I'd given you one.'

'It was in the box in your hall.'

'I'll see you later, then.'

'Same room as last time. Oh, and chocolate biscuits in the bedroom would be good. No apples. No pears neatly sliced on a plate with a stupid white napkin. I am allergic to sliced pear with napkin.'

'Are there any other instructions you'd like to give me before you hang up?' I used all of the irony at my disposal.

'I'll text you if I think of anything,' said Elsie.


I was even more certain of my facts when later that day Joe gave me a call.

'Thanks for sending Tom Gittings over to do a DNA test. That should prove who the body in the Herring Field was.'

'I didn't send him.'

'You must have put the idea into his mind.'

'Maybe.'

'We've also got a bit more information on Robin Pagham. My two drug smugglers are a bit vague about dates, but they think that on the day Robin died they'd given him some Rohypnol and some cocaine to take ashore.'

'And they think he might have sampled the goods en route?'

'Well, that would be the last piece in the jigsaw, wouldn't it? He takes too much, loses control of the boat. It explains everything, really.'

'I'll tell Elsie not to come down, then,' I said.

'What?'

'Don't worry,' I said. 'I think she's just coming to get away from the diet her assistant is trying to put her on.'

Coincidentally I ran into Tom a little later in the village – I say coincidentally, but it's a small village and we know each other's habits. So it just happened that I was standing outside the pub at six o'clock.

I told him what I'd heard about Robin. He nodded absently. 'I suppose I'm not that surprised he was involved in something of the sort,' he said. 'It's funny the things that come out after somebody is dead.'

'By the way,' I said. 'Did Martina Blanch ever mention that she was distantly related to Robin?'

'Oh yes,' he said. 'One of the reasons she first visited West Wittering was that her family came from this part of the world. She pointed out a gravestone to me – Morgan Blanch – her great-great-great-grandmother, I think. We later worked out that Morgan would have been Lancelot Pagham's sister.'

'She might have stood to inherit something if Robin had died without making a will,' I said.

'Really? You can go that far back?'

'Apparently.'

'I didn't know that.'

'But Martina might have known?' I asked.

'She was interested in history and genealogy and stuff. I think she once mentioned she'd done a family tree back to the 1660s. If she'd married Robin, she'd have got it all anyway, but she didn't. Well, the past is coming back to haunt all of us at the moment – I mean the body in the field.'

'Did you decide to go ahead with that DNA test?' I said.

He looked at me slightly suspiciously. 'Yes, I did. If the body is an ancestor of mine, I feel I ought to ensure that he's properly buried.'

'Does your dad know?'

Tom's face was a bit sheepish. 'I'll tell him later.'

'He wouldn't approve?'

'God knows. He's been a bit odd lately. Moody.'

'The field's still yours?' I asked.

'Oh yes, the plan to sell it to Robin is obviously dead.'

'One thing I don't understand,' I said. 'Your father was annoyed when Robin changed his mind.'

'Who told you that?'

'Sophie,' I said. 'Well, indirectly.'

'Yes, he was. Furious.'

'Why didn't your father just go ahead with the wind farm himself, if it was such a good scheme?'

'I asked him that. He said it wouldn't work that way. He said he'd explain one day, but he couldn't now.'

'It had to be Robin?'

'Yes. Nobody else. He was cross because he said that Robin was hoping to get the field for nothing one day.'

'He hoped your father would just give it to him?'

'Yes.'

'There's no chance Robin was blackmailing your father?'

'Blackmail? No, of course not.'

'Something in his past? Something from his time in Ireland, say?'

'He was in the army. Everything he did was totally legit.'

'But a lot of it was secret?'

'I suppose so.'

'So, why else would he just *give* Robin the field? What hold did Robin have over him?'

'I've no idea. But whatever it was, Robin will never lay his hands on it now that he's dead.'

# CHAPTER TWENTY-EIGHT

## Elsie

I wasn't sure which flower bed I'd parked on last time, so I just steered the mini onto the nearest one available, avoiding the daffodils that seemed to have sprung up everywhere.

In the middle distance I could see somebody working away with a spade, so I wandered round to the side of the house. Catarina was digging the vegetable patch. She worked efficiently and methodically, only partially hampered by the fact that her high heels were sinking into the mud. She paused, swore briefly in what I assumed was her native language, then set to again.

'Isn't it a bit early for that?' I asked.

She looked up at me. 'Is spade there if you want to help.'

I walked over and fetched the second spade, which had been thrust into the earth a short way off.

'OK, Cat, what do you want me to do?' I asked.

'Dig,' she said. 'Then put cocaine in pile by lilac and heroin in pile by azaleas.'

I noticed that there were already two neat little piles on the lawn – packets wrapped in oilcloth and stained with mud.

'Are you sure this is the right time to harvest heroin?' I asked. 'I'm sure my old man used to leave it in the ground until Easter. Said it had a better flavour.'

'We dig now. By Easter police come back with sniffing dogs.'

Though I like it to remain my little secret most of the time, I do know how to use a spade, having helped my dad on his smallholding many years ago, before I worked out that it was easier to buy it all ready-chopped in plastic bags at Waitrose. After I'd removed a foot or so of soil I struck drugs – the spade made contact with the outer covering of another package.

'Careful!' Catarina called across to me, 'don't tear fabric. If bag leak, heroin not good for cabbages.'

I dug more carefully and gathered in a fine crop of narcotics. 'There must be thousands of pounds-worth of stuff here,' I said. 'Did you grow it all from seed?'

'Robin buries it,' said Catarina. 'He thinks I not see, but women take an interest in their husbands' gardens. Is natural.'

'So, he wasn't just bringing it ashore, then?'

'He go out in boat. Bring back packages. Sometimes men come to collect. Sometimes he hide here if not safe to collect straight away. When Robin die, much drug in garden. Too much drug. Police come to house and search. They find nothing. But I think – next time may search garden. So I phone gang boss.'

'He's in the Yellow Pages?'

'This is your irony?'

'No, I'm genuinely curious. Life is full of surprises.'

'Is that your irony?'

'Yes.'

'Not Yellow Pages. I have number already.'

'As you do.'

'Police catch some smugglers. They bring photographs to me and say do I know them? Of course I do not say it – do police think I am some sort idiot girl? – but I know them. And I know who they work for. So, I phone him. I say get your ass round here, moron, or police take all your drugs. He come tonight with white van and man with AK47.'

'Is this package heroin or cocaine?' I asked.

Catarina felt it briefly. 'Cocaine, obviously,' she said.

'I'll put it by the lilac tree, then,' I said.

Later, over coffee and yummy cakes, Catarina said: 'Maybe you not tell Ethelred about heroin.'

'You think he might not approve?'

'I think not.'

'I agree. He wouldn't grass you up, but knowing that he had condoned a felony would trouble him, poor thing. He would lose sleep. Now that the drugs have gone, by the way, do you think that the stories of ghosts in your garden will also stop?'

'You think I spread ghost stories to keep peasants away from vegetable patch?'

'Not if you say you spread the rumours for some other reason. Do you mind if I help myself to another cake or two by the way? You can't get these in London – or at least, I can't.'

'You have secretary?'

'I have an assistant.'

'You must get her to go out and buy. I give you address of good baker.'

'What an excellent idea. I'll do that. Digging certainly gives you an appetite. Did you hear, by the way, that they'd dug up a body in the Herring Field?'

'Old body. Just bones.'

'Ethelred thinks it's an ancestor of Tom Gittings. Do you know why Robin didn't buy the Herring Field when it was offered to him?'

'No, but Field is useless. I wonder if he wants field to bury stuff in – much better than garden – police not look there – but maybe too close to path. People walk there and see. That man, Whitelace. He is always there. Watching.'

'Colonel Gittings apparently said that Robin was the only person it was worth selling the field to. Colonel Gittings wouldn't have been involved in drugs too?'

'I think colonel is like Ethelred. Not take drugs.'

'True, it was only a thought. Maybe he just meant that only Robin had land adjoining it. I know what else I wanted to ask you: did you know somebody named Martina Blanch?'

'She girlfriend of Robin's. They have fight. But she come back.'

'She visited Robin after they broke up?'

'Yes. Once. Maybe twice. I do not know how often. You cannot watch your man all the time. You try, of course, but is not possible. Even with CCTV. I say to Robin, you not see that woman again. She on make. You screw her again and I kill her.'

'But you didn't kill her,' I said.

'Not even acid,' said Catarina tolerantly. 'I go fetch more cake.'

# CHAPTER TWENTY-NINE

'You could have saved yourself a journey,' I said to Elsie. 'There's nothing to investigate. Robin died when he was smuggling heroin.'

'Catarina doesn't think it's the drug smugglers.'

I smiled. 'Why, does she know them personally?'

'A bit,' she said.

'Really?' I joked. 'She's got their phone number or something?'

'It's probably in the Yellow Pages,' Elsie said enigmatically. 'Don't you think it's interesting, though, about Martina?'

'That she kept in touch with Robin? Yes, I suppose so. But she'd already said that she no longer bore him any ill will. Catarina clearly saw her off.'

'She stood to inherit a lot of money if Robin died without a will.'

'But he did make a will,' I said. 'He left his money to

Catarina. Then he died smuggling drugs. He wasn't killed by Martina or Derek Gittings or Sophie or Barry Whitelace or anyone else in the village.'

'Your problem, Ethelred, is that you lack imagination.'

'I thought that, as a writer, imagination was one thing that I did have.'

'Don't take this the wrong way,' said Elsie, 'but your problem is that your books are all very similar – I mean that they have the same stock characters and standard plots, continually working the same theme of a mysterious death that could only have been committed by a closed group of between six and twelve suspects, all of equal suspectability. Their motives are invariably ones that Agatha Christie would have recognised and had, in many cases, already rejected as too improbable. So, imagination? No, it's not your strong suit.'

'Sorry,' I said, 'when you say "don't take this the wrong way", you mean that there is a right way to take all that?'

'It is offered in the spirit of honest, constructive criticism. You probably haven't had much of that lately.'

'There are some advantages in not having an agent,' I said.

'But very few,' said Elsie. 'As for your last agent . . . that Janet person.'

'Janet Francis,' I said.

'Precisely. That Janet person, as she is better known in the book trade. Completely wrong for you.'

'I liked her,' I said.

'Well, you slept with her, so obviously you did. She only wanted you for your body.'

'Do you think so?' I said.

'You're right,' said Elsie. 'I've absolutely no idea why she wanted you. Except to steal you from the excellent agency that you were then contracted to. The one that had nurtured your career since you were a baby.'

'Not quite since I was a baby.'

'Trust me,' said Elsie, 'you were a baby. It's a shame that my list of authors is full to bursting or I would suggest you wrote to me begging to come back. But sadly it would be pointless.'

'You were going to take Tom Gittings,' I said. 'Your books can't be completely full.'

'An exceptional talent,' said Elsie.

'And I'm not?'

'Don't take this the wrong way . . .' said Elsie.

'OK, I get the picture,' I said. 'Anyway, I don't need an agent.'

'All writers need an agent,' said Elsie. 'But some need an agent more than others. You fall into the extreme and very needy end of the spectrum.'

'But you don't have room for me, anyway.'

'Let me reconsider that. Hmmm. Do I need an author who is high-maintenance and whose pathetic book sales will bring in microscopic amounts of commission for the agency? Nope. I've got lots of them already.'

'Thank you for reconsidering,' I said. 'I'm grateful.'

'My pleasure,' said Elsie. 'Would you like me to send you a letter confirming that in writing?'

'No thanks,' I said. 'I'd better go out and buy some biscuits if you're staying.'

\* \* \*

I noticed Tom's car parked outside the shop, so I was not surprised to find him inside.

We exchanged the usual greetings, then I said: 'Are the police keeping you informed of progress in your field? Will you go ahead with the test drilling when they've finished their investigations?'

Tom looked around cautiously. 'Some time ago, before Robin died but after he'd made it clear he didn't want the field, Dad was approached by a company that wanted to put down a drill hole or two to see if there was any oil shale down there. They're trying to build up a picture of the whole area. They were willing to pay us for allowing them to drill. Later Dad went off the idea, but we'd signed the contract so the planning application went ahead. We've no intention of doing anything more than the test drilling. It's all pretty small-scale – nothing like as big as most of the other sites. Fortunately we've managed to avoid the demonstrations they've had elsewhere.'

'At least they discovered your ancestor,' I said.

Tom shook his head. 'We've had the results back. Not related to me in any way.'

'So, it isn't George?'

'It can't be.'

'How odd, I was convinced that was who it was. The year was right. The place was right. It all fitted in with the rest of the story.'

'You sound disappointed.'

'Yes, I am a bit. You don't think . . . It isn't possible that Barry Whitelace just planted a few random bones down there to hold up the drilling?'

'If he was going to fake it, he'd have faked Bronze Age, not Victorian. Anyway, I doubt if he could have fooled the police pathologists. They'd know recently dug ground when they saw it. You were pretty certain it was going to be George?'

'Yes, but it can't be, can it? I'm as sorry for you as anyone – it would have been quite a good twist in the tale. Elsie is down, by the way, in case you need to speak to her about your book.'

'Yes, she emailed to say she was coming.'

'Did she?'

'We just need to finalise the contract.'

'You're definitely signing with her, then?'

'Absolutely. If she'll take me. Who wouldn't? Every writer needs an agent.'

A feeling flooded over me, a bit like homesickness, though West Wittering was now my home as much as anywhere ever had been. It was a sort of emptiness – the chill you feel, suddenly and quite unexpectedly, on a summer evening that sends you hurrying back into the house for a pullover – the realisation, on waking up, that it is the last day of the holidays – opening the door of your flat and then remembering that there is nobody there to greet you because your wife left you the previous week to go and live with your best friend. It was all of those things.

'Are you OK, Ethelred?' Tom asked.

'OK? Yes, I'm fine,' I said. 'Absolutely fine.'

Tom was wrong about one thing. The following day demonstrations started. For about a week television vans squeezed down Ellanore Lane to film the small group of protestors who had been bussed in from London. One or two locals joined the protest, including Barry Whitelace, briefly one afternoon. Then the signs were taken down, and the oil company that had planned to drill there announced an indefinite postponement. The field was left with a mound of bare earth where the body had been removed, but with the birdsong and the wind in the trees unchanged.

I often walked out in that direction now. The field, as I say, looked no different, but what I knew about it drew me back over and over again. There in 1848, a man had killed his brother. There in 1875 somebody had been buried at the dead of night (when else could they have done it?) with lanterns giving out just enough yellow light for the gravediggers to work. And over the years it had, for I believed the tale that I had read, become a millstone round the necks of the Gittings family, in a way that I still did not understand. How odd that, when they had sold almost everything else, they clung to this one boggy, reed-clogged bit of marsh, miles from their house or any other land that they owned.

I saw Barry Whitelace there only once, on a cold blowy morning, when the sun had only partially melted the overnight frost, leaving the reeds standing stiff and brittle amongst the withered foliage.

I asked how he was.

'Bearing up,' he said. 'The funeral's next Tuesday. Eleven o'clock, if you can make it.'

'Of course,' I said. 'Thank you.'

'Won't be many there. Jean . . . she fell ill you see quite

soon after we arrived . . . didn't get out that much towards the end . . . her sister's coming from Margate. David's in Wisconsin, of course.' He fell silent leaving me to speculate on who David was. The 'of course' suggested I ought to know, so I couldn't really ask.

'I'll be there,' I said.

'At least they're leaving this alone for a bit.'

'Yes,' I said. 'You don't know who could tell me about the past ownership of the field – I mean who sold it to whom and when? And why it might have been transferred?'

'Derek Gittings, since he's the current owner.'

'And if I didn't think I'd get much out of him?'

'You could try their lawyers – Chettle and Smallbrook. They're in Chichester. They'd have something, I'm sure. They were the Paghams' lawyers too. I know because Robin threatened to sue me for slander.'

'I'll give them a call,' I said.

# CHAPTER THIRTY

'I regret to inform you,' said the young lawyer brightly, 'that I am neither Mr Chettle nor Mr Smallbrook.' He paused, a smile on his lips. It was clearly one of his standard jokes. 'Mr Chettle died in 1882 and the last Mr Smallbrook – young Mr James as he was known – retired from the business in 1990. He now lives in Selsey.'

I suspected that all new visitors to the office were given this introduction. The lawyer who was neither Chettle nor Smallbrook had rattled it off fairly glibly. His name was Morton, if I'd caught it correctly, and he was quite chatty. He seemed inclined to be helpful if he could.

'It's a shame about Mr Chettle,' I said. 'If he'd still been around, he would have been able to answer my questions from first-hand knowledge.'

'Quite,' said Morton. 'Your research is purely historical and, as I understand it, relates to a murder that took place in 1848?'

'Yes. Purely historical. So, I hope I don't need to take up too much of your time.'

'We are always happy to help out local historians if we can. I got my assistant to dig out some papers. I should explain that there are *two* archives – one relating to the firm of Chettle and the other to the firm of Smallbrook and Dawson – the two amalgamated in 1948. Chettle represented the Gittings family as far back as we can trace our records. Smallbrook and Dawson is a relatively new concern – it dates back only to 1846. The original Mr Smallbrook and his successors dealt with the affairs of the Pagham family.'

'So today you are the lawyers for both families?'

'Yes. They deal with different partners. But there are no immediate conflicts of interest – neither is suing either at present.' He laughed.

'Robin Pagham did, however, sue Barry Whitelace,' I said.

Morton frowned. 'That is another matter entirely,' he said. 'In any case, you said your query related to the nineteenth century . . .'

'So it does,' I replied.

'Good,' said Morton, relieved that I had not tricked him in some way. He opened a buff-coloured envelope and took out some yellowed documents. They emerged with a faint rasping noise of old paper on old paper. He unfolded the brittle sheets carefully.

'1848?' I said as I glanced at the date.

'Precisely. The transfer of the freehold of the property known as the Herring Field from Perceval Pagham to George Gittings, signed by both gentlemen.'

'In return for a payment of £500 and "in recognition of the lease",' I said. 'What does that mean, exactly?'

'This is clearly intended as the final part of a larger transaction, by which one party granted the other a lease. £500 would have been a lot to pay for the Herring Field alone. Extortionate, you might say. But if a lease had also been granted on some other property, then the payment makes more sense.'

'But Perceval Pagham would have had no other land to lease to George Gittings.'

'I think that must be right. I happen to know that the Paghams have lived at Greylands since the mid-nineteenth century, which they must therefore have purchased shortly after the events you are investigating, but I don't think they owned any other land then, not in 1848.'

'So the reference to a lease remains a mystery.'

'Quite. There's no lease here. Wait a minute, though – do you see that?'

I looked at the corner of the document that Morton was indicating.

'Two small holes,' he said triumphantly. 'And, between them, a thin brown line. What do you make of that?'

'Something was previously pinned to the document?' I said.

'Yes,' said Morton, slightly disappointed that I had spoilt his great revelation. 'That's the mark of a pin that once attached this to something else. And the faint line of rust suggests that the pin was in place for a few years – long enough for a bit of oxidation to take place. As a lawyer you become a bit of a detective. I'd call that a pretty convincing piece of evidence.'

'So you're saying the lease may once have been attached to it? Where is it now, then?'

'It must have become accidentally detached at some point – or even deliberately transferred to another file, which may have been lost. The Smallbrook archives took a direct hit from a German bomb in 1942. A great deal of historic interest was lost for ever. This is from the Chettle archives, which were frankly less well kept. Anything could have gone missing from those.'

'I think that Perceval Pagham may have been blackmailing George Gittings,' I said. 'The lease could have been lost, as you say, but it wouldn't surprise me if it never existed at all. £500 was simply the price for keeping quiet about what Perceval had seen or worked out.'

'Which was?'

'That George had murdered his brother. Another man had hanged for it.'

'You don't say? How exciting. And that's the murder you're researching? £500 sounds quite cheap to cover up a homicide, even in 1848.'

'There were further transfers of property in 1875 and 1876?'

'Yes, I looked those up too, as you requested. I can see why you wanted them now, but I don't think they take you any further forward. Straightforward transfers of leasehold agricultural land at about the price one would expect. Nothing furtive or underhand. If there was blackmail, as you say, it's not apparent from those deals. And George died in 1875, so would have been beyond blackmail.'

I paused for a moment. 'Leasehold land?' I said. 'I'd assumed the Gittingses held the freehold.'

Morton consulted the papers again. 'Held on a very long lease by the look of it – over nine hundred years still remaining. Every bit as good as freehold, really, though there may have been some ground rent to pay.'

'Does it say who the freeholder was?'

'Nope. You'd have thought it might, wouldn't you? But if the land was properly identified – and there are maps here – then they may have thought that was irrelevant. It was probably the Church – they owned a lot round here. We still have to look out for chancel repair obligations in leases and freeholds. The bishop had a palace on Cakeham Road.'

'I know,' I said. 'The grandest beach hut in the area. And then there were later transfers of property in the twentieth century?'

'I believe so. But I had understood your query related only to the earlier ones? Land transfers are, of course, matters of public record, but I would have needed to consult the families concerned before showing you anything that might relate to a living person. So, I could go up to the nineteen fifties, say . . .'

Morton flicked through the file and frowned.

'Something interesting?'

'How odd. A letter to Colonel Gittings' grandfather, I think. It says that he could appeal to a Lands Tribunal if he wished, but there would be a danger of losing the entire lease – it therefore had to be his decision. That doesn't sound at all likely. Very bad advice from us, I think. We must have known that was wrong.'

'Why would he go to a tribunal anyway?'

'Oh, if he thought that the terms of the lease were unfair in some way. But even if the tribunal found against you, you'd just be back where you were. There wouldn't be a penalty of any sort.'

'Anything more on that in the file?'

'No, just the letter from us to him. They'd obviously spoken before and wanted to put it on record. A bit of a mystery. Still, it doesn't seem to relate to your project and it's none of my business, anyway.'

'You don't deal directly with the Gittings family yourself?'

'No. The Paghams and the Gittingses each deal with one or other of the partners. I am some way yet from being that.' He smiled again. 'I should say "dealt" of course. The Pagham family sadly no longer exists.'

'I know,' I said. 'But you are presumably still dealing with Catarina over the estate?'

I saw him shudder slightly. 'Not I, I am pleased to say, but the relevant partner does. Yes, an interesting lady. She does not seem to understand that our role is to advise her on the law as it stands – not the law as she wishes it to be.' Then, deciding he might have said rather more than he should about a client to somebody who clearly knew Catarina, he started to stuff the papers back into their respective envelopes.

'I suppose that work relating to the will is now more or less complete?' I said.

He looked up and shook his head. 'Oh, no. Another month or two until probate is granted,' he said. 'At least. Are you by any chance a beneficiary?'

'No,' I said. 'Not in any way.'

Morton nodded, reassured. 'It's just that we've had one or two queries. One lady has been very tenacious.' He frowned as if trying to remember something. 'Actually, her enquiry was not unrelated to what you are doing,' he said. 'She claimed to be descended from Perceval Pagham's sister. Interesting, no doubt, but of no relevance. Robin Pagham had made a will and she was not mentioned. End of.'

'Martina Blanch?' I asked.

Morton stopped stuffing envelopes, realising perhaps that he might just have breached yet another confidence. Then, deciding that Martina was neither a client nor anyone else to whom he owed a duty of care, he continued: 'That's right. I keep forgetting what a small world it is down here. Everyone knows everyone. Not like London. Of course, she would have been correct that, if there had been no will, we'd have needed to cast back several generations to see if there was an heir. Nobody likes to see money going quite needlessly to the Treasury. But there *was* a valid will, properly signed and witnessed. She was very insistent on the last point. She implied that it might be a forgery. A forgery! Well, we put her right on that, I can assure you. We are executors, so there could be no doubt at all of its validity. Cast iron.'

'I'm very pleased for Catarina's sake,' I said.

'Quite,' he said. 'Have you made a will, by any chance, Mr Tressider?'

'No,' I said.

'Do let us know if we can help you with it.'

'I'm not planning to die in the near future,' I said. 'But I'll give it some thought.'

'Okey-doke,' he said, 'I wouldn't leave it too long if I were you.'

Morton's request was one of those random reminders of your own mortality that ambush you from time to time. It was also a reminder that, if I made a will, I had no idea who I would leave my wealth (such as it was) to. My old college? The Crime Writers' Association? The National Trust? Or should I leave no will and give some lawyer the pleasure of casting back through generations of Tressiders to discover some unknown third or fourth cousin that I'd never met? My father had occasionally spoken of an uncle of his in Cornwall – he might have had children and, by now, grandchildren and great-grandchildren, but I had no idea where they were to be found. My mother had had three sisters, but all had died childless. Like Robin Pagham I was the end of the line that stretched back to Adam and Eve but would go no further – a sort of evolutionary dead end, like the pterodactyl or the steam locomotive.

Jean Whitelace's funeral was another reminder. It was, as Whitelace himself had predicted, a small gathering. We occupied only the first two rows of pews in the church, and did not fill them entirely. It seemed a small recompense for sixty-odd years of life and friendship. The service was short, the sky overcast and undecided for the interment. Jean was buried quite close to Robin's grave, where the earth was still fresh and a simple wooden cross marked the spot, awaiting a more permanent memorial stone in due course.

Whitelace turned – we had just finished the prayers for his wife and the coffin had been lowered – to look at Robin's grave.

'Bastard,' he muttered under his breath.

'He had his moments,' I conceded, thinking of his treatment of Martina as much as anything.

'Did his lawyers have anything to tell you about the Herring Field and when it was transferred?'

'It looks like blackmail,' I said, replacing my hat on my head. The wind was still cold. 'George Gittings paid Perceval £500 to keep quiet and was given the Herring Field as a reminder of his crime. So, the story you showed me seems more and more accurate. The Gittings' land is all leasehold, by the way – probably with the Church as freeholders, according to the man I spoke to.'

'Same with the Herring Field? Leasehold? That would be useful.'

'Would it?'

'Of course. If there's a freeholder, their permission would be needed for any development. If it's the Church they might think twice about granting it for a wind farm or gas field.'

I thought about it. 'True, but the Herring Field was definitely transferred freehold. I'm sure of that. How odd that that one field should have been different from all the surrounding ones.'

'It probably doesn't matter now.'

'Tom says there are no plans to take it further.'

'I should think not.'

I looked across the churchyard to where Tom was talking to the rector. There was to be no food, no drinks following the funeral. Either it had not occurred to Whitelace that it was expected of him or he had despaired of the task of making sandwiches, even for so few. Another mourner approached and I said my goodbyes to him and made my way over to Tom.

'I didn't know her well,' said Tom. 'But I thought I should come – I knew there wouldn't be many here. Those who knew Jean liked her a lot, but Barry Whitelace hasn't endeared himself to the village. He jumps into things without realising what effect he has on people. He blunders through life like an absent-minded elephant.'

'I guess so,' I said.

'Almost the first thing that he did after he arrived was to put round a letter accusing Robin of setting up an illegal wind farm without planning permission – that was when he and my father were talking about the sale of the field. Of course, he wasn't at a stage where he needed permission for anything. Robin might have laughed it off. But it was the language Barry Whitelace used. He called Robin a failed actor, which really hurt. He also drew people's attention to his criminal record and questioned whether he was a fit person to run anything. Robin went straight to his lawyers and Whitelace backed off. Maybe elephant is the wrong comparison – rhino might be better. Clumsy, short-sighted and about to become extinct, but better not to get in his way.'

'Where was he on the day Robin died?' I asked. I'd never

really followed up the idea that he might have been the coffee drinker who had given Robin a lift. It had seemed improbable at the time, but maybe not now.

'At home looking after Jean, I imagine. He couldn't travel very far by that stage. Not that Jean would have known whether he was there or not towards the end – I mean, if you're suggesting he needed an alibi.'

'No, I'm not suggesting anything,' I said. 'I went to see your solicitor yesterday, by the way, to ask about the Herring Field.'

'Did you? I suppose I should have thought to suggest that. Did you see Hepplewhite? He's the partner we normally deal with.'

'No, I spoke to somebody called Morton.'

'Ah,' said Tom, with a smile. 'Sean Morton's fairly new – a refugee from a firm in London, I think. Could he tell you anything useful?'

'He was quite chatty. Had time to delve back into the records for me.'

'I don't think they work them as hard in Chichester as they do in big City firms.'

'One thing he said that you may be able to confirm – the Herring Field is owned freehold?'

'Yes, of course. For what it's worth.'

'But the rest of your land is leasehold?'

Tom looked at me, puzzled. 'No, that's wrong – that's freehold too.'

'Are you sure?'

'Yes. Of course. We've had it for years and years.' Tom shook his head. 'I mean, Dad's never mentioned having to pay ground rent or anything. He'd have said something at some stage.'

'He's said nothing at all?'

'No.'

'Nothing about the terms of the lease being unfair?'

'No. Why do you think there's a lease?'

'Some time ago, your solicitors advised your family not to appeal to a Lands Tribunal over the terms of a lease in case they lost the whole thing. Morton thought that was bad advice – maybe deliberately bad advice.'

Tom shook his head. 'I think Morton's just got it wrong. That firm has advised my family and Robin's for generations. The Paghams might have been more important clients, but we would have been older ones. They'd have advised us to the best of their ability.'

'Fair enough,' I said, not wishing to press the point. It was difficult to see how Morton could have been mistaken. 'The other thing is this: after Robin's death, Martina Blanch started asking questions about the estate. She thought that there might have been some hanky-panky with drawing up the will that left everything to Catarina.'

'There's no question of the will having been tampered with after Robin's death. Robin actually told Dad that he was leaving everything to her,' said Tom. 'And he was quite sober when he said it. It was one of many things that have annoyed Dad over the past year or so – Catarina getting the whole thing. He was furious for days.'

'So, who should he have left it to? Martina?'

'I've no idea,' said Tom. 'I've honestly no idea.'

\* \* \*

Later, looking back, I realised that, that morning, I had finally been given all of the information that I needed to tell me who had murdered Robin Pagham. But I still hadn't put all of the pieces of information together and I left the churchyard feeling that I was no further forward than I had been a week before.

But I was wrong.

# CHAPTER THIRTY-ONE

It was the following morning that the first phone call came.

'Dad's furious,' said Tom.

'Again? What about this time?'

'Your visit to Chettle and Smallwood. Morton shouldn't have told you what he did.'

Morton had certainly been indiscreet. With regard to Catarina, I didn't entirely blame his brief outburst. My experience, too, was that she was impatient with any advice that didn't fit her existing prejudices. But I couldn't see why Colonel Gittings would have strong feelings about that. Nor did what Morton had said about Martina touch him in any way. That Chettle and Smallwood had misadvised his grandfather might have been of interest to him, but should hardly have called down his ire on me personally.

'Which bit of what he told me?' I asked.

'The lease.'

'But he couldn't tell me about the lease. He didn't have

it. I rather thought that the lease was pure invention – a ploy to cover up Perceval's blackmailing of George. You mean it really exists?'

'Apparently.'

'And the advice about the Lands Tribunal?'

'When I told him about Morton's opinion, Dad just looked blank and then said: "bloody hell".'

'So the missing lease – or maybe some other lease entirely – was unfair in some way. But your family was badly advised not to try to get the terms changed. I don't understand what I'm supposed to have done wrong.'

'I don't understand it entirely myself. But Morton shouldn't have told you any of that. It apparently relates in some way to Dad's offer to sell Robin the Herring Field. If it got out then, according to Dad, it could ruin us. But it wasn't clear which bit. Dad wasn't as coherent as I would have liked.'

'But that deal's off. How could it still matter – whatever the lease says?'

'Have you told anyone else about this?'

'Not really.'

'OK. Maybe it's not so bad, then. I'll try to reassure Dad that whatever the secret is, it's safe. I'll also see if I can get to the bottom of what this is all about.'

'Let me know if you do,' I said.

Tom gave an ironic laugh.


The second call was from Barry Whitelace.

'Ethelred? I've tried your number a couple of times but it was engaged.'

'I've been talking to Tom,' I said.

'Oh,' he said. 'Fair enough. Look, I need to say something to you. About Robin Pagham.'

'Go ahead,' I said.

'I must admit, I haven't slept all night thinking about it.'

'Because . . . ?'

'Sorry – I'm not telling this story well, am I? I saw Catarina yesterday. She says you're investigating Robin's murder?'

'Not exactly . . .'

'I didn't know anyone thought it was a murder.'

'Catarina mentioned it at the funeral service.'

'Really?'

'The whole village has been talking about it ever since.'

'I'm sorry – I was looking after Jean – I sort of missed a lot of the things that were going on in the village. They didn't seem important.'

'They weren't. You missed nothing except a lot of speculation. And I'm not investigating anything for Catarina. I'm just looking at the Herring Field murder back in 1848.'

'That's a relief. You see, after I spoke to Catarina, I remembered all of the things I'd said to you about Robin – I mean, I called him a bastard. I told you I'd threatened to kill him.'

'No you didn't. You never said you'd threatened to kill him.'

'Didn't I? I thought I had. You see, when I first heard about the wind farm idea, I was told that Robin was talking of going ahead but had no authority to do it. I think they

259

meant that he didn't actually own the land – well, I know that now. But at the time I thought it was because he was pushing it through without proper consultation. I called him a few things, I can tell you.'

'Yes, I've heard.'

'So, he threatened to sue me. So I told him I'd kill him if he put a single windmill in place.'

'When did you do that?'

'During the meeting with his solicitor.'

'A little rash if you wanted to do it undetected.'

'Well, exactly.'

'I'm sure you didn't mean it.'

'Oh no, I meant it. But one of the paralegals managed to disarm me before I could stab him.'

'You actually took a knife to the meeting?'

'Of course not. There was a paperknife on the table. So, I thought, why not? Never get a better chance. Go for it.'

'Well, I doubt you'd have killed him with that.'

'On the contrary. It was really sharp. One of the earlier Chettles had brought it back from Peking after the looting of the Summer Palace. As I said afterwards, they should keep dangerous things like that locked away. Or return them to China. They had to accept some of the blame, I told them.'

'But nobody pressed charges against you?'

'I signed a paper saying that I revoked my slanders about Robin, admitted they were false, malicious, utterly without foundation and I would not repeat them. Also that I would not set foot on his land or go within a hundred yards of his house. Or within a hundred yards of Chettle and Smallwood's office. Well, I had to sign. I still felt he was in the wrong over planning permission, but I'd rather lost the moral high ground.'

'I can see that,' I said.

'Of course, when I heard that people thought that Robin might have been murdered – well, I immediately thought of what I had said. Didn't sleep a wink, as I say.'

'It's perfectly possible his death was an accident,' I said.

'Really? I was rather hoping somebody killed him,' said Whitelace. 'I'm just letting you know it wasn't me.'

The third call was from an irate lady.

'Is that Ethelred Tressider?'

'Yes. And you are . . . ?'

'Martina Blanch. You have an agent called Elsie Thirkettle, who sometimes claims to be a lawyer?'

'She is no longer my agent. I'm quite willing to believe she claimed to be a lawyer. In what way can I help you?'

'Don't send her to hassle me again.'

'I didn't.'

'I've spoken to Sophie. Though I wasn't aware of it when I was interrogated by Elsie, I now know you're investigating Robin's death.'

'Also untrue. I'm researching another murder entirely . . .'

'Which doesn't interest me in any way. Mr Tressider, I am a busy woman. I am currently up to my eyeballs in a management buy-out. I do not have time to talk to the police. I do not have the time to talk to literary agents who imagine they are doing the police's job. I certainly do not want the publicity that might result from becoming involved in a murder investigation. If the press got wind of it, it would be all over the financial pages. Tell this Elsie woman to back off. Or my lawyers will be writing to both of you.'

'I wish I had the sort of influence you imagine I possess—' I began.

But the phone had gone dead.

The final call was from Elsie.

'Have you signed the contract yet?'

'What contract?'

'The one I emailed you this morning.'

'I haven't had a chance to check my emails. Why would you send me a contract?'

'I told you, I'm signing you up again. You need to sign a new contract with revised terms.'

'Better terms?'

'For one of us, yes.'

'But I never said I'd sign.'

'Well, clearly you have to sign. Otherwise I can't take you back. On revised terms. Do try to keep up, Ethelred.'

'I've been busy,' I said.

'Tell me about it,' she said.

'Do you mean you are also busy or do you actually want to hear? Are you eating a biscuit?'

'Maybe.'

'I thought Tuesday had you on a diet?'

'She's busy with other things. I've promoted her.'

'In order that you don't have to eat apples?'

'There are worse reasons.'

'The diet wasn't such a bad idea.'

'Look, Ethelred, let's do a deal. You tell me about your day.

I'll eat biscuits so that I don't have to interrupt you – OK?'

So, I told her about my day.

When I finished, she said: 'What you need to do is to gather all of the suspects together in one place.'

'Gathering all of the suspects together in the drawing room doesn't work in real life,' I said.

'Yes, I know that *now*,' she said. 'But it won't be like last time.'

'In what way?'

'This time we'll gather everyone together at your place.'

'It still won't work. Or are you planning to drag them round the house as if it were a giant Cluedo board, until you get to the room in which the murder took place? Then, under the rules of the game, they have to confess?'

'That's not a bad idea,' said Elsie. 'Not bad at all.'

'I wasn't serious,' I said.

'Of course not. I just mean, you've given me a great idea. Get some food in. You're going to give a dinner party.'

'For how many guests?'

'Are you trying to be ironic?'

'Yes.'

'Well don't. About eight guests plus the two of us. Chips and chocolate.'

'What would you like with the chips?'

'Nothing too green.'

'I wasn't seriously suggesting—' I said.

But she too had rung off.

# CHAPTER THIRTY-TWO

It was three days after that that Elsie's Mini arrived unannounced in my drive.

'I hope you have the menu sorted,' she said as she pushed past me and into my hall.

'You *were* serious about the dinner,' I said.

'Of course. I sent you an email.'

'Did you?'

'No, maybe not. I meant to. I've been very busy, Ethelred. Contracts. Deals. Lunches. Everyone is coming, by the way.'

'Who is "everyone"?'

She counted them off on her short, fat fingers. 'Tom. Sophie. Catarina. Martina. Barry Whitelace. I haven't heard from Colonel Gittings yet, but he's invited.'

'So that's the complete list of suspects?'

'Plus Mr Morton from the solicitors. I asked for a couple of representative drug smugglers but the police wouldn't release them. Even though I said you would guarantee their conduct. We can manage without. Maybe you could play a drug smuggler? No, maybe not. We'll have to imagine them.'

'So, you are going to accuse them all, one by one, over dinner?'

'You have invited them,' said Elsie patiently, 'to a murder mystery dinner. They are expecting an evening of fun and games. And that is what you will give them. During the course of the evening, one of them will crack and admit to the murder of Robin Pagham.'

'How?'

'That's down to you. You're the writer.'

'If I were preparing something like this – just a normal evening with no real murders involved – I'd spend a week coming up with a scenario. I can't be expected to produce something in . . .' I checked my watch, '. . . five and a half hours.'

'Call that five. They're invited for quarter to seven and you'll need to change into a dinner jacket.'

'It can't be done, Elsie.'

'OK, I was going to give you the easy bit, but we'll do it as you prefer. I'll write. You cook. And I'll need chips. Lots of them.'

Tom arrived first, slightly before the appointed hour, in a dinner jacket and a red bow tie. 'Dad couldn't make it,' he said. 'Well, to be honest, I was surprised he even considered it.'

'But he did consider it?' I asked. 'I suppose that's a compliment of sorts, in view of all that's happened.'

'He seemed to think that there was more to the invitation than met the eye. Is there?'

'I wish I knew,' I said. 'Elsie is organising the entertainment. Expect the unexpected.'

'I hope I'm properly dressed, anyway,' said Tom. 'The invitation said black tie – but I rather like this red one. It depends who I'm playing, I suppose. Are you allocated a role too?'

'Mrs White, the cook,' I said. 'Pour yourself a drink. You know where to find the beer. I need to check on the onion soup.'

I'd adjusted the heat under the pan when the second guest arrived. Barry Whitelace thrust a bottle at me.

'I'm not sure of the form at these things, so I bought a bottle of wine, just in case. I got it at the Co-op. It was surprisingly cheap. Sorry I'm not in a dinner jacket, by the way. When I dug it out it was covered in mildew. I don't get to wear it a lot these days – last time must have been about five years ago, before I retired. I knew this suit was all right, though – I wore it for Jean's funeral. Is everyone else here?'

I left Whitelace talking to Tom while I fetched him a dry sherry. I returned to find them discussing the Reverend Sabine Barclay-Wood.

Whitelace turned to me. 'Did you ever read his *Happy Recollections of a Sussex Clergyman*?'

'Yes. It was in the library.'

'Did you read the postscript?'

'I'm not sure I got that far.'

'Perfect example of how to throw away a winning position. For years Barclay-Wood had wanted promotion to a position at the cathedral but had never got it. Then, in the late thirties he decided to publish his memoires. Nothing wrong with that, but at the last minute he added a postscript in the form of a fairy tale about a church mouse that, purely in passing, accused the Bishop and Dean of Chichester of malice, corruption, embezzlement and neglect of their duties. The irony was that the new bishop had, unknown to the vicar, finally managed to get him nominated to just the post he'd always coveted. Then the book came out and they cancelled the whole thing. The libel case was still working its way through the courts in 1945 when Barclay-Wood died.'

I nodded. This was exactly the sort of anecdote that I could use in some future book, but I could smell burning from the kitchen and had no time to take notes.

Elsie emerged, just as I was rescuing the main course, having showered and changed.

'How is the mystery evening coming on?' I asked, stirring frantically. 'Everything planned?'

'Planned? Sorry – I went back to my room and fell asleep. But I've got a pretty good idea what to do.'

'So you've held one of these events before?'

'No.'

'But you've been to one organised by somebody else?'

'No.'

'So, your plan is . . .?'

'To wing it. I've done that before, plenty of times.'

'Would you like to serve drinks while I finish cooking, then? I'm finding it a bit tricky doing both, especially when you have to listen to Barry Whitelace's anecdotes.'

'What have you got? Drinks, I mean.'

'Sherry. G and T. White wine. Whisky. Beer. Orange juice. I think just offer those to keep it simple.'

'Nibbles?'

'There may be crisps in that cupboard over there.'

'Is that all?'

'I've only had a few hours' notice.'

'Planning, Ethelred. That's the secret,' said Elsie.

She took a bag of crisps from the cupboard, ate a couple of handfuls and tipped the last few sad fragments into a bowl.

'You really needed more of these,' she said.

When I next checked the guests, Sophie and Martina had arrived, as had Mr Morton and his wife. 'I'd assumed you meant both of us,' he said. I nodded. I reckoned I had enough food if Derek Gittings wasn't coming.

Catarina arrived half an hour late, heavily made up and in a tight dress of red satin. She surveyed the room and demanded vodka. I remembered I had a bottle in the fridge. Elsie took it and served her a vodka that would have made the Guinness Book of Records. The other guests were already on their second or third drinks by this stage, and Elsie had been generous with the measures there too. Most people had been allocated one crisp to soak up the alcohol. It would be a lively evening. It was with some trepidation that I finally sat everyone down at the table and served the soup.

The murder mystery evening had begun.

\* \* \*

'So,' said Tom, as I was clearing the last of the soup bowls away, 'when does the murder bit begin? Or has it already? Are there clues we should have spotted?'

'That's right,' said Elsie, taking out a sheet of paper and glancing at it quickly. 'There are clues we should all have spotted. But did we? That's what we need to find out.'

'So, who has been murdered?' asked Tom. 'Or is that yet to happen?'

'Let's call the murder victim Robin Pagham,' said Elsie.

'That's rather in poor taste,' said Martina. 'Most of us here knew Robin – in fact, now I think about it, we all knew Robin . . .'

'I didn't know him well,' said Morton.

'Nor me,' said Mrs Morton.

'Does that make it in good taste?' asked Martina.

'Fine,' said Elsie, reluctantly crossing something out on her sheet of paper. 'We'll call him Rob Black.'

'Rob Black?' asked Catarina, waving her vodka glass. 'Who is this person?'

'A former actor and sailor,' said Elsie. 'And we'll say he drowned. Because one of you killed him.'

The room had gone completely silent. Then Catarina said: 'Is true. First they kill Robin, now they kill Rob Black. They are bad people.'

'All right,' said Tom brightly. 'So who are we all supposed to be?'

'You,' said Elsie, glancing at her paper, 'are Tom . . . er . . . Green.'

'And me?' asked Martina.

'You are Martina Peacock.'

270

'Am I anyone?' asked Whitelace.

'You are Professor Barry Plum.'

'Professor of what?' he asked suspiciously.

'Professor of Local History,' said Elsie.

Whitelace nodded.

'Can I be Miss Scarlet?' asked Sophie.

Elsie paused. I knew this was a role she coveted for herself, but she nodded.

'And us?' asked Morton.

'Mr and Mrs White.'

'Don't I get to be a separate character?' asked Mrs Morton.

'You are in it together,' said Elsie.

'I suppose my father is Colonel Mustard,' said Tom. 'Which is odd, if I'm Tom Green.'

'Not as odd as some of the things we will reveal tonight.'

'What about Ethelred?' asked Sophie. 'Isn't he anything?'

'Not much,' said Elsie. 'Anyway, he's busy.'

It took me a few minutes to get the fish and chips out of the oven and the vegetables drained and into a bowl. By the time I had returned, everyone was trying to remember who they were – from a games point of view, I mean. But there were four empty wine bottles on the table. Since Elsie and Sophie weren't drinking wine, the rest were getting through it fast. I fetched another couple of bottles and hoped it would last. Elsie immediately topped everyone up. I was beginning to see what her plan was. I just wasn't convinced it would work.

'So,' said Elsie. 'Rob Black is in need of money. He refers to a mysterious "old man", who will provide him with some cash when he dies. Then he sails off one day and never comes back. Just beforehand, however, somebody visits him. They drink a cup of coffee together. Rob's car has broken down, so the visitor gives him a lift to the sailing club. Not many people are around that morning. Rob likes sailing in difficult conditions but perhaps today he doesn't want anyone to see him leave. Because we know he's gone to meet some smugglers . . .'

'Smugglers? How exciting! But why aren't they here?' asked Mrs Morton. 'They must be suspects.'

'Ethelred can be the smugglers,' said Sophie. 'Blackkerchief Dick and Dirty Harry.'

Catarina shook her head. 'Vladislav and Bogdan,' she said. 'I know them. Are not good men. But I think not kill Robin.'

'OK,' said Elsie to me. 'You get to play after all. You are now Vladislav.'

'Thanks,' I said.

'He did not do it,' said Catarina. 'Not Vladislav. Is guilty of much – torture, extortion, genocide – but did not kill Robin.'

'Genocide?' I said. 'I did that?'

'Just a little. Not too much.'

'So, let's look at the motives of those who might want him dead,' Elsie continued. 'Martina Peacock, for example. She is distantly related to him and stands to inherit everything if he dies soon – but not if he marries.'

'Who says Martina Peacock is related to him?' demanded Martina.

'Tom Green,' said Elsie.

'What! Tom! How could you?'

'I didn't mention it to Elsie at all,' said Tom.

'No,' said Elsie. 'Tom Green told one of the smugglers . . .'

'Which one?' I asked.

'Bogdan,' said Elsie.

'Thanks a bunch, Bogdan,' said Martina, looking in my direction.

'I'm Vladislav,' I said. 'I just do a bit of genocide. Don't blame me.'

'As it happens, Martina Peacock is in the area on the day that Robin Black dies. In fact, she is seen in West Wittering. Her visit is on the unlikely pretext that she is accompanying Sophie Scarlet who is going on a date with Tom Green. Sophie thinks Tom Green is a bit of a prick and that he may stand her up.'

'Really?' said Tom, looking at Sophie. 'You thought that? And you brought Martina along on the date just in case? Bloody hell. Well, at least I know what you think of me.'

'Oh, for goodness' sake, Tom. One moment we're going out – the next I'm dumped without any explanation at all. What do you expect? As for backup plans, if I hadn't shown up you'd have gone running home to daddy.'

'Meaning what, exactly?' demanded Tom.

'Anyway,' said Elsie, smiling benignly at the scene before her. 'Martina checks that all is well with Sophie – Sophie sends her a text saying she was having a great time, smiley face, xxx . . .'

'Martina! You told Elsie about texts I sent you?' demanded Sophie.

'Oh, chill out, Little Miss Scarlet,' said Martina, reaching for the Pinot Grigio. 'At least I didn't claim that you've got a motive for killing Robin.'

'But Martina *has* got a motive,' said Elsie. 'The inheritance . . .'

'Let's be clear about one thing,' said Martina. 'I have no motive at all.'

'Money,' said Elsie. 'I'd call that an excellent motive.'

'I didn't need his money,' said Martina with contempt. 'Do you have any idea who I am?'

'Mrs Peacock?' volunteered Whitelace. 'This wine's much nicer than the bottle I brought, by the way. Mine was probably better value, though. Two for seven pounds. I left the other one at home.'

'I am the chief executive and majority shareholder of Blanch Capital,' said Martina. 'I could have bought Robin out a hundred times over. He needed me for my money – not the other way round. I had no reason at all to risk killing somebody and losing the firm that I've spent my life building up.'

'That's right,' said Sophie. 'Though her father spent a bit of time building it up too before he handed it over.'

'Yes,' said Tom. 'That's right.'

'Well, you'd know all about inheriting stuff from your father, Tom,' said Martina. 'At least I make my own decisions now.'

'So why is it called Blanch Capital if she's Mrs Peacock?' asked Whitelace.

'That's a very good point,' said Mrs Morton. 'Maybe it's a red herring.'

'Moving on,' said Elsie, 'we now come to Professor Plum.'

Whitelace looked round. 'Who's that?'

'You,' said Mrs Morton.

'Professor Plum was an environmental campaigner,' said Elsie.

'Excellent,' said Whitelace, looking very pleased.

'He'd had a run in or two with Rob Black about a wind farm,' Elsie continued. 'He'd threatened to kill him.'

'That's a coincidence,' said Whitelace. Then he stopped abruptly. 'Hang on,' he said, 'you're not saying that I really . . .'

'*Did* he really?' asked Mrs Morton. 'I mean, did he try to kill somebody in real life?'

'He certainly did,' said Mr Morton. 'Came to our office. Tried to stab Mr Pagham. Darren disarmed him.'

'Your Darren?'

'Yes.'

'Thin Darren?'

'That's right.'

'I didn't think he had it in him.'

'He caught me off guard,' said Whitelace huffily.

'So where was Professor Plum on the day Robin was killed?' Elsie demanded.

'How should I know?' asked Whitelace. 'He's an imaginary character.'

'All right. Let's say he did *exactly* what you did that day. Where would he have been?'

'At the hospital in Chichester, taking his wife to chemotherapy.'

'Really? All day?'

'Yes. We had a long wait. We arrived around nine, but we didn't get away until mid-afternoon.'

'The hospital would vouch for that?'

'For me, yes. I don't know about Professor Plum. He could have been anywhere.'

Elsie looked at the piece of paper in front of her. I noticed that quite a lot was now crossed out.

'So is that it?' asked Whitelace.

'Yes,' said Elsie, folding the paper away.

Whitelace turned to us. 'I bet it's not,' he said. 'That's the sort of trick they use – make you think Plum's got a watertight alibi, then at the last minute you discover he could have got away for an hour and killed Mr Black.'

'And could he?'

'What?'

'Get away.'

'Me or Plum?'

'You.'

'No, of course not. I told you. I couldn't have left Jean on her own.'

'Right. That's it for Plum, then,' said Elsie. 'So, we turn to Colonel Mustard.'

'Am I Colonel Mustard too?' asked Tom.

'I suppose so.'

'I could be,' said Mrs Morton. 'I don't really want to be Mrs White. She seems simply to be an adjunct of Mr White, who is a bit dull anyway. Trust me on that, I know him well. Could I be Colonel Mustard?'

'No, you couldn't,' said Elsie. 'So, Colonel Mustard is an old friend of Mr Black's. He's sailed with him. He's dined with him. But Black has reneged on a deal to build a wind farm.'

'Thank God,' said Whitelace.

'Colonel Mustard is furious,' said Elsie. 'He's ruined, for reasons I don't quite understand. Anyway, he visits Black and then drugs him, puts him in a sailing boat and pushes him off.'

Tom glared at Elsie. 'The business deal was fairly insignificant,' he said. 'More to the point, my father was a very good friend of Robin's. And he was so upset at his death that he didn't even attend the funeral. Look, Elsie, I'm not at all happy with this. If you're going to accuse somebody it's better to do it to his face.'

'Well, you're Colonel Mustard,' said Mrs Morton. 'You are apparently two characters while some of us are only half a character. So, you'll just have to answer for him. Would anyone like to accuse me of being half the murderer?'

'No,' said Elsie. 'We wouldn't. Now let's turn to Tom Green and Sophie Scarlet.'

'Sophie can't possibly have done it,' said Tom. 'She was with me all day.'

'And Tom was with me,' said Sophie.

'How touching,' said Mrs Morton. 'Don't they make a lovely couple? Does this end with their getting married? Agatha Christie always ends with a wedding, if possible.'

'I don't do that sort of ending,' said Elsie. 'But therein lies their motive. I think they were genuinely in love. Colonel Gittings split them up. And why? Because Tom had stolen Sophie from Robin. So Robin talked to the colonel and the colonel made Tom drop her. But neither of the two lovers ever forgave Robin. So they got together again in secret. Of course, whenever they met in public

277

they had to pretend they hated each other – hence their improbably not speaking at the funeral. But they were working hand in glove. They hatched a plot by which one of them went to the museum – not a likely place for a date, after all – and the second one crept back to the village to kill Robin. Then the first one – whichever the first one is – provided a false alibi, even to the extent of eating two lunches.'

'Two lunches? That's improbable,' said Mrs Morton.

'No it isn't,' said Elsie. 'It absolutely depends what's on the menu. Say they had egg and chips and burger and chips for example and you couldn't make up your mind—'

'If I thought you really suspected Sophie,' Tom interrupted, 'I would admit to the murder myself. But it was neither of us. We were at the museum all day. I remember every moment of it.'

'Do you?' asked Sophie.

'Yes, of course,' said Tom.

'You see,' said Mrs Morton. 'It's all going to end with a wedding. I think that's lovely. I just hope there's no silly misunderstanding that gets in the way. You often get that when the writer wants to pad the story out.'

'What about Catarina?' asked Martina, pointing a wine glass in her direction. 'Which character is she playing?'

'She's not,' said Elsie.

'Why not? She's the one who's collected the money, after all. The family money. *My* family's money. The money that was none of her damned business. She breezes in, snares Robin. Gets him to leave her everything. Then Robin dies. Where was Catarina Green on the day?'

'We've already used Green,' said Mrs Morton.

'It's a common name,' said Martina.

'You say I common?' demanded Catarina.

'Where *were* you, Catarina?' Martina repeated. 'We've all provided alibis so far. For some reason nobody's got you to produce one yet.'

'I was shopping,' said Catarina.

'Do you have proof of that?'

'Robin is mean. Not give me enough money. I buy some small things – not worth keep receipt.'

'It's Catarina who asked me to investigate,' I said. 'Why would she do that if she had killed Robin? She was already in the clear.'

'Because she didn't kill Robin herself. She got Bogdan and Vladislav to do it. But she knows that her two stooges will get themselves arrested sooner or later and may spill the beans. So, she sets up this enquiry to frame somebody else in the village. Fortunately, she comes across two idiots willing to do just that – a talentless and largely unknown crime writer and his agent.'

'She's not my agent,' I said.

'Otherwise, fair comment,' said Elsie.

'Well, you're not going to frame me,' said Martina.

'Nor me,' said Tom, 'and certainly not my father.'

'Quite,' said Sophie. 'Certainly not daddy.'

'What do you mean by that?' asked Tom.

'You know perfectly well what I mean. Elsie was right. It was your father who split us up. That's the way he operates. I bet you said nothing.'

Tom looked at her.

'And don't say what you are planning to say about my mother,' Sophie added.

'How do you know I'm planning to say anything?' asked Tom.

'Because I know you, Tom Gittings,' said Sophie. 'To think I might have—'

'Green,' said Mrs Morton. 'He's called Tom Green. I was afraid this was the way things were going but if this is to be a convincing lovers' tiff, then you'd better get each others' names right.'

'Might have what?' asked Tom.

Sophie opened her mouth, then closed it again and shook her head.

'Might have what?' repeated Tom.

'I've had enough of this,' said Sophie. 'I'm going. You can get a taxi home, Martina, unless you want to come now.'

'It's just getting interesting,' said Martina.

'Right,' said Sophie. 'Thank you for inviting me, Ethelred. I hope you all enjoy the rest of the evening.'

We all turned to watch her go. Nobody spoke at all until the front door had slammed.

'Well, Tom,' said Mrs Morton, 'if you need any of us to tell you whether to follow her, then the answer is probably that you shouldn't.'

'Thank you,' said Tom. 'Let me know the result tomorrow, Ethelred.'

We watched a second (and I suppose, since he was also Colonel Mustard, third) suspect escape.

'I think it may work out for them,' said Mrs Morton. 'It did for us.'

'Under slightly different circumstances,' said Mr Morton, thoughtfully.

'Yes, slightly different,' said Mrs Morton. 'You never were much of a runner.'

I surveyed the room. Whitelace was asleep in his chair, snoring gently. Martina was checking her phone for texts. The Mortons had started a discussion, about two hours too late, as to which of them should have abstained from wine in order to drive home. Catarina had gone to the loo.

'Well, that was a great success,' I said to Elsie. 'We're no closer to knowing who the murderer is.'

'Maybe you should interrogate Mr and Mrs White,' said Mrs Morton.

'Yes,' said Mr Morton. 'Otherwise, why are we here?'

'Oh, Ethelred thought there was something odd about some lease having gone missing in 1848,' said Elsie. 'I was going to let him question you on it, but I forgot.'

'The lease is interesting,' said Mr Morton. 'I've never known such a fuss about what is really just a piece of history.'

'Sorry if I got you into trouble,' I said.

'Oh, that doesn't matter,' said Morton.

'He's always shooting his mouth off,' said Mrs Morton. 'One day he'll get into a real mess.'

'But not this time,' said Morton, 'because whatever the big secret is, I failed to reveal it to you. At least two of the partners presumably know – one representing the Gittings family and one representing the Paghams. But nobody has ever told me. I can't help feeling that if we knew what was in the lease – and why we advised against a tribunal – we'd know a lot more about the feud, and why it all still matters now.'

'I did wonder who the freeholder was.' I said. 'I mean, who owns the freehold to the Gittings' house now. They'd have gained from the advice not to challenge the terms of the lease.'

'I do,' said Catarina, coming back into the room. 'Lawyer says is mine. I say, what is freehold. He says means Colonel Gittings only owns lease. I say, so he pay me rent? They say – not any more. Not now Robin dead. Before they pay big rent. Massive rent. But not now Robin dead. No more rent ever. Thousand-year lease and no rent ever.'

'This thousand-year lease, when does it date from?' I said.

'I too ask that. Dates from 1848.'

And then I saw it. How it had all been done. It was ingenious. Evil, but ingenious.

'What?' asked Catarina.

'I've just realised how you can set up a blackmail that will deliver cash at regular intervals for a hundred and fifty years,' I said.

Catarina nodded. 'Cool,' she said.

# CHAPTER THIRTY-THREE

The following morning, I drove up to the Gittings' house and parked the car on the gravel drive. Black clouds scudded across the sky above me. We would be in for a storm very soon.

As before, the door opened a crack. 'You can clear off, Mr Tressider. I've tried to help you and you've repaid me with insolence and disloyalty. You're not welcome here and I've told Tom to have nothing more to do with you.'

'I know you killed Robin Pagham,' I said. 'I know how you did it and I know why.'

For a long time two steel-blue eyes observed me. Derek Gittings' expression did not change. 'Go to the police, then. They investigate murders, don't they?'

'I'd like to talk to you first. I've plenty of evidence against you. But it doesn't incriminate Tom.'

Again, a long unblinking stare, then: 'Fine. Have it your way. Let's talk.'

He shuffled ahead of me in his old carpet slippers,

switching on lights as he went. The strawberry thieves still decorated the wallpaper in the study, but there was a new sense of order. Two large black plastic sacks in the corner bulged with waste paper. On the desk was a single pile of letters to be dealt with – the circulars and junk mail had vanished. The bookshelves too seemed to have been pruned and rationalised. But a lot of the defiance had gone out of Derek Gittings. He dropped into his chair, his shoulders hunched, and looked at me. 'So, where do you want to start?'

'In 1848,' I said, brushing away some dog hair before I sat down. 'Robin's death makes sense only in the context of the Herring Field murder and what happened immediately afterwards. It explains why he had to die and why his death couldn't wait.'

Derek Gittings laughed. 'You've got it all worked out, then?'

'A lot of it. So, to begin at the beginning, the death of John Gittings benefitted one person and one person only – his brother George. George gained the estate and John's fiancée. The fiancée, Jane Taylor, was what would then have been described as a flighty piece. She was leading both men on – and possibly not just them. I think that John had discovered what had been going on behind his back and arranged to meet George at the Herring Field to have it out with him. George killed him with Lancelot's knife.'

'It's not a new theory,' said Derek Gittings. 'I suspect that a lot of people at the time thought Pagham had been stitched up. And a local historian took a look at it a few years back and said he reckoned that George had been the one who had gained. Tom wasn't giving away any family

284

secrets when he suggested you might turn it into a book. If he'd known the whole story I doubt he'd have let you go anywhere near it, but he didn't. He couldn't have.'

'But you do know more than that?'

'If it helps you at all, then yes. What you say is correct. There was apparently a deathbed confession of some sort – thirty years too late to save Lancelot Pagham. George did it all right. And it was much as you describe. George claimed he had met John there to talk things over, they'd argued and then he'd discovered in his pocket a knife he'd found on the green the day before.'

'So, he hadn't intended either to kill John or frame Lancelot?'

'You think not? Well, you've read the evidence. Somebody sent the note to Lancelot sending him over to Itchenor on a wild goose chase. And, as you say, the testimony of George's future wife, at Lancelot's trial, suggested that there might have been something going on between her and Lancelot. George may have had a good reason for wanting the blame to fall where it did and put a second rival out of the way. His own intervention at the trial appeared to support Lancelot but actually damned him. Very clever, you might say. Maybe even the deathbed confession wasn't as frank as it might have been, or maybe it's been edited a bit over the generations. There are some things we'll never know.'

'But Perceval Pagham knew George was the killer?'

'He told George he'd seen him, thought he was acting oddly and followed him to the field.'

I thought of the devil's sudden appearance in the tale of *The Murderer and the Devil*.

'So, he preferred to blackmail George rather than save his brother?'

'Again, apparently so. It depends a bit whether he really was a witness or whether he worked it out later, after the trial, and just claimed to have seen it. However he did it, he certainly convinced George that he had the dope.'

'And Perceval's price was the Gittings' estate,' I said. 'Bit by bit. How did they come up with the scheme?'

'Perceval went to George and initially demanded the lot,' said Derek Gittings. 'George's reply was that he could scarcely hand over the whole estate without exciting a great deal of suspicion. He might as well go to the authorities straight away, make a confession and get it over with. Perceval went away and consulted a lawyer – a man named Smallwood – and came back with a plan that he thought was watertight. Perceval was to sell George the Herring Field. In return George was to make over to him the freehold of the Gittings' estate. Perceval then sold George, for £500, a thousand-year lease. So George got it all back again, minus just the £500 and gained the Herring Field.'

'That's the lease that was missing from the file at Chettle and Smallwood?'

'I have a copy and I assume Robin had a copy. I think my grandfather demanded ours back from the solicitor – he never quite trusted them not to let the cat out of the bag. As young Morton did.'

'And the lease specified some ground rent?'

Derek Gittings smiled bitterly. 'Of course it did. That was the whole point of it. I think you've already worked it out pretty much, though perhaps not the exact percentages.

The ground rent was one quarter of the value of the estate whenever the current leaseholder died. It was payable to Perceval and his heirs for ever – or rather until the Gittings family was completely ruined.'

'His heirs being defined as . . .'

'Precisely, you mean? "The heirs male of Perceval Pagham and his descendants" was the wording. Believe me, the words are etched on my brain. The eldest son was to inherit first, failing which the second, and so on. No daughters.'

'And if there were no male descendants?'

'Generations of lawyers at Chettle and Smallwood have pondered that one. The consensus was that if there were no legal heirs, the lease was still good for the remaining term, but that no ground rent was payable because there was nobody entitled to it.'

'So, as long as there were Paghams, one quarter of the remaining estate was lost each time the owner died?'

'Exactly. George died – according to the records – in 1875, so Perceval lived to collect. He'd already put the £500 to good use and bought a small farm. Now he was able to add a substantial chunk of land to it. Then the following year George's eldest son, John, also died. That was another big slice out of the estate – one quarter of the remaining three-quarters. John had a young son, also called John – maybe guilt made them try to keep the murdered man's name alive. John Gittings III, as I shall call him, survived until the nineteen thirties, just to spite the Paghams, but further deaths in 1950 and 1984 meant all that was left was the house and a few acres around it. And the Herring Field, of course – that is ours freehold and always will be.'

'The death in 1875 – there was a story that George was taken away by the devil.'

'You've read *Curious Tales of Old Sussex*?'

'Yes.'

Gittings laughed. 'You want to know what happened?'

'I'm curious.'

'George had kept the whole story from the rest of the family – for obvious reasons. Maybe he'd hoped there'd be no surviving Paghams to collect by the time he died. But in 1873 or '74, his son John became seriously ill – cancer, I think. George was getting old. He knew that if he died and John succeeded, then passed away shortly after in his turn, almost half of the estate would vanish just like that. But he had a good chance of outliving John and handing over to John Gittings III direct, thus losing only a quarter. He also had a Plan B, which was that, if he died first, his death was to be concealed until after the elder John had died, limiting the damage to the same amount. At some point there must have been a family gathering at which he revealed to the horrified family what he had done.'

'And George did die first?'

'Yes, in 1874. So Plan B went live. The family simply told everyone he was sick and unable to appear in public. And they waited for John to die. But he didn't.'

'And people started to ask questions about where George was?'

'Precisely.'

'So what then?'

'I think you know – it's as you discussed with Tom.

Their options were limited. They couldn't keep George's corpse around the house indefinitely. According to family tradition, they buried George in a desolate and lonely place, where there was no chance of it being found. Until Whitelace interfered, I had no idea where, but it transpires it was the Herring Field. I suppose it was obvious, when you think about it.'

'But the DNA results . . .'

'What DNA results?'

'Tom did a DNA test. The body wasn't an ancestor of his.'

'I wish he'd asked me before he did it. I could have told him who it was . . .' Derek Gittings paused. 'The tests are sometimes wrong. In this case they must be. It was George. I can promise you that.'

'So, when was the secret burial?'

'I've no idea. Probably very shortly after he died. It would have been awkward if the body had been found. They may have thought they could just claim he had gone away.'

'But the rector got the truth out of them?'

'So it would seem. To prevent a scandal, they reluctantly announced his death, about a year after he had actually died, and held a funeral but with no body.'

'Then when his grave was opened again to bury his wife, they found it empty.'

'Is that right? I didn't know that little detail. John died a few months later and the Paghams got the second chunk of the estate.'

'But the lease could have been challenged in court, surely? It had been signed under duress. It was in effect a sort of fraud.'

'Yes, but there was a further clause. If the contents of the lease were ever made public by the leaseholder or his representatives, then the whole lease was forfeit. It all had to be handed back to the Paghams. That might have been overturnable too, but none of my ancestors felt quite confident enough to make the challenge in open court and risk losing the lot. I knew about that advice back in the fifties not to go to a tribunal. I'd assumed it as the final word on the subject until I heard what Morton had told you. I'd always suspected that if there was ever any conflict of interest between us and the Paghams, Chettle and Smallwood would know which side their bread was buttered on . . .'

'So, whatever the case may have been in law, none of the leaseholders *believed* they could tell anyone about the terms of the lease – not even their own family?'

'Some probably did tell them – George must have done, as I said. Others felt that it was a burden they had to bear alone until they could hand it over to the next generation. I didn't learn anything until my father was dying. We had a long talk in which he explained it all to me: why there would be very little for me to inherit, why the loss of land over the years hadn't been down to poor management and gambling debts – the story that was generally believed – but to the steady attrition of an ancient blackmail.'

'Does Tom know?'

'Not yet. His turn would have come in due course. I'd better tell him straight away. He needs to know.'

'So, you were the "old man" Robin was waiting for to die, so that he could collect.'

'I suppose I must be.'

'Couldn't a deal have been struck? There must have been a point when it would have been worthwhile for everyone if your family had just bought back the freehold?'

'If the Paghams had been willing to sell. But I think they rather liked taking their revenge for Lancelot's death a slice at a time. There was no love lost between the families. Actually, I'd tried to do a deal with Robin myself. We knew each other well. We sailed together. He was a friend. I knew he needed cash and he knew I could last another twenty or thirty years before he could collect on the blackmail again. It might not happen in his lifetime, the way he was living it. And there was less and less, as the years had gone by, for the Paghams to collect a quarter of. Tom stood to inherit a small fraction of the original estate. So, to end the feud, I offered Robin the Herring Field, with the prospect of planning permission for a small wind farm – in return for releasing us from the terms of the lease and letting us keep what little remained. I'd done all the research, spoken to all the right people. It wasn't such a bad deal. And he was a friend.'

'But he wasn't interested?'

'At one stage . . . but then he decided it wasn't worth it. I was cross to begin with. I'd expected better of him. Couldn't we just lay the whole thing to rest after all these years? But then I began to wonder whether I needed to do a deal at all. The Paghams were not lucky with their offspring, as you may have gathered. Cecil Pagham had five boys, four of whom died in the First World War and a daughter who died in the 1919 influenza pandemic. His only surviving son, Gawain, had three children. Two died in the war –

one in North Africa, one on D-Day. The third was Roger, Robin's father, who was much younger than the other two. For years the whole contract had hung by the slenderest of threads. Just one death would end the whole thing. Robin, as you know, was the last of the line. He showed no sign of marrying and producing legitimate heirs and every sign of killing himself with alcohol or drugs. The chances were we'd made our last payment, anyway.'

'Then Robin got engaged to Sophie?'

'That's right. Lovely girl. I'd known her for years – she spent family holidays in West Wittering as a child. I almost saw her as one of my own. But totally wrong for a wife-beater like Robin. I knew what he'd done to other girlfriends. I had to stop it.'

'So you got Tom to intervene?'

'He's a good lad. I sang Sophie's praises to him. Encouraged it in every way possible. Made sure I got them together.'

'And you split Robin and Sophie up?'

'Best thing from every point of view.'

'But it didn't work out between Tom and Sophie?'

'Once she'd left Robin, it was job done. I didn't discourage Tom, of course . . .'

'Didn't you?'

'Well, maybe a bit. It didn't seem quite right in some ways . . .'

'While they stayed together it reminded you of what you had done?'

'Of what I'd *had* to do,' he said.

'Then Catarina arrived on the scene?'

'It wasn't just that. I knew the wording of the lease back to front. What worried me increasingly was the definition of "heirs male". I wasn't sure that a court wouldn't rule now that illegitimate children could inherit as well – indeed, if somebody had tested it back in the nineteenth century the courts might even have taken the same view. The lease didn't, after all, actually specify *legitimate* children. Just the eldest male child. That made a successor far more likely – a real and present danger, in fact.'

'So, Robin had to die before he had any children at all.'

'Yes. He had to die. He was a good friend, of course. But he had to die. I did try to reason with him – put forward the Herring Field scheme again. But he was having none of it. So, my thoughts turned to more direct routes. The whole bloody business started with a murder. It could end with a murder too – only this time I'd make sure that there would be no witnesses. At first, I wondered about a drug overdose – easy enough to arrange and not likely to create much of a surprise. I actually got Robin to supply me with some cocaine and other things, ostensibly for my own use, so that I could administer them to him at a later date. But there was always a chance that some meddling person would find him in a coma and get him to hospital in time. And anyway, as I say, he was a friend. I didn't want him to die quite so sordidly. I reckoned, however, that I could rig up a sailing accident that would be much better from every point of view. I waited for a day when the weather conditions were right and when I knew Robin would be going out – when you can sail from Snow Hill depends a lot on the tides – I could predict his

293

sailing times. I watched the tide tables and the weather forecasts – it didn't take too long. A day or so before, I went down to the sailing club and made a few alterations to his rudder. It would get him out of the creek, but as soon as it was under any pressure the whole thing would sheer off, leaving him helpless.'

'Wouldn't that have been obvious when the boat was found?'

'Trust me – I know about sailing and I know about making deaths look like accidents. On the day, I'd invited myself over to talk to him about the Herring Field again – there might be money to be made from fracking – though I knew he really had no interest in doing a deal. I'd asked him to make sure we were alone and could talk properly without being overheard – sensitive stuff – big profits to be made. His natural greed and curiosity made him send Catarina off to Chichester for the day. Of course, when I explained it all, he saw that the revised scheme was just the old scheme with a few bells and whistles. He got the field and planning permission. Nothing more. So it was nothing doing. Strange to think that if he'd just said "yes", or even prevaricated a bit, he'd still be alive today. As it was, I just had time to slip the Rohypnol into his coffee when he was out of the room. I wasn't sure how well he'd drive after that, so I'd already disabled his car by disconnecting the battery. When it failed to start, I kindly offered him a lift. I'd already delayed him more than enough, so he quickly accepted. I actually helped him get the boat ready. We were the only ones down there. Nobody else fancied going out on a winter's afternoon with a stiff breeze blowing.'

'What if somebody had seen you?'

'I'd have had a bit of explaining to do, but Robin would have been dead for all that. However bad the outcome for me, I'd have been able to hand over to Tom what remained of the estate, unencumbered by the terms of the lease. That was the main thing.'

'Unless Tom was implicated too.'

'I did everything I could to avoid that. Tom knew nothing of the lease. And I arranged for him to be out of the way that day. I phoned Sophie and told her that Tom would like to meet up with her again but was too embarrassed to ask. She knew Tom well enough to know that was possible. I said he'd suggested the museum – that was the sort of place that Tom would suggest, bless him. Then all I had to do was to tell Tom that Sophie had called *him* and left a message. He got back to her and confirmed it all. They must have both found it a bit odd, but the result was right. They went off to Singleton together. He had a witness.'

'That explains the confusion between Tom's account and Sophie's – both thought the other had made the first move and that they had some specific motive for doing so.'

'I also told Tom to make sure he kept the receipts, just in case he decided to write an article on the museum for the *Observer*. He could reclaim them as expenses. Of course, more to the point, they would also prove where he was – and where Sophie was – if things had gone wrong. I wasn't having either of them caught up in it all.'

'I used the same idea in a book of mine,' I said.

'Did it work for the murderer there?'

'For a while. Then somebody spotted a discrepancy. Murderers usually get caught in fiction. They'd get nobbled on page two if it wasn't for the red herrings. There were a few red herrings in this case too. For a while I suspected Barry Whitelace. I actually think he would have killed to prevent the wind farm. He tried to kill Robin himself, but was less determined than you. I also suspected Sophie – perhaps in collaboration with Tom. And finally there was Martina Blanch.'

'Martina?' asked Colonel Gittings.

'Yes. Did you know that she was descended from Perceval's sister, Morgan Blanch – Morgan after Morgan le Fay, I assume, and Blanch after whoever she married. She was well aware that she stood to inherit the estate if Robin died childless and without making a will.'

'Yes, she'd have got most of it, but not being a descendant of Perceval himself, she couldn't have collected on the lease. That would still have been at an end. I think she'd have still married Robin, oddly enough. Women think they can tame a man like that. She'd have found out that she couldn't, though Catarina might have done it.'

'I also thought that Robin might have been killed by drug smugglers. He was heavily involved in smuggling it would seem.'

'I know. Robin had quite a loose tongue. He told you all sorts of things when he was drunk. He was stupid to get involved with people like that – they could have bumped him off without a qualm of any sort. But in the end the killer was me and me alone.'

'Yes,' I said.

'And what proof do you intend to present to the police? I assume you have something?'

'No, not a lot. I sort of lied about that – a bit like Perceval Pagham, perhaps. And I haven't recorded this conversation on my mobile phone. I'm not sure I know how to. But I can tell them about the lease, which I imagine you or your lawyer will be obliged to disclose. You've admitted you keep one copy. My guess is there is at least one more, locked away in a safe, guarded by Robin's lawyers at Chettle and Smallwood. From what you said, the police will find traces of drugs around this house, even if you've disposed of the bulk of them. And you won't be able to account for your whereabouts at the critical times because you were exactly where I shall claim you were. Since this is a village, I suspect that more people will have noticed you going about your business than you might imagine. Martina and Sophie were certainly spotted at the sailing club that morning. Somebody will have seen you, whatever you believe. It's just that the police haven't yet asked the right people the right questions.'

'If the police show up, I've no intention of denying anything. Robin beat up his girlfriends and, whatever Tom may have told you, used Rohypnol on women whenever he felt it might be to his advantage. He was also charming, generous and great company, but that's beside the point. I've killed plenty of men over a long career – they were necessary, unavoidable deaths. This is merely my first in a civilian capacity. It's strange to discover now that, if Morton is right, there was always another way out of the lease. But for all that, I don't regret killing Robin. He knew how much the terms of the lease hurt me. He called himself a friend and could have saved me and my family all that pain at a stroke. He could have accepted my offer of the Herring Field. He could just have torn up the lease if he wished. But he couldn't be bothered. On that last morning he literally laughed in my face. It was with great pleasure that I watched him sail away. Anyway, whatever happens to me, Tom inherits the house and the rest of it. And he'll have an eight-hundred-year lease that is perfectly marketable if he wishes to sell, as he may. He'll be the first owner of this house for a hundred and fifty years who could actually dispose of it on the open market. Of course, I'd still rather save him the embarrassment of a trial for murder and having to give evidence. All I'd ask is a few hours' notice if you're going to have me arrested. I've still got to finish clearing my desk and putting things in some sort of order. I've made a start. This wasn't entirely unexpected.'

'Tom put me onto it,' I said. 'He suggested I researched the Herring Field murder.'

'Don't blame him in any way,' said Derek Gittings. 'When he came back from the funeral and told me that Catarina had asked you to investigate Robin's death, I told him I thought that was a bad idea. There was plenty in Robin's past that, as a friend, I didn't care to see dug up. Better let sleeping dogs lie. I asked him to divert you in some way. In one sense his choice was inspired – offer you a real-life mystery set in the village in which he lived. What he had no idea of was that it was connected to Robin's death. And the more I pushed you back to the 1840s, the more you seemed to want to find the links through to the present day.'

'I need to think about what I'm going to do,' I said. 'I'll phone you when I've decided.'

'Thank you, Ethelred. That's kind of you. I'll await your call with interest.'

Colonel Gittings looked at me. There was no fear in those eyes. There was not even much curiosity. He seemed to have made up his mind what he would do, regardless of my own decision.

I went for a walk to clear my mind. What was right? Derek Gittings was a murderer. But Robin had, frankly, had it coming to him – a blackmailer, a minor drug dealer, a rapist, a man who thought that it was OK to slap women around a bit and break a nose or two. The police weren't looking for anyone. Nobody else was going to get arrested by mistake. And yet, it wasn't my decision. I ought to hand him over and let the DPP decide what to charge him with.

A couple of minutes' brisk walking brought me to Snow Hill. On the green, the ragged winter grass was waterlogged and deserted. Over by the sailing club a small depression was becoming a pond, on which the water rippled. I looked over towards the dunes of East Head, where I had planned to go, and wondered if I was wise to venture that far. A stiff breeze was now blowing. The grey surface of the creek, normally placid, was being whipped into angry little waves that crashed against the shingle, making it sing. The South Downs, crystal clear on a fine day, were no more than a watercolour smudge on the horizon. The storm that I had felt approaching earlier was almost upon me. But I needed to keep walking. The first drops of icy rain hit my face, but

I plodded on, my jacket darkening with the moisture and my trousers dampening and clinging to my legs.

By the time I reached the beginning of the dunes at East Head, with its great arc of dog-walkers' sand, grey waves were thudding against the sea wall. A solitary gull rose above me, struggled for a moment in the gale and then, accepting the inevitable, allowed itself to be carried sideways, in one great swoop towards the sodden fields.

On an impulse, I turned left, away from the dunes, following the beach eastwards, along the line of bleak, padlocked beach huts. The wind threw a spray of sand in my face, leaving me blinking and wiping my eyes. I sheltered for a moment in the porch of one of the huts.

Taking out your phone once you are stationary is now almost a reflex action. The first thing that I noticed was that I had missed a call – Tom Gittings. He'd obviously heard I'd been to see his father. I'd call him as soon as I got back home and out of this storm. I took the shortest route back, via the ruler-straight estate road and past the church. I was still no clearer what I ought to do, but I had no immediate plans to contact the police. I supposed I ought to let Derek Gittings know that, at least.

In a carefully nuanced assessment of urgency, I had hung up my wet coat but was still in my soaking corduroy trousers when I got out my phone to return Tom's call. Just as I did so, however, it rang again.

'Where are you, Ethelred?' Tom demanded.

'Back home. I've been for a walk. Sorry I didn't reply to your first call. Is it urgent?'

'Dad phoned me. He's told me everything. Your visit – the lease – Robin's death. Did you pass Snow Hill on your walk?'

'Yes. On my way out. I came back the other way.'

'Did you see Dad there? Or did you see his car parked by the sailing club?'

'I was there maybe forty-five minutes ago. I didn't see anyone around. The weather was foul, even then. He'd hardly be going sailing today.'

'When I got home a few minutes ago I found a note saying he was planning to take the boat out. He's not answering his mobile.'

'But it would be suicidal,' I said. 'Even if he was planning to take the boat out, he'll have changed his mind when he sees the conditions. I can't see how he'd even get it launched. It'll only take me a couple of minutes to get to Snow Hill and check. I'll ring you back but I'm sure it will be absolutely fine. He won't do anything silly.'

I didn't stop, not even to lock the front door. I ran down the road towards Snow Hill, my freezing fingers fumbling with the buttons on my coat as best I could, the rain dripping down my face.

The storm lasted three days. The coastguards called off their search the following evening. The boat was washed up a couple of weeks later, somewhere in Hampshire.

# CHAPTER THIRTY-FOUR

It was not the worst of memorial services.

It was one of those Aprils when winter suddenly passes into summer without missing a beat. A week before, patches of dirty, pockmarked snow had still streaked the churchyard. Now the sun shone down on glistening clumps of daffodils and primroses. The trees were that delicate, pastel shade of green that marks new growth and new hope.

At Tom's request, nobody wore black. When he moved towards the lectern, some of us wondered if he really had the strength to get through the ordeal but, apart from an overlong hesitation before he began speaking, he was completely composed. He spoke movingly of his father – a man who had contributed much to the community, a man who had demonstrated his bravery in Northern Ireland and Iraq, a man who never ducked a challenge of any sort, a man who would do anything for his family. Anything at all. There were those who said that he had never truly recovered from the death of his great friend, Robin Pagham, who as everyone knew, had also died in a sailing accident only weeks before. Some had even gone so far as to claim that his father had been overcome with remorse for not being able to prevent Robin going out in his boat on that fateful day. Tom did not think, however, that had anything to do with the second tragedy. His father had always relished sailing in difficult conditions. He had simply miscalculated either the weather or his ability to deal with a rough sea and high winds. But he had . . . Tom paused for a moment . . . died doing what he enjoyed most. He had achieved all he had wished to do. We should all be happy for a life well lived. Tom's only regret was that his father had not lived to hear that he and Sophie were now engaged. That would have pleased him.

The rector also said a few words and we sang a hymn or two – I don't remember which. And that was that. There was no body to bury, no grave to stand over. As we emerged again into the sunshine, I and many others felt a weight lift from our shoulders. I was aware of the warmth and the birdsong and the very distant hum of traffic on the road to Chichester. We all chatted in a pleasant way about this and that. Nobody seemed to have anything more important to do.

'That was a good speech,' I said to Tom, when I managed to catch him alone. 'Nicely judged. And you were right that he would do anything for the family.'

'Even murder?'

'That's the interesting thing about murder,' I said. 'You don't have to be dishonest. You don't have to be malicious.

You don't even need to be particularly violent. You just have to be backed into a corner and think there's no other way out. It could happen to anyone. That's why it's murder we write about rather than fraud or theft.'

We were standing beside one of the older graves – George Gittings 1830–1875 and his loving wife, Jane 1831–1900. Except, according to the tale, only Jane was actually buried there.

'The one thing I still don't understand about all this, though,' I continued, 'was that the DNA test showed that you were not related to the body from the Herring Field, but your father insisted it was George.'

'I think I've worked that out,' said Tom. 'I'm surprised you haven't too. Think back. Half the village seems to have been courting Jane in 1848. John and George were not her only admirers. Don't you remember her rather defensive evidence at the trial about talking to Lancelot Pagham?'

'You mean George's elder son was in fact Lancelot's?'

'It could be. But there's a more interesting possibility. Perceval Pagham stood godfather to John Gittings II. I think there's every chance that the father was actually Perceval. It may not have been only the Gittings brothers who fell out over Jane – which may in turn explain why Perceval wasn't keen to save Lancelot. In short, it's quite possible I'm not really a Gittings at all – I and my father and my grandfather and my great-grandfather and my great-great-grandfather were all Paghams, if we had but known it. So, it's not surprising that the DNA test showed no relationship between me and George Gittings. It's not the Paghams who have died out – it's the Gittingses who died out when Albert, George's other son, was

305

buried in the 1930s. And there's a further point that you will not have missed. If the last few generations of Gittingses are descended from Perceval . . .'

'John Gittings II was actually Perceval's *eldest* son.'

'Precisely. He was arguably the heir male of Perceval's body to whom, under the lease, the payments were due thereafter. Forget any appeal to a Lands Tribunal – we never needed to pay a penny to anyone except ourselves. Of course, if we wanted to reclaim our money, we'd need both to prove beyond reasonable doubt who was the father and to establish that illegitimate children were always eligible to inherit. I suspect that even Jane Gittings wasn't sure who the father was, or she might have told George there and then. That would have stopped everything in its tracks. She didn't have the DNA evidence that I have, of course.'

'If you'd included all that in your funeral address, you'd have got the congregation to sit up,' I said. 'You'd have beaten by a head Catarina's intervention at Robin's funeral.'

'You think so?' said Tom. 'Shame I didn't say it, then.'

'I think what you said was absolutely right,' I said. 'And ending with news of the engagement was nice.'

Tom pulled a wad of paper out of his pocket, as if to double-check he really had made no reference to murder, then smiled sheepishly at what he had actually produced for my inspection.

'I think that's a contract,' I said with a laugh.

'Yes, the speech must be in the other pocket.'

'So, you've signed with Elsie?'

We both looked across the churchyard. Elsie had taken the instruction not to dress in black to the letter. She wore a pale-pink dress and short white cardigan that nowhere near met in the middle. Large, very dark sunglasses with thick red frames were perched on her head. She was in an animated conversation with Catarina. I heard her exclaim, 'that's crap, that is' – and then the conversation proceeded in a friendly manner as before.

'Yes,' said Tom. 'I signed the contracts yesterday. I need to give this one to Elsie. That completes the legal formalities.'

'You won't regret it,' I said. 'Or only occasionally.'

'And you?' asked Tom.

I felt the bulge of paper in my inside pocket pressing against my chest. My pen, I knew, was in the other pocket. Elsie was right in front of me.

'I haven't decided,' I said.

'When will you decide?'

'In the next few minutes.'

'So, you're going back to her?'

'Maybe,' I said.


For the moment I was content. The story had in a sense ended well. But, as the good vicar of Selsey had discovered, you could still ruin everything with an ill-considered postscript.

I looked up at the cloudless blue sky and allowed the stripling sun to warm my face for just a moment or two longer.

# POSTSCRIPT TO:

## *HAPPY RECOLLECTIONS OF A SUSSEX CLERGYMAN*

# THE HONEST MICE

*Once there was a clergyman who lived in the remotest depths of the county of Sussex. He was poor and obliged to live on a miserly stipend that would have shamed the least of his parishioners to own it. He was a learned man, however, who had studied the folklore of the good people of that part of the country and had written a book and several hymns, and he thought that perhaps his talents might be the better recognised if he moved to the great city of Ch------r and became a canon of the famous cathedral there. Many a time and oft he wrote to the Dean and to the Bishop begging to be considered for the next position amongst the residentiary canons that fell vacant there. But they turned him away with soft words, assuring him that he was always in their minds but that such-and-such a post had already been reserved for another cleric and that his turn would doubtless come. But it did not come and the good clergyman grew old but no richer than he was before.*

*Now it came to pass that, one day, he had prepared for himself a fine supper – a crust of dry bread on a wooden trencher and a little milk in a cracked glass. But before he set to, he prayed most earnestly to God, thanking him for his goodness and mercy. Thus he sat, with his eyes closed, for many minutes. When he opened them, however, all that he could see on the trencher was a little brown mouse and a few crumbs. And the glass was empty.*

*'Bless you, little mouse,' said the clergyman sadly, 'for your need was greater than mine and all I could offer you was stale bread that the baker had given me out of pity. You do not know right from wrong and had no idea you were depriving me of my only meal today.'*

*The brown mouse looked at him with his big black eyes. 'Actually we do know right from wrong,' he said. 'It was just that, tonight, you prayed for a minute less than last night, so you caught me in the act. Another thirty seconds and I'd have been back in my hole in yonder wainscot and you'd have been none the wiser.'*

*'Nevertheless,' said the clergyman, 'I forgive you, little mouse. Tomorrow, if I have any bread at all, I shall set aside half for you and we shall dine together.'*

*'Actually,' said the mouse, 'I can eat better elsewhere, but since you have been so kind to me, which humans rarely are, I will attempt to grant you one wish.'*

*'You have magical powers?' asked the clergyman.*

*'No,' said the mouse, 'because I am quite clearly only a mouse. I'm actually shocked that, as a clergyman, you even thought that possible. However, sometimes mice can achieve things that human beings cannot. If I could grant*

you any wish, and I'm not saying I can, what would it be?'

'Well,' said the clergyman, 'I should like to be a residentiary canon of Ch------r Cathedral. But due to the malice and duplicity of the Bishop and Dean each of my applications has failed.'

'Let me see what I can do,' said the mouse. 'I rarely go to Ch-------r these days, but I have cousins who live much closer. I shall send them and they shall spy on the Bishop and Dean and report back to you on what they say. Nobody notices us mice but we have very sensitive ears. Perhaps you will learn something of value and perhaps not. We shall see.'

'Thank you. And in return I shall buy the very best cake from the baker and leave it out for you and your cousins.'

'That will not be necessary, but thank you, nevertheless,' said the mouse.

So, the clergyman used his meagre savings and started to leave out plates of cake every night, and every morning the plate was empty, except for a few crumbs. After a week or two the mouse appeared again.

'You are right,' he said. 'My cousins report that the Bishop speaks very slightingly of you. He and the Dean mock your learning. They plan to give the next post, promised faithfully to you, to the Dean's wife's sister's cook's nephew. In a day or two you will receive a letter saying that the position was unfortunately awarded to another candidate with a greater claim to it.'

And so it happened. The letter's honeyed words did not deceive the good clergyman, but he bided his time, waiting for the mouse's next report. It was not long coming.

'My cousins tell me that the Dean and Bishop neglect their flock shamefully. They think of nothing but eating and drinking and strutting around in fine vestments with borders of gold lace. They are proud and cruel.'

'And am I to suffer this without being able to do anything?' asked the clergyman.

'No,' said the mouse. 'My cousins say that they will soon have information for you that will give you power over the Bishop and over the Dean of Ch-------r. Be patient! Soon all will be revealed.'

'Thank you,' said the clergyman. 'And is your cousin happy with the cake I provide?'

'Reasonably,' said the mouse. 'But perhaps you might provide some with butter icing next time?'

So the clergyman sold some of his precious books and purchased cake with butter icing for the mice and left it out. And every day it vanished, except for a few crumbs. By and by the mouse returned.

'My cousins say that their dossier on the Bishop is almost complete. He draws a large salary but does nothing for it. The Dean is even worse, as you would expect, for he is much cleverer than the Bishop. Every day parcels arrive from Rome, containing perfumes that the Bishop and Dean burn in secret. One parcel contained a hat with many strange tassels, the purpose of which my cousins could not guess.'

'It is worse than I ever suspected,' said the clergyman. 'I have dreamt of such things and awoken crying out . . .'

'We know,' said the mouse. 'We know and understand. Your very worst fears of the Bishop are true. But if the

314

Archbishop were to be informed, then he would be removed at once. My cousins are now investigating the Archdeacon, who may harbour Arminian doctrines. Have courage, my good sir! Soon your dearest wish will be granted!'

'And the cake is satisfactory?' asked the clergyman.

'It is quite nice,' said the mouse, 'but Black Forest gateau would be even nicer.'

So, the clergyman sold his remaining books and bought Black Forest gateau and left it out for the mice. After a few weeks he found a note written in very small writing.

'Thank you for the cake, which we have enjoyed. While we lived in a country parish, we were honest mice, for honesty was all we saw and knew about. Having lived in a cathedral, however, we now know that what we should do is to receive the largest reward we can and then do nothing for it. I am sure that you have it in your heart to forgive us, and that is why you will never be suitable for any post at the great cathedral at Ch-------r. Yours sincerely, the Mice.'

# ACKNOWLEDGEMENTS

My thanks are due, as ever to the team at Allison & Busby – in particular Susie Dunlop, Sophie Robinson, Kelly Smith, Lesley Crooks, Kathryn Colwell, Simon and Fliss Bage – to my agent David Headley and to David Wardle for another stunning cover illustration.

I am also indebted to John Ll Williams FRCS for his advice on how to sabotage a sailing boat; but, after several glasses of wine, I confess I may have missed some crucial details. I have also added some embellishments of my own. I can therefore offer readers no guarantee that the method as described would actually work, but would be interested to hear, in strict confidence, from anyone who employs it successfully.

I must repeat my apologies to the people of West Wittering for again implying that the village is a hotbed of crime, a home to Mafiosi, drug dealers or (worse still) incompetent sailors. My fictional West Wittering bears increasingly little resemblance to the real one, and my fictional population no similarity at all to its actual inhabitants, who harbour no murderous intentions that I am aware of.

Finally my thanks, gratitude and love to my family for their support – my wife Ann, our son and daughter-in-law, Tom and Rachel, and our daughter Catrin, to whom this latest volume is dedicated.